Brewer, Steve.

Monkey man.

$24.00

STEVE BREWER

INTRIGUE
PRESS

MADISON | WISCONSIN

Published by Intrigue Press,
an imprint of Big Earth Publishing
923 Williamson St.
Madison, WI 53703

First Edition: September 2006

Library of Congress Cataloging-in-Publication Data

Brewer, Steve.
 Monkey man / by Steve Brewer.
    p. cm.
 ISBN 1-890768-73-1
 I. Title.

 PS3552.R42135M66 2006
 813'.54--dc22

                                                    2006023451

Design by Kevin Glidden

Printed in the USA

To Frank Zoretich, my partner in crime

Chapter 1

Nothing interrupts a nice chat like the arrival of a gorilla. Jeff Simmons and I were locked in conversation, leaning across the yellow Formica tabletop, our faces only inches apart as we discussed the investigation he wanted me to undertake. But once the big ape entered the café, even someone as intense as Simmons had trouble maintaining his concentration.

The whole place went quiet as the person in the shaggy gorilla costume grunted through the door. Such sudden hushes are rare at the Flying Squirrel cafés that dot Albuquerque. Usually, the colorful coffeehouses are cacophonous with conversation, crowded with students and suits and tourists and artistes and other loafers. The first Flying Squirrel opened fifteen years ago in Nob Hill, a trendy zone near the University of New Mexico, and it was a huge hit. In the years since, the owners have opened a dozen locations. These days, half the business deals in this town get inked over coffee, under the buck-toothed logo of the Flying Squirrel.

I use the cafés a lot. I run Bubba Mabry Investigations out of my home near UNM, but I rarely see clients in my pigsty of an office. Better to meet on neutral territory, preferably in a noisy place where we needn't worry about being overheard. Even better, a place with strong coffee and yummy desserts.

Jeff Simmons hadn't objected when I'd offered to meet him at the Flying Squirrel's downtown location. It was fairly close to the city zoo, where he worked, but he apparently wasn't worried about being seen talking with a private eye, even though the case might end up costing him his job.

Simmons looked every inch the whistleblower, furtive and feverish and idealistic. His blue eyes danced behind thick eyeglasses with gold wire rims. He was perhaps ten years younger than me, in his late twenties, still young enough to be an optimist. He dressed like an Ivy Leaguer in a frayed blue Oxford shirt over baggy chinos and penny loafers. Simmons was a few inches shorter than my six feet and slightly built, but he had a square, masculine jaw with two days' growth of blue-black beard. His side-parted hair was short on the sides, but enviably thick on top. Bobby Kennedy hair.

"I know this isn't your normal sort of work, Mr. Mabry," he said. "It's not the kind of case where you can learn much by 'tailing' people like a 'gumshoe.'"

He made those little air quotes with his fingers as he spoke. I tried not to hold it against him.

"All the numbers are in there." He slid a fat envelope across the table toward me. "I've run the data repeatedly, and there's clearly something wrong. We're losing animals at a rate far beyond what's normal for a zoo this size. I put some comparisons with other zoos in there. If you examine the numbers, you'll see for yourself."

I didn't have the heart to tell him how little numbers mean to me. I barely passed algebra in high school. I always tip waitresses too much because I can't figure the math. The thick envelope might as well have been full of alphabet soup.

"I'm sorry," I said, "but I don't see how I can help you. If you had some suspects, people I could check out, maybe we could get somewhere. But a bunch of numbers about how many critters croaked each month—"

"I do have suspects. Only certain people are in a position to track these deaths. Every time a zoo animal dies, we're required to perform a necropsy—"

"Neck-who?"

"Necropsy. It's like an autopsy, but for an animal rather than a human."

"Ah."

"Cause of death must be recorded. All the information goes into a nationwide database so we—"

That's as far as he got. He stared past my shoulder, distracted, and I swiveled around and saw this big black gorilla bobbing through the coffee shop.

Everyone else turned to look, too. Customers gaped and chuckled and elbowed each other. A rustle of whispered speculation: Was it a singing telegram? A fraternity prank? An advertising stunt?

The costume's jutting face, with its fake white teeth and red rubber tongue, gave no clue about the person inside, and its scowling brow shadowed his eyes. Furry black gloves covered his hands.

The ape carried a purple valise with big yellow daisies on it, like something a circus clown would use to carry oversized shoes. With his free hand, the grunting gorilla gestured at grinning customers and thumped his plastic chest. He walked with a rolling gait, veering between tables, headed our way.

Simmons'ss face flushed. Did he recognize the guy in the ape suit? Or, was he just flustered over King Kong coming toward our booth? I know I felt embarrassed, with everybody looking our way.

The gorilla stopped beside us and the repeated grunt turned into a hoot of excitement. The ape had found the people he was hunting, and it was us.

I could think of no reason for the simian attention. It was Monday, February 6th. Not my birthday. Too early for Valentine's Day. If the ape was here to deliver a singing telegram or something, it must be for Simmons.

"Hey," I said, "is it your birthday?"

He didn't answer. His eyes went round, and he fearfully scooted away from the gorilla. I don't know where he thought he was going. We were trapped in the wooden booth.

The ape opened the valise and reached inside. Here it comes, I thought. The bouquet of fake flowers. A rubber banana. A cream pie.

But no. The ape pulled a pistol from his bag.

I assumed it was a gag, a toy gun that would spit out a flag that read, "BANG!" I was expecting comedy, not gunplay. But after a second or two, it sank in: That was a real revolver, about a .38-caliber. Four-inch barrel of blued steel. A black hole in the end that seemed to grow larger as I stared at it.

"Holy shit!" I shouted, which left something to be desired as a warning to others but got my point across.

I fell backward on the wooden bench and tried to slither under the table. The tabletop wouldn't offer much protection, but it was better than nothing. I'm allergic to bullets.

It was a tight fit, and my belly got stuck between the sharp-edged table and the bench.

The gorilla's gun roared, and a hot red mist spattered me. I flattened further and slid under the table. The gun boomed again, sounding like a cannon.

I couldn't see Simmons because I was on the floor, but he'd clearly been hit. His feet kicked a couple of times, then lay still.

The gorilla's shaggy legs hustled away. I crawled out from under the table and cautiously clambered to my feet, my head snapping around as I searched for our assailant.

He was halfway to the exit, fully upright now, walking like a human in a hurry. Customers cowered on the floor or crouched behind furniture as the gorilla swung his gun back and forth, keeping them at bay.

Then the ape was out the front door and sprinting away to the left, past the tall windows at the front of the coffeehouse.

As soon as he was out of sight, a clatter and jabber arose from the multitudes. People screamed and cried and yelled for an ambulance. One brave soul opened the front door and leaned out, looking for the ape, but came back shaking his head. The gorilla was gone.

I turned to Simmons, dreading what I knew I'd find. Too late for an ambulance to do him any good. He'd taken one bullet to the chest, and bright blood soaked his shirt. The other shot left a round hole squarely above his earnest eyebrows. His glasses were askew and blood trickled down past his wide blue eyes.

My lunch roiled in my stomach. The table and our ceramic coffee cups were speckled with Simmons'ss blood, as was the unopened envelope he'd given me. I looked down at my clothes, saw that my poplin jacket and blue T-shirt were peppered with blood, too.

People gathered around, staring at Simmons, whispering and mumbling and weeping. Sirens wailed nearby.

On impulse, I plucked the envelope off the table and slipped it into the inside pocket of my jacket. If the others saw, nobody said anything. The envelope was clearly mine; it was on my side of the table. It didn't have anything to do with someone in an ape suit plugging a guy in one of the busiest restaurants in town.

Or did it?

Chapter 2

The downtown Flying Squirrel sits only a few blocks from Albuquerque Police Department headquarters, so it soon crawled with cops. They herded customers into groups and took down names and addresses and phone numbers. Witnesses who'd had the best view of the shooting were corralled near the checkout counter so detectives could take first crack at us. Since I was the one spattered with Simmons'ss blood, I'd be first up.

Before the grilling could begin, Lieutenant Steve Romero lumbered through the front door. The top homicide detective at APD, it was only natural that he'd draw what was certain to become a high-profile murder case. But the square-shouldered detective's also an old friend—my best man when I got married a few years ago—which meant he'd zero in on me like a swooping hawk. I tried to hide behind some other witnesses, but it didn't work.

"Hello, Bubba," he said as he approached my group. "Imagine finding you here."

I muttered, "Lieutenant."

Romero wore a long tan coat over a gray suit and striped necktie, much fancier than his usual jeans-and-bomber-jacket winter ensemble. He stuffed his hands in his pockets as he looked me over. "You were with the victim?"

I nodded. No sense trying to dodge it. Everyone in the place could identify me as Simmons's bloody seatmate.

"Come tell me about it."

The lieutenant cut me out of the herd, and we crossed to the booth where Simmons's body still lay sprawled on the hardwood bench. After taking their initial photographs, the cops had covered the body with a sheet. Blood had soaked through in places, making Rorschach butterflies on the white cloth.

Romero lifted the sheet and studied Simmons. I looked away.

"Damn." He let the cloth drop back into place. "Chest and head. Shooter knew what he was doing."

"A professional hit?" I asked.

"You ever hear of a pro wearing an ape suit?"

Good point.

"Shooter wasn't monkeying around," Romero said.

I shot him a look, but his face split into an innocent grin. Cops.

"You were sitting over there?"

"Yeah. Face to face. The dead guy, Jeff Simmons, was trying to hire me."

"Ouch," Romero said. "That won't be good for business."

I hadn't considered that. The thought of the publicity to come made me want to weep.

"Why'd he need a private snooper?"

"He didn't get a chance to say." I don't know why I was being evasive. I guess it's second nature with me. A cop asks a question, I lie and dodge and divert.

Romero just stared at me, waiting.

"It had something to do with his job, I know that much," I said.

"What job?"

"Simmons worked at the zoo. Data processing. He thought he'd found some kind of mismanagement."

"And he wanted your help?"

"Hey, don't blame me. I tried to tell him it wasn't my kind of case."

"What did he say to that?"

"Nothing. That's when the ape walked in."

Romero nodded thoughtfully. He glanced around the coffee shop, measuring distances and calculating angles, before letting his raptor gaze settle on me.

"If there's misconduct at the zoo, he should've talked to your wife, not you."

I'd had the same thought. My wife, Felicia Quattlebaum, is an ace reporter with the Albuquerque Gazette. Give her a story like that and she'd chase down every lead until the zoo animals weren't the only ones behind bars. But I hadn't gotten the chance to tell that to Simmons, and I told the lieutenant so.

"No idea who was in the ape suit?" Romero's prone to changing the subject without warning. His way of tripping people up.

"What? No! How would I—"

"Did Simmons recognize him?"

"No," I said, while thinking: Maybe.

"Shooter took off the costume outside. Big furry pile out back, between two parked cars. Probably had a ride waiting. He peels off the ape suit, leaves it where it falls, jumps in his car, and he's gone."

"Maybe somebody saw him out there," I offered.

"We're asking around, but not so far. You didn't go after him?"

"Shit, no. I was busy hiding. Just like everybody else in here. We didn't know who the gorilla would shoot next."

Some people muttered behind me, agreeing. Romero ignored them.

"You weren't packing?" he asked.

"You know I almost never carry a gun. Why would I bring one today? Sitting in a public place, talking to a potential client."

Romero stuck out his lower lip and tilted his head, thinking it over. He's probably never without a gun. I bet his pajamas have a holster sewn into them.

"I had no reason to think there'd be shooting," I added.

"Guess you were wrong about that, huh?"

I glanced at Simmons's covered corpse. "Guess so. Damn."

"We're going to need you to come over to headquarters. Give a full statement."

I nodded. It was what I'd expected.

"You want to meet me over there? Or do we need to give you an escort?"

"I know where your office is." I turned away to trudge toward the door.

"Hey, Bubba?"

"Yeah?"

"Go wash your face first. You've got blood all over you."

Yuck. I'd forgotten that. I must've paled at the thought of Simmons's blood freckling my face because Romero grinned.

"Sure sign of a bad day, huh?" he said.

I had a feeling it would only get worse.

Chapter 3

Outside, the winter sunlight was glaringly bright but bore little warmth. Orange sawhorses and strands of yellow tape labeled "Crime Scene—Do Not Cross" blocked Silver Avenue in front of the café, and a few uniformed officers made sure people obeyed. Thirty or forty gawkers had gathered outside the tape, and their breaths clouded the air. Reporters and photographers flocked together nearby. News vans from the local TV stations had already galloped to the scene and their satellite dishes beamed signals skyward.

I wanted nothing to do with any of it. Bad publicity would hurt business, and my business was no great shakes already. Word would get out; there was no stopping it. I'd be named in investigative reports, and the news media would glom on. But I didn't need to cooperate in my own ruination.

Trying to avoid the reporters, I ducked under the tape and nearly ran right into my own wife.

Felicia somehow had wriggled her way to the front of the crowd, popping clear just as I straightened up. I don't know how she manages it. She's a relatively tiny woman. She doesn't look fierce. She wears oversized glasses and her straight dark hair often hangs in her face. Yet she gets people to bend to her will, or get out of her way. I sometimes wonder if she slips through crowds by jabbing butts with her ballpoint.

"Bubba, we need to talk."

"Not here," I said. "Not now."

She had her notebook and a pen in her hands. I flinched, anticipating that she might jab me, too.

"What's all over your shirt?"

"Blood."

When, oh when, will I learn to keep my freaking mouth shut? Uttering that one word, "blood," caused the curious crowd to gasp and press closer, everybody trying to get a gander at the gore. Worse yet, it proved to Felicia that I was definitely involved in the tragic homicide or, as she would put it, "the big story."

Pen poised, she said, "What happened in there, Bubba?"

There was no escape. The crowd had closed around us. Suddenly, a young blond woman squirted between two whiskered loiterers and sided with Felicia.

"Did you say 'Bubba?'" she squealed. "This must be your husband! The private eye!"

She thrust her hand out. I took it automatically and gave it my usual one-pump handshake. She didn't seem in any hurry to let go. She looked me up and down, a big smile on her face. She had the best teeth money could buy. They were so white, it hurt to look at her.

She was maybe twenty years old, slender and tan and perky as all hell. Her blond hair was wrapped around her head in some kind of a work-intensive hairdo, what I think they call a French twist. She wore a navy blue business suit with a close-fitting, knee-length skirt, like something Audrey Hepburn would've worn in the movies. High heels, too, which made her about five inches taller than Felicia, who was dressed in her usual reporter garb: jeans and sneakers and a jacket with lots of bulging pockets.

"Felicia's told me all about you!" the blonde gushed, and I could only imagine how that conversation might've gone.

I know better than to hold hands with a lovely young woman, especially when my wife is watching. As I pried my hand loose, Felicia made a show of rolling her eyes.

"Who's this?" I asked.

Felicia opened her mouth to answer, and I anticipated sarcasm, but the youngster spoke up first.

"Julie Keen," she chirped. "I'm an intern at the Gazette. I'm following Felicia around, learning the business."

Oh, shit. This is the one. Felicia had bitched about her for three weeks. Julie Keen was in the journalism department at UNM, which had a program where students were assigned to shadow reporters as part of their training. This was the first time anyone dared stick my sweetie with an intern. Felicia figured she was being punished for something, which wouldn't have surprised me one bit. My strong-willed wife can be hard to get along with, just living under the same roof as more-or-less equals. I can't imagine what it must be like to be her boss.

"So that's real blood on your clothes?" Julie dug in her suitcase-like handbag and came up with a pen.

Felicia said flatly, "No, it's fake blood. He just does that to get attention."

Julie blinked at her, looking puzzled.

I was getting more anxious by the second. I didn't want Romero to catch me out here, talking to not one—but two—reporters, before I'd been officially interrogated at headquarters.

I tried to sidestep them, but Felicia cut me off.

"Who got killed, Bubba?"

I quickly told her the basics—victim's name, the ape, the gun, the resulting chaos. She furiously scribbled it all down. Beside her, the intern did the same.

I didn't give them anything they couldn't easily get from the police. I didn't tell them that Simmons suspected malfeasance inside the zoo. I didn't say the cops had already found the gorilla suit. I sure as hell didn't mention the envelope I'd concealed from Romero, the one currently burning a hole in my pocket.

"Hey!" A man's deep voice erupted behind me.

I turned to see a lacquered TV reporter fighting his way through the crowd, a pony-tailed cameraman hard on his heels. Apparently, they'd spotted me being interviewed and wanted a piece of the action. The reporter had a microphone in his hand, ready to thrust it into my face as soon as he was close enough.

"Gotta go now," I said to Felicia.

"Right," she said. "Follow me."

She turned and elbowed people out of her way. The crowd tried to close behind her, but I stuck tight to my baby's back. Behind me, Julie Keen pushed and pouted her way through the rubberneckers.

As soon as we broke free, I hurried to my car, which was parked at a curbside meter half a block away. Felicia and her intern followed.

"I've got to get over to the cop shop," I said over my shoulder. "Romero's orders."

"Okay," Felicia said. "I'll call your cell later, fill in any gaps in my story."

I made a mental note to not answer my phone for the next few hours. The less mention I got in Felicia's article, the better.

"Nice to meet you!" Julie tweeted.

I climbed behind the wheel and cranked the starter a couple of times before the engine caught. Spun the wheel and did a U-turn to avoid the blockage in the street.

I'm driving a ten-year-old Cutlass these days. I had a great truck, a big red Dodge Ram, but it got wiped out in a wreck on a snowy street back around Christmas. The insurance money hadn't gone as far as I'd expected, so a used Oldsmobile was the best I could do. I'd picked the most anonymous car possible, better for surveillance work. It was in pretty good shape—though its gray paint was sun-bleached in spots—and it had a big V-8 under the hood. The engine was a little temperamental when cold, but it was a barn-burner once it got going.

I could've strolled over to police headquarters. Would've been a nice walk in the crisp winter air. But I wanted the car nearby for later, and I needed to hide the envelope Simmons had given me. I didn't expect to be searched at the cop shop, but you never know. I might say the wrong thing and end up under arrest. It's happened before.

The four-story cop shop sits on Roma Avenue, diagonally across the concrete expanse of Civic Plaza from the pointy high-rises that dominate Albuquerque's skyline. Signs said the underground parking garage below the plaza was full, so I circled the block four or five times until I finally spotted a space by a meter. Did a nice job of parallel parking, bumping the truck behind me only twice. I shut off my engine and looked all around to make sure the coast was clear before I fished the envelope out of my pocket and hid it in the glove compartment.

I leaned toward my mirror and checked my hangdog face to make sure I hadn't missed any specks of blood when I washed up in the Flying Squirrel restroom. Slicked back my thinning brown hair with my hand. Checked my teeth. The modern private eye, groomed and ready for anything.

I locked up the car, and put my every nickel of loose change into the parking meter. Then I zipped up my dappled jacket and walked to headquarters, more or less ready for interrogation.

Keep it simple, I told myself as I went up the broad front steps. Keep it brief. Don't mention the envelope or the reporters. Stick to the story you told Romero at the café. And, if things take a wrong turn, lie your ass off.

Chapter 4

Four hours later, Romero finally sprang me. My ears rang from all the questions and my butt ached from sitting on a hard chair and my brain hurt from trying to keep everything straight as the cops made me tell the story again and again. But I was free now, and glad to breathe the cold night air.

A parking ticket fluttered under the windshield wiper of the Olds. Bound to happen this close to headquarters. The cop probably made his quota during his cigarette break.

Muttering curses, I ripped the ticket off the windshield, unlocked the Olds, and climbed inside. I put the ticket in the glove compartment and Jeff Simmons's envelope back in my pocket.

Took a few tries to start the car, but once it caught, I revved the engine to warm up the heater. Cold air blew on my ankles. I sighed and steered the car out of its parking spot.

I was halfway home before I thought to check the messages on my cell phone. I try not to use the phone while driving; I've already got more than my share of everyday risk. But there wasn't much traffic at this hour on a weeknight, so I took my chances.

I punched buttons until I got the little lighted window that showed the calls I'd missed. They lined up in a nice, even column: "Felicia. Felicia. Felicia. Felicia. Felicia."

Shit. I'd hear about that later. But surely she'd understand why I'd turned off my phone's ringer during my interviews with the police. I couldn't just say to Romero, "Hang on a minute, Lieutenant. I've got a call." His answer would be: "Can you hear me whapping you upside the head now? Good!"

More messages waited on my answering machine at home. A couple from Felicia, both along the lines of, "Maybe you didn't get my earlier messages on your cell. Maybe you're at this number now. Maybe you'd better call me if you want to stay married." Like that.

The other message was from Marvin Pidgeon, a lawyer for whom I'd done a lot of work lately. Pidgeon was a slip-and-fall specialist, suing corporations and government entities on behalf of clients who'd suffered life-threatening, career-ending injuries by tripping over a sidewalk crack or slipping on a freshly waxed floor. At least that was Marv's version. The way I saw it was that Marvin and his clients were committing insurance fraud, and I was abetting them. But, hell, the work mostly consisted of taking photographs of sidewalks and helping half-wits prepare for interviews, so it was light duty. It paid okay. And no apes had shot anybody in my vicinity over a slip-and-fall.

Marvin apparently was hot after a new case because he sounded excited on his phone message and instructed me to call him immediately. I made a mental note to get right on that. Soon as I drank a beer or two to wash the taste of the cop shop out of my mouth.

I cracked open a Heineken, flopped into a chair, and leaned my elbows on the kitchen table. I was beat. It's exhausting, running around in circles with Romero nipping at your heels. I took a few slugs of beer, then stripped off my jacket and hung it over the back of my chair.

Jeff Simmons's envelope jutted up from the inside pocket. I slid it out and set it on the table before me.

The envelope was still sealed, blank front and back except for the blood spatters, and I was tempted to throw it away. Wasn't like there was anything inside that envelope for me. Simmons had never been my client. He'd been a potential client, one who hadn't even given me a retainer before the gorilla croaked him. No reason in the world for me to get further involved.

I tore it open. Inside was a sheaf of computer printouts. I unfolded the six pages and spread them flat on the table. Columns and rows of numbers and letters swam before my eyes. Crap, I didn't need this.

Two beers later, the spreadsheets started to make sense. Down the pages' left side were the names of animals—"black lemur" or "collared lizard" or "three-toed sloth"—each followed by its Latin name, then a six-digit number that I took to be some kind of an identification code. Then these columns: Birth date. Date of death. Date of necropsy. Cause of death. Under "Disposal," all of them were labeled "C," which I took to mean "cremated."

According to the numbers, the zoo lost three or four animals, on average, every week. That didn't seem particularly high to me. Hell, everything dies. And we're talking exotic animals here, ones far away from their native climates. They're probably susceptible to a wide range of diseases. And it would be easy to make mistakes. Somebody supplies the wrong food or sets the thermostat for the wrong temperature, and you've got another dead critter. But the last sheet of numbers Simmons included was a comparison with other zoos, and it showed that others—even much larger ones—had better rates of survival.

Somebody was doing a lousy job of keeping our animals alive, or something sinister was going on at the zoo. Either way, it was the kind of thing Felicia would be great at uncovering, but I couldn't see myself handing these numbers over to her. Simmons had entrusted the papers to me. Maybe he had good reasons to hire a private eye rather than going to the media with his findings.

The doorbell rang, startling me. I grabbed up the papers to hide them from Felicia before I caught myself. Felicia wouldn't ring the damned doorbell. I told myself to calm down. I stacked the papers neatly, tucked them behind some canisters on the kitchen counter. Then I walked through the living room to the front door.

I expected reporters, maybe the same TV vermin I'd escaped outside the Flying Squirrel. Or cops, ready to haul me in for more questioning. Maybe even Marvin Pidgeon, clamoring for me to run out and investigate a sidewalk.

The last thing I expected was a new client. Naturally, that's what I got.

Chapter 5

Clearly, she'd been crying. She had eyes as large and brown as a spaniel's, but they were bloodshot and her eyelids were puffy. Her nose glowed red and her lips looked swollen. Despite all that, she was beautiful. Lean and leggy and young. Coppery skin. Glossy black hair that fell past her shoulders. She wore snug black jeans and a denim jacket studded with silver stars.

"Bubba Mabry?"

I couldn't deny it, though the look of her, those recent tears, made me cringe. "Yeah?"

"I need to talk to you."

I'd only opened the door partway, in case the dinnertime caller had been shooting news video or selling Fuller brushes or pushing Jesus. I was tempted to shut it in her sad face, just as I'd been tempted to get rid of Simmons's envelope, and for the same reason. I didn't need more problems. Sure, other people's problems are my business, but I felt full up at the moment.

Registering my hesitation, she said, "My name's Loretta Gonzales. I'm Jeff Simmons's fiancée."

The last word caught in her throat and her eyes flooded. Damn. I'm no good at saying "no" to a weeping woman.

"Won't you come in?"

I didn't want her to see the mess in my office, so I led her across the living room to our battered corduroy sofa. We sat at opposite ends, turned so we more or less faced each other. She took a ragged tissue from her leather purse and dabbed at her eyes.

"Sorry," she said. "I'm still shook up."

"You're probably in shock. You should be home, resting."

"I'll never rest until I know why Jeff was killed."

Oh, hell. Here we go.

"The police are pursuing every—"

She cut me off, shaking her head. "They won't tell me anything. They asked a bunch of questions, but said they could only give out information to next of kin. Since Jeff and I weren't married yet—"

She broke down, sobbing into her hands. I fetched a box of Kleenex from an end table and handed it over. She pulled tissues from it, wiped her face, and took shuddering breaths, trying to get herself under control.

Hysterics I don't need. I mean, she had every right to grieve. Love of her life gunned down by a gorilla, et cetera, et cetera. But she should do this at home. What did she want from me?

"I need to hear," she said between gulps, "exactly what happened."

So I told her. I kept it quick and clinical. No embellishment, little detail. She didn't need to know about the mystery envelope or how I'd ducked for cover or how surprised her fiancé had looked to be dead.

By the time I was done, she'd gotten hold of herself. She nodded and said, "Thank you."

"Sure."

I cleared my throat and scooted forward on the sofa and slapped my hands on my knees, as if preparing to stand. All the subtle signals that it was time for her to go. But she just sat there, studying me.

"Do you know why Jeff approached you?"

"Not really," I said. "Something going on at the zoo—"

"I work at the zoo, too. That's how we met. We're really not supposed to date our colleagues, but we'd been seeing each other on the sly for more than a year. We hadn't announced yet that we were getting married, but we were thinking about having the ceremony right there at the zoo."

I nodded and sighed. Couldn't she take a hint? I didn't want to tell her to hit the bricks, but I was tired of talking about Jeff Simmons. I was tired, period. And I hadn't eaten since lunch. And the beers had gone straight to my head.

"I know about Jeff's suspicions," she said. "About the mysterious deaths."

That surprised me, but I tried not to let it show. Naturally, he'd told her. They both worked at the zoo. They were engaged, still at that stage of the relationship where they tell each other everything.

"I didn't actually mention all that to the cops," I said. "I told them he'd contacted me because of some possible misconduct at the zoo, but he really hadn't given me the details before the, um, shooting occurred."

"But that's the reason," she said. "That's why Jeff was shot. Somebody wanted to stop him before he could tell anybody."

Okay, I'd considered that. I'm sure that was one avenue of investigation being pursued by Romero. But people get killed for lots of reasons. It didn't necessarily follow that Simmons was onto something so significant at the zoo as to merit a homicide. Of course his girlfriend would think so. She'd make him out to be a crusader, a martyr even, given half a chance. But I didn't see how it had anything to do with me.

"You came highly recommended," she said. "That's what Jeff told me."

I couldn't imagine who might've made such a recommendation. I have a few satisfied clients, sure, but my reputation's not exactly sterling. Before I could ask her who'd referred Simmons, she hit me with this: "I'd like to hire you. Just as Jeff was going to do."

Whoa. Took me a second to get my head around that.

"Look, I understand you're upset right now," I said. "But I don't know that I can do you any good. I was telling your boyfriend the same thing when the, um, ape came into the Flying Squirrel today. This just isn't my cup of—"

"If you were good enough for Jeff, then you're good enough for me. I believe what he said. Somebody must investigate the zoo. If we find out what secret's being covered up, then we'll find out who killed him."

"Not necessarily—"

"Why else would someone shoot him?"

Tears welled up in her eyes again. Aw, hell.

"But it's a police matter now," I said. "They don't appreciate private investigators nosing around in homicide cases."

She straightened her spine, looked me right in the eye.

"I've got a good feeling about you, Mr. Mabry. I'm sure you can find a way."

"But—"

"Please. I need this. I need you to help me."

"It could get expensive, you know. I don't exactly come cheap, and who knows how long—"

"Money's no object," she said, a phrase I found startling and splendid and enviable, all at the same time. I wondered how it would feel to be able to say that, just once in my life.

"My family's very wealthy. Have you heard of ArGon Foods?"

I nodded. Who in New Mexico hadn't heard of ArGon? It was one of the biggest employers in Albuquerque, with huge factories producing salsa and tortillas and frozen green chile and refried beans. Probably every fridge in town was stocked with ArGon products.

"ArGon was started by my dad, Armando Gonzales. My sister and I own pieces of the company."

Holy guacamole. This lovely young lady, in her denim and grief, was likely worth more than I'll ever make in my whole life.

"Excuse me for asking, but if you're part of that Gonzales family, what the heck are you doing, working at the zoo?"

"I love animals, especially the big cats. When I was a little girl, I went to the zoo every weekend. It's what I've always wanted to do. I'm still at UNM part-time, earning my master's degree in biology. But I'd be perfectly happy working at the zoo forever."

"But isn't it hard work? I mean, what do they have you doing, throwing steaks to the leopards, stuff like that?"

"How's that any different from throwing tortillas to the masses?"

One pays a helluva lot better than the other, but I didn't say that. My brain was busy, trying to accept the idea that I could tear off a little piece of the ArGon fortune for myself, if I were willing to go sniffing around the zoo.

"All right, I'll do it. But I can't guarantee results. I don't have much to go on. Your fiancé gave me some numbers about the dead animals. I didn't give them to the cops. In fact, I was looking them over when you rang the bell. But there's not much there that will help me. I deal in people, not numbers. I need to know who might be behind those animal deaths and why they would try to cover them up. I told this to Jeff. He said he had suspects, but he, um, didn't have time to give me any names—"

She teared up again. Jeez. How to talk about this without coming back, again and again, to the fact that her boyfriend had been blown away?

"I can give you names," she said, her voice quavering. "I know everyone there."

"But what will that tell me? Do you know who Jeff suspected?"

She shook her head.

"He wouldn't talk about that part. He said it might be dangerous." She took a deep breath. "Clearly, he was right. I know he thought the necropsy results were being manipulated in some way. So that would mean Buck Tedeski. He's the head veterinarian at the zoo. Does all the necropsies."

I fetched a pen and pad from a drawer in the end table, asked her how to spell "Tedeski."

"Then there's Noah Gibbons. His title is curator of mammals, but he's really like the number two guy at the zoo."

"Who's number one?"

"Carolyn Hoff's the director, but she doesn't have much to do with the day-to-day care of the exhibits. She's administration, you know? A paper-pusher."

"Okay." I wrote Hoff's name down anyway.

"Most of the suspicious deaths were mammals," Loretta said. "That's why I'd put Gibbons near the top of the list."

"There were some reptiles, too," I said, remembering the "collared lizard" and "albino rattlesnake" from the list.

"Perry Oswalt is curator of reptiles and amphibians. I can't see Perry involved in something like this, but you should check him out, I guess."

"Who else?"

"Jeff mentioned something about Cristina Tapia at one point, but I don't know if he really thought she might be involved. She's director of outreach, which is a nice way of saying she's in charge of volunteers and public relations at the zoo. If there's some kind of monkey business going on, Cristina would be the first to try to cover it up."

I wrote down Tapia's name. Hell, at this point, everybody was a suspect.

"If you're going to look at Cristina," she said, "then you might as well check Jim Johansen, too."

"Jungle Jim, the guy who's on TV all the time?"

Johansen was the public face of the zoo, a handsome, tanned guy who decked himself out in safari garb. He regularly appeared on local television shows, talking up exhibits, bringing live parrots and snakes and baby crocodiles from the zoo, sometimes scaring the toupees right off the news anchors.

"Jim has the run of the place," Loretta said. "He's been at the zoo for decades, and he probably knows where all the skeletons are buried."

Her turn of phrase caused a thought to flash through my mind: The skeletons of all those dead animals, all those unfamiliar shapes and structures. What the hell did a lemur's skeleton look like, for instance? Or a fruit bat's? Were the bones all burned up in the crematorium? Were they put on display somewhere?

While I was off thinking those morbid thoughts, Loretta was saying, "That ought to be enough to get you started."

She got out her checkbook. I always love this part of the investigator/client relationship.

"Would two thousand dollars be enough to get you started?"

Two thousand? That was four times what I would've asked for. I nodded, tried to keep from giggling. The poor girl was in mourning, after all. I felt bad for the late Jeff Simmons, too, but I was feeling better about my bank account by the second.

I made a lot of reassuring noises about how I'd get right on the job while I pocketed the check and walked Loretta to the door. Went to shake her hand, but she leaned in to me and gave me a trusting hug. Her sweet-smelling hair pressed against my nose as I awkwardly returned the embrace. When she stepped back, her eyes were wet again.

"You gonna be okay driving home?" I asked.

She nodded. "Thank you. Thanks for everything. My cell phone number's on the check. Call me as soon as you know anything."

I pledged that I would, and she went out the door. I followed her onto the porch, watched her drive a sleek Lexus into the night.

The check was enough to earn my loyalty. But that hug was an expression of her faith in me, her new hero. I'd need to do a good job to merit that trust.

Damn.

Chapter 6

9 went to the kitchen and stared into the open refrigerator in hope that something tasty would jump out and hit me in the mouth. Never works, but I always try it. After two minutes, I gave up and pulled out bread and sliced roast beef and mustard so I could assemble a sandwich to soak up the beer I'd been drinking.

I arranged everything (including a fresh beer) on the kitchen counter, but got no further before I heard the front door whoosh open and the thud of my sweetie's sneakers on the hardwood floor.

"Jesus Christ on a bicycle!" Felicia shouted demurely. "What a shitty day!"

This is my wife's version of the traditional "Hon-eee! I'm ho-o-ome!"

I went to the living room to greet her, grinning over the big check in my pocket. No matter how bad her day was, two thousand bucks ought to cheer her right up.

"There you are!" she shouted. "I've been calling and calling."

"Yeah, I know—"

"You got my messages?"

"Sure, but I—"

"Then why the hell didn't you call me?"

"Well, I was with the cops—"

She flailed her arms around the living room. "Cops? I don't see any cops. If they've kept you from calling, they must be here somewhere. Are they in the kitchen?"

No one truly enjoys being on the receiving end of sarcasm, but this wasn't the time to mention that to Felicia.

"I just got home a few minutes ago—"

"What about your cell phone? Don't you still have a cell?"

There's no arguing with her when she gets like this. I shut up, prepared to wait her out.

"See, Bubba, there was a reason I kept phoning. It's called a deadline. You might've heard of it. I know you don't have them in your business, but, hey, it's different in the newspaper game. Every day, we put out a whole new product. The paper's full of stories. I write those stories. To do that, I need fresh information. And to think my own husband has that information and won't cough it up—"

She stopped to glare at me, her hands on her hips. Uh-oh.

"What the hell are you smiling about?"

"Who, me?"

"Yes, you. I'm chewing your ass out here, and it takes all the fun out of it for you to stand there, grinning like an idiot. What is it?"

"Nothing." I tried to wipe the smile off my face, but it was difficult. "Go ahead. Finish chewing."

She narrowed her eyes. "What's the matter with you?"

I couldn't contain myself any longer. I fished the two-thousand-dollar check out of my pocket and handed it over.

A confession: I live for these moments. My business is rarely what you'd call lucrative. Much of the time, I can barely justify continuing. There's always subtle pressure to chuck it all and get some kind of a real job. I like being my own boss, but Felicia thinks I'm not motivated enough to be successful. This usually comes up when she finds me snoozing on the sofa in front of *Oprah*. I've tried to explain that the private eye biz is cyclical. At times, there's nothing going on and no money coming in. Other times, I'm hardly home at all because I'm so busy doing surveillance and interviewing witnesses and taking pictures of sidewalks.

Once in a while, I score big. At those times, I have to lord it over Felicia a little. I can't help myself.

She looked at the check. Handed it back to me, unfazed.

"Yeah? So?"

"Big retainer," I said. "More where that came from."

"Who's Loretta Gonzales?"

"My new client. A very wealthy young woman. Her family owns ArGon Foods."

"Why's she retaining you?"

"She's Jeff Simmons's fiancée. She wants me to find his killer."

That pulled Felicia up short. Hee-hee.

"Doesn't she know the police do that job for free?"

"She doesn't trust them. Plus, she thinks the ape bumped off Simmons because he was about to tell me about some kind of scandal at the zoo."

Her eyes lit up. "A scandal? Like what?"

"I can't say."

"Horseshit." She took a menacing step toward me. "You'd better spill it."

I'm eight inches taller than Felicia and at least fifty pounds heavier, but when she gets that look in her eyes, I get a chill down to my socks. It's not that I'm afraid of my wife, exactly. Let's just say that pissing her off reaches a point of diminishing returns in a hurry. I make her mad, and I hear about it for days. Some women, when they get angry, give their husbands the silent treatment. I should be so lucky.

"Okay, okay." It was past her deadline now. Too late to get it into tomorrow morning's newspaper. Maybe, by the time she could get it confirmed and in print, there'd be no need for secrecy.

I told her about Simmons's dead zoo animals and the numbers being off and the comparisons with other zoos around the country.

"Wait a minute," she interrupted. "You think the ape killed this guy because he knew something about dead lions, tigers, and bears, oh my?"

"Not exactly. We're not talking about the big, popular animals like that—"

"Bubba. Have you lost your mind?"

"Huh?"

"If somebody's got something to hide at the zoo, they're not about to kill Jeff Simmons in a such a public place. You don't cover up a secret by generating front-page headlines."

When she put it like that, it didn't make much sense that someone would snuff Simmons to keep him from blowing the whistle. But it was all I had so far.

"My client thinks that's why her boyfriend was killed."

"Yeah," Felicia snorted. "And she's thinking real clearly at the moment."

Okay, she had a point there, but I couldn't concede the argument.

"It's possible," I protested. "Why else would somebody kill him?"

"For any of the hundred reasons people kill each other. He pissed somebody off. He stole from somebody. He's cheating on his girlfriend. Hell, Bubba, maybe your client bumped him off herself. No reason to think it had to be a man in that monkey suit, right?"

Yipes. I hadn't considered that. But why would Loretta—

"Maybe Simmons owed somebody money," Felicia continued. "Maybe his drug dealer was inside the ape suit. Maybe Simmons was a spy, and Homeland Security hired a gorilla to get rid of him."

I rolled my eyes.

"Hey," she said. "Makes as much sense as saying dead animals at the zoo led to a dead guy in a café."

"I looked at the numbers. There's definitely something screwy going on at the zoo."

"Yeah? Show me."

Uh-oh. I thought of Simmons's sheets of data, tucked away in the kitchen. Could I hand them over to her? Wouldn't she scurry right back to the newspaper and put them in print for all the world to see?

"I can't do that," I said. "But if I prove it, you'll be the first to know."

She pushed up her glasses and looked me up and down. I tried not to squirm.

"Fine," she said. "Frankly, I'm too bushed to have this argument anyway. Worked my ass off today, that little intern yapping along behind me the whole time."

Ah, a diversion. I said, "Boy, she seemed like a pain."

"You have no idea. She never, and I mean never, shuts up, not even for a second. I'm trying to work, trying to get information out of people, and I've got her barging in and asking questions and derailing my train of thought."

"Tell her to hush."

"Believe me, I have. Nothing fazes her."

"Can't you shake her? Sic her on somebody else?"

"Not so far." Felicia got a glint in her eyes. "But I just got an idea about a way to get rid of her. I'll try it tomorrow."

"Good. Maybe that'll make you feel better."

I ventured closer, put out my arms for a hug. She stepped into my embrace and I gave her a squeeze.

"You want some dinner?" I said to the top of her head. "I was just making a sandwich."

"I'm too tired to eat. Maybe a hot shower."

"That would help. Wash away your bad day."

She leaned back and looked up at me, her hands at my waist.

"You just want me in a better mood," she said. "You're hoping I'll forget about how you didn't return my calls all day."

"Now, hon, I—"

She grabbed a couple inches of fat at my waist and gave it a vicious pinch.

"Yee-ouch."

"You'd better think twice next time," she said as she let me loose. "I don't believe your investigation will turn up anything, but if it does, you'd better run to the nearest phone and alert me. You hear?"

"Yes, dear." Always the right answer.

She stomped off to the bathroom. I rubbed at the newly sore spot at my waist. Soon as I heard water running, I hustled to the kitchen and retrieved Simmons's documents. Folded them up and hid them in my pocket. They weren't much, but they were all I had.

I couldn't let Felicia take them away from me.

Chapter 7

It had been a few years since I last visited our local zoo. It's a good one, modern and clean, or at least I'd always thought so. But when I went there Tuesday morning, it was to uncover dirt, to search for cruel secrets.

The official name is the Zoo In Albuquerque, but everybody calls it either "the zoo" or by its initials, "ZIA." Half the stuff in New Mexico is named Zia or decorated with the zia symbol, which is a sun sign we stole from the Native Americans. Looks like a circle with fork tines sticking out of it in four directions. Our state flag features a red zia on a bright yellow background, and our license plates look the same. You can find zia symbols on the KiMo Theatre downtown and on guardrails along Interstate 40 and on trinkets in the tourist traps in Old Town. It's freaking everywhere. Naturally, it looms large over the entrance to the Zoo In Albuquerque.

The real sun was halfway up the sky by the time I arrived, but it still was too chilly for many people to be outdoors admiring the exhibits. Albuquerque usually gets a false spring in February, a couple weeks of sunshine and warm temperatures that trick trees into budding and flowers into bloom. Then March blows in, frosting everything in ice, resulting in an unofficial fifth season we call the Time of the Frozen Daffodils. This year's warm spell was another week or two away, and for now we still suffered the kind of cold, dry weather that makes you apply chapstick six times a day. I zipped up my twenty-year-old leather jacket, and shoved my hands in the pockets while I roamed the zoo, re-familiarizing myself with the place.

First thing you encounter at the zoo is the low-slung, anonymous administrative building, which sits to the left of the main entrance. Most zoo visitors probably never even notice the dung-colored offices. They're too busy lining up at the glass-walled ticket booths at the main gate. Once you buy a ticket, you pass through chrome turnstiles and then you're inside the zoo's wild world.

Broad sidewalks lead past a gift shop and a shallow pond surrounded by stands of bamboo. Normally, the pond's full of pink flamingos, the zoo's living lawn ornaments. But they must put them someplace warmer in the winter because the flamingos were nowhere to be seen.

Just ahead, the concrete pathway forked. One sidewalk went to a building that holds the Tropical Rain Forest exhibit, and beyond to the birds and the reptiles and other small animals. The other fork trooped off past a small lake and a winter-bleached meadow to large enclosures where they keep the big cats and the camels and the dusty elephants and the splashing seals.

I skirted the Tropical Rain Forest building. It would be warm in there, but I preferred the chilly outdoors today. Besides, the exhibit's dense foliage and squawking birds give me the heebie-jeebies. I watched too many jungle movies when I was a kid. Even though there was absolutely no chance there'd be a snake or a tiger or a monkey loose inside that building, I still feared that some beast could be hiding in the trees, waiting to pounce. If nothing else, the free-flying birds lived to poop on whoever dared to pass. If they were waiting on me, they'd just have to hold it.

Not much to keep a person entertained at the zoo during the cold months. The giant tortoises wouldn't come out of their shells. Pheasants and parrots hunkered in their nesting boxes. Even the furry animals were curled up against the cold, sleeping.

I could've entered the reptile house, which was always kept a comfortable temperature, but I try to avoid snakes. I got my fill during my youth in Mississippi, where there are poisonous vipers every ten feet or so and walking through the piney woods is an exercise in twitchy wariness. One nice thing about living in a city is you don't have to always watch your feet. Sure, you might step in something nasty, especially if there are pets nearby, but it's not likely to kill you.

There are very few cages at the Zoo In Albuquerque. Most enclosures are designed to look as natural as possible, with lots of shrubs and vines and gnarly cottonwoods. Walls are constructed of big fake boulders formed of gray concrete or tan stucco. In the big cat area, where Loretta Gonzales worked, humans walk on a skyway, looking down on the lions and cheetahs that snooze in the dirt below. The path's only ten or twelve feet above the ground, which made me curious about how high a cheetah could jump. Other snoozing big cats were behind fences made of heavy wire. The fences bore signs warning against sticking your fingers through the mesh. I wondered how many idiots ignored those signs and ended up being called "Stumpy."

At enclosures holding animals on the verge of extinction, zookeepers had posted silver signs with black letters that said ominously, "Vanishing …" I thought about Jeff Simmons's suspicions. Some animals were vanishing, all right, but perhaps not for the reasons we'd thought.

I wandered around until lunchtime, then ate a "ZiaBurger" at the zoo café, which sat near the duck-dotted lake. The diner was pretty empty, like the rest of the zoo on this wintry day, and before long I was back out among the animals, finishing my tour.

The walkways through the zoo connect in big loops, so it's possible to see every exhibit without covering the same ground twice. The last section before you're back at the main gate is devoted to everybody's favorites, the primates. Monkeys and chimps and gorillas and orangutans, all hominoid and active and disgusting.

I can't stand them. I know they're supposed to be the stars of the show, but monkeys—or apes of any kind—give me the creeps. Those furry fingers, those grasping hands, those frank stares. Brrr.

I trace this aversion to a traumatic childhood experience. When I was eight years old, my mother took me to the zoo in

Jackson, Mississippi. The zoo was supposed to be the highlight of our trip to the capital, but it turned out badly because of some goddamned monkeys.

I think they were spider monkeys, but I can't be sure now. Some kind of black hairy things with outrageously long arms and sour faces. A family of them cavorted in a cylindrical cage, and the little baby monkey was just about the cutest thing anybody had ever seen, so naturally the laughing crowd was thick as flies. I wriggled my way to the front so I could see, pressed up against a rail that was chin-high to me, only six or eight feet from the smelly monkeys.

People threw peanuts through the bars, and the monkeys snatched them up and pushed them between their long, hairy lips. Even the baby monkey got in on the action, chewing and staring unblinkingly at the humans all around.

Attracted by the peanuts, a few sparrows flitted about the cage; the bars were spaced far enough apart that the dusky birds could zoom between them like fighter jets. One sparrow hit the deck and pecked up a peanut. Quick as a flash, the largest monkey snaked out his long arm and grabbed the bird. Before the sparrow could even squirm, Daddy Monkey twisted its little head. The snap of its neck was audible to all.

The humans gasped. The other monkeys shrieked with delight. I projectile-vomited all the popcorn and cotton candy and other junk I'd consumed that day, all over the rail, my shirt, my shoes.

That really got the monkeys to howling. The horrified audience scurried away, their day at the zoo ruined.

Daddy Monkey gnawed on the dead bird. I witnessed that through tear-filled eyes, and it set off a whole 'nother round of puking. By the time I was done spewing, I never wanted to see another monkey the rest of my days.

The primate path at ZIA goes a long way, curving past the large habitats, and I hurried along, hunkered in my jacket, barely glancing over at the glaring apes, which were separated from the humans by fences and empty moats. Those damned primates were liable to do something disgusting, involving genitals or tongues or excretion, and who needs it, you know? I see enough yucky displays from winos and hookers in the red-light district along East Central Avenue. I don't need to watch apes do the same.

Back at the main gate, I decided my tour had confirmed my initial suspicion: Everything important at the zoo goes on behind the exhibits. The public's so busy oohing over the animals, we never think about the effort it takes to present them. Once you start paying attention, though, you notice gates and driveways and little paths that dead-end at blank, locked doors. Much of the year, these service entrances are hidden by foliage, but they're quite visible in winter. I'd kept note of them as I walked among the exhibits, with the growing knowledge that I needed to get into that behind-the-scenes world. Whatever Simmons had stumbled across, it happened back there. That's where the secrets were kept.

But how to gain access? Backstage was strictly off-limits to the public. I needed an ally, somebody who had the clout to give me carte blanche to wander.

I tugged at my jacket and ran a hand through my breeze-jumbled hair, getting presentable. Then I took a deep breath and entered the zoo's administrative offices.

The warm reception area was just like your average doctor's office—chairs and tables spaced around the carpeted room, a gum-chewing receptionist behind a desk. But no sick people, actually, no one waiting at all. And the aquarium built into one wall was much larger and more exotic than anything your doctor might offer. All the magazines had wild animals on the covers.

I approached the bleached-blond receptionist and waited for her to notice me. Then I handed her a business card and asked to see zoo director Carolyn Hoff.

Why not go straight to the top? Worst the director would tell me would be "no," and I've heard that before. A lot.

Chapter 8

One look at Carolyn Hoff and I saw why Jungle Jim Johansen was the public face of the zoo. Johansen was the type of rugged outdoorsman associated with sun-scorched savannas. Hoff, on the other hand, looked as if the closest she ever came to sunshine was weak fluorescent lights.

She was in her sixties, and she looked ill. Her face was pasty and wrinkled, and she was broomstick skinny, a scarecrow wearing an Anne Klein suit and clunky heels. Her hair was a copper-colored bouffant that had "wig" written all over it. Her eyebrows were painted on halfway up her forehead, which only served to accentuate the bags under her eyes, and her thin lips were a bright red, which made her teeth look yellow.

She smiled and acted interested in my arrival—though I'd shown up without an appointment or even a phone call first—and I got over my initial reaction, which was to cover my mouth and run from whatever germs were eating at her.

"A private investigator," she said, still looking at my card. "I don't think I've ever met one before."

"We're just like the ones in movies," I said. "Only less so."

That made her smile again, which gave me a little shiver, and I followed her down a corridor to her spacious office.

The office was decorated in modern, efficient style, except for an antique desk of weathered brown wood. Its corner posts were carved into lifelike monkeys standing on their hind legs, arms extended over their heads, holding up the desktop. Yeesh.

Carolyn Hoff perched on a swivel chair behind the desk, barely making a dent in the cushions. I sank into a comfy chair across from her.

"So, Mr. Private Investigator," she said, that eerie smile reappearing. "What is it I can do for you?"

I wasn't exactly prepared for this interview, since I hadn't planned it in advance. But no sense dancing around.

"I'm looking into the death of Jeff Simmons," I said. "I was with him yesterday when he was killed."

Her smile vanished. A crease above her nose pulled the painted eyebrows into a head-on collision.

"You're the one mentioned in the newspaper," she said.

"That's right."

"I didn't recognize your name."

I wondered how many "Bubbas" trooped through her office every week, but let it go. I was in here now. That's what mattered.

"Tell me," she said. "Did Jeff suffer?"

"Not more than a second or two. It was like, bang-bang, that fast. He probably didn't feel the second shot."

"That poor boy. I wonder if he even knew what was happening."

I flashed back to that moment at the Flying Squirrel. The look of alarm on Simmons's face, the way he involuntarily recoiled in the booth. He'd known something was up. Had he somehow recognized the guy in the ape suit?

"I don't know much about private investigators," Hoff said, "but I know homicides are handled by the police."

"That's right," I said. "And I don't want to do anything that might jeopardize the police investigation. I don't want to get in their way."

A passing thought: When Romero finds out I'm poking around in Simmons's death—and he will—he won't be happy. My ears twitched in anticipation of the lecture to come.

"My client believes Jeff's death had something to do with his employment here at the zoo. So I'm trying to look into that."

"Your client. Who would that be?"

"I can't say. That's where the 'private' part comes in."

"Ah." She fiddled with a letter opener on her desk. About the cleanest desk I'd ever seen, by the way. No papers sitting out. No in-and-out trays. Just a blotter and a plain cup holding a few pens and the letter opener with its carved wooden handle. If Carolyn Hoff was a paper-pusher, as Loretta said, then she kept the papers hidden away between pushes.

"Did your client say how the zoo might be involved?" She gave me a level look, and I got the message: She wouldn't tolerate any bullshit on my part. Naturally, I lied like hell.

"The client doesn't have any idea. All we know is that Jeff Simmons was meeting with me at the Flying Squirrel because he had some sort of problem here at the zoo."

The eyebrows climbed toward her hairline. The wig didn't move.

"He didn't get a chance to explain it to me. Before we got to it, the guy in the ape suit arrived and started shooting."

Carolyn Hoff absorbed that.

"I'd like to think," she said, "that if Jeff had a problem here, he would've brought it to me."

"Maybe he didn't feel it was safe."

That look again. This time, it said: "Like it was so much safer for him to talk to you." She sat back and clasped her bony fingers together. Her fingernails were painted the same bloody shade as her lipstick.

"I have to tell you, Mr. Mabry, I have only one concern here. I can't let you make the zoo look bad. Our public image is all we have going for us. People love the zoo. The politicians know this, which is how we survive the budget cuts that plague the city every few years. And the public overwhelmingly votes in favor of the bond issues that fund our construction and renovation projects."

I nodded.

"So, no matter how bad I might feel about Jeff's death, I will not—repeat, will not—let you damage our reputation. Am I making myself clear?"

"Perfectly. Nobody said the zoo killed Jeff Simmons. Someone connected to the zoo, however? That's a distinct possibility. Anytime there's a murder, co-workers are one group the police check out."

"We had police here all morning, pursuing that very thing," she said. "But as I told them, Jeff got along with everyone. Nobody held any grudges against him, as far as I know."

"Then you've got nothing to worry about. If his murder really didn't have anything to do with the zoo or your employees, then I think you'd welcome any investigation."

She said, "Hmm." Unconvinced.

"It's no secret that Jeff worked here," I said. "It was in the Gazette this morning. The sooner his murder gets solved, the sooner people stop making that connection to the zoo. Worst thing for you would be a police investigation that drags on for months with no resolution."

She dropped her hands to her lap and stared at me for a long time before she said, "I see your point. And you think, by cooperating with you, we can make this all go away faster?"

I shrugged. "Can't hurt."

The crashing eyebrows again. "It had better not."

I didn't like the threat, but I said nothing. I wasn't exactly making an ally here, as I'd hoped, but I'd gotten past the first lines of defense.

"What is it that you want?"

"Tell me about Jeff Simmons," I said. "For starters. Then, if it would be okay, I'd like to see his office. Maybe talk to some of his colleagues."

She shook her head slightly. "The police have already covered that ground."

"I'd like to see it for myself."

Again, the iron will rose in her face, and I guessed that this woman must be absolute hell to work for.

"All right," she said. "You can see his office. But I'm not authorizing you to talk to our other employees. They're busy. They don't need the interruption."

"What about Jeff? Was he always busy?"

"Always," she said. "He was a top-notch numbers cruncher. Put in a lot of long hours. Built the computer programs that we use to keep inventory around here."

"He do much with the exhibits?"

She looked puzzled. "Almost nothing. He was an office rat, not a zookeeper. There's not that much crossover between the two. The administrative side of ZIA is like any other nonprofit corporation or government agency. We've got reports to write and fundraising to do and fires to put out. The other side is more touchy-feely and public, sort of a cross between a loving farm and show business."

"But Jeff cared about the animals, right?"

She leaned forward in her chair, resting her arms on her desk. Her narrow shoulders folded up toward her ears, made me think of the wings of a bat.

"We all love animals. That's why we do this, when something else would be more lucrative. We love the public. We love bringing the two together. It's an important mission. And that's why I'm not letting anything, even a murder, screw that up."

Chapter 9

For someone who looked so unhealthy, Carolyn Hoff walked at a pretty fast clip. I followed her down a long corridor that veered off to the left beyond her office. Doors lined the corridor. Many were closed, but name tags on the walls labeled them as various employees' offices.

One thing I could tell right away about the zoo: All its decorating money went to the exhibits. The hallway and offices were unadorned, aside from the tacked-up clippings and family photos and Dilbert cartoons that decorate every cubicle in America. The floors were bare concrete. The walls were plain vanilla, and bore enough grime and scuffs to indicate it had been a long time since they'd last been painted.

In one open office, behind a cluttered desk, sat a plump young man with round glasses that were too small for his Pillsbury Doughboy face. What caught my attention was the bright green boa he had draped over his shoulders. The snake's head was turned to face him and it looked almost as if we'd interrupted them kissing. The guy saw me looking. He blushed. The snake didn't.

I glanced at the label by his door: "Perry Oswalt, Curator of Reptiles/Amphibians." One of the names Loretta mentioned. I hesitated, wanting to talk to him, but Carolyn Hoff was hot-footing it ahead of me and I had to hurry to catch up to her.

The corridor ended at a T intersection with another hall, and Hoff pulled up. She wasn't even breathing hard.

"Jeff's office is just down here to the right."

"What's that way?" I pointed to the left.

"Medical facilities. It takes a lot to keep all the animals healthy."

"Is that where the necropsies are done?"

Her eyebrows did that train-coupling thing again. She probably wondered how a goober like me even knew the word "necropsy."

"Yes," she said. "Why do you ask?"

"No reason."

Her eyes narrowed, looked as if they were being packed away in the bags under them. But after a second, she shook her head and we moved on.

Jeff Simmons's office was even more devoid of ornamentation than the rest of the administrative area. Just a desk and a chair and computers and snaking cables. Rectangular machines with blinking lights were stacked on racks behind floor-to-ceiling glass.

"Climate-controlled area," Hoff said. "We're all linked to those servers."

I nodded, pretending I knew what she was talking about.

Computer printouts were piled high on Simmons's desk. They looked similar to the ones I had in my pocket, and I itched to go through them, but Hoff wasn't giving me a minute alone. She stood just inside the door, her arms crossed, watching me so closely you'd think I was a shoplifter.

Now that I was here, I had to make it look good, so I sat in Simmons's chair and opened drawers and acted like I was looking for something. All I found were the usual office supplies and a few software manuals and lots of files that I couldn't rifle with Carolyn Hoff watching over me. I noticed that there was no photo of Loretta Gonzales displayed anywhere. I closed all the drawers and swiveled the chair around until I faced Hoff.

"Funny," I said, "but from in here, you can't even tell you're at the zoo. This could be a data processing office at an insurance office or a bank."

"It's like I told you," she said. "The functions are largely separate."

Just then, Loretta walked past in the hallway behind Carolyn Hoff. She froze when she recognized me in her boyfriend's office. Loretta was dressed all in khaki and she was wearing rubber boots that came up to her knees. Her face was puffy from crying all night, and I wondered what she was doing back at work one day after her fiancé took two deadly slugs.

Hoff caught me looking and glanced over her shoulder. "Oh, hello, Loretta. How are you today?"

"Just fine, Ms. Hoff." Loretta walked on, disappearing from the doorway before Hoff could introduce us or explain what we were doing in Simmons's office. Just as well. The chief executive seemed pretty astute. She probably would've caught on if Loretta and I started exchanging signals.

Hoff turned back to me. "One of our keepers. Loretta Gonzales. Good worker. Goes right in those pens with the big cats as if they were little kitties."

"Huh. You wouldn't catch me going into those cages. I have no desire to become lunch."

Her red lips stretched wide, and I cringed against the yellow smile. She said, "Same here."

I tried to imagine how disappointed a lion or tiger would be if scrawny Carolyn Hoff were served up for dinner. An appetizer on a toothpick.

"You about done here?" she asked.

"Not much to see, is there?"

"Like I told you. I think it will turn out that Jeff's death had nothing to do with his work here."

"Maybe so. But I'm trying to cover all the bases."

"Right." She glanced at the watch that dangled loosely on her wrist. "I really need to get back. I've got a staff meeting coming up in a few minutes."

I followed her back out into the corridor.

"Guess you'll talk to the staff about Jeff Simmons's death," I said.

"It's bound to come up. But I don't want people to wallow in it. We need to move on, take care of business around here. That's the way Jeff would've wanted it."

I nodded, thinking: Not me. When I go, I want every business in town to shut down. I want flags at half-staff. I want a national day of mourning.

I'll be lucky to get an obituary in my wife's newspaper. Maybe a handful of people will skip work to attend my graveside service. A few friends who'll miss me, and lenders I'll never pay off and enemies who'll show up just to make sure it's really me in the coffin. A depressing thought.

We were nearly back to the reception area when a big bronze guy stepped out of an office and filled the hallway. Jungle Jim Johansen, dressed all in khaki from his chukka boots up to his Aussie-style hat with one side of the brim pinned up. He was so lantern-jawed and buffed and manly, he could've been a GI Joe.

"Hiya, Carolyn," he said, his voice deep and friendly. "What's shaking?"

"Just showing this gentleman around. We're on our way out."

We stopped walking. No way to get past Johansen's wide body unless he turned sideways to let us pass. He thrust a hand out at me and took mine in a crocodilian grip. I felt sure the feeling would come back within a day or two.

"Jim Johansen," he barked. "Good to meet you."

"Bubba Mabry."

"Getting the grand tour, eh?"

"No. Just looking at Jeff Simmons's office."

That took some of the bonhomie off him. He pressed his lips together.

"Simmons, eh? Damned shame what happened to him. You a cop?"

"Private investigator."

"Is that right? What's your angle?"

"I don't have an angle. I'm just trying to—"

"Mr. Mabry was just leaving," Hoff said firmly.

"All right." Johansen tossed her his locally famous grin. "I can take a hint. Here."

He fished in one of his many pockets and came up with a business card. Handed it to me.

"If you need to talk to me, or if I can help in any way, let me know," he said. "I liked old Simmons. Mousy little guy, stuck in that computer room, but he was always decent to me."

I thanked him and assured him I'd call. Only after he'd observed me put his card in my pocket did he pivot so we could squeeze by. It was like slipping past a swinging door.

Before I got out of range, he clapped a big hand on my back, knocking the wind out of me.

"I mean it," he said. "Give me a call."

I sputtered that I would and he marched away. I trailed Hoff the rest of the way to her office, but she stopped before I could follow her inside.

"I've got that meeting now," she said, checking her watch again.

I looked around, didn't see any staff members clamoring to meet with her, but I let it ride. I'd gotten all I could out of Carolyn Hoff.

"That Jungle Jim seems like a friendly guy," I said.

"That's his job. He's paid to be our ambassador of goodwill. He hands out business cards like he's running for office."

I nodded. "Guess I'll call him and—"

"I wish you wouldn't. As I said before, my people don't know anything about Jeff's death and they're busy doing their jobs. I'd appreciate it if you didn't come nosing around here anymore."

"But he said—"

"Trust me. Jim Johansen knows damned little about anything. He certainly doesn't know anything about this. He'll just pump you for gossip, then spread it among our other employees. We don't need that."

"Jim? A gossip?"

"You have no idea." She gave me a chilling smile. "One of the many crosses I bear. Please, don't make my job any more difficult than it already is."

"That's not my intention—"

"Good day, Mr. Mabry. You can show yourself out?"

I said sure, and she went into her private office and closed the door behind her.

Not exactly the bum's rush, but close. I briefly entertained the idea of knocking on office doors, seeing who I could raise, but the gum-smacking receptionist peeked around the corner and cocked an eyebrow at me.

What could I do? I showed myself out.

Chapter 10

Zoo employees might've been real busy, as Carolyn Hoff said, but some certainly seemed willing to squeeze me into their workdays. First, there was Jungle Jim, who practically wrote his phone number on the bathroom wall for me. Then another guy came chasing after me before I reached the parking lot.

"Hey!" he shouted. "Hey, you!"

No one else around on the breezy sidewalk. Pretty clear he was talking to me.

The ferret-faced man puffed to a halt and looked me up and down, same as I was doing to him. He frowned, so I guess he didn't like what he found any more than I did.

He reeked of money, from the top of his razor-cut blond hair to the tips of his Italian loafers. He wore slacks and a blue shirt and a striped tie—nothing special—but the shirt had cufflinks, which put him into the category of sniffing dandy, as far as I was concerned. The cufflinks were gold-and-onyx beauties, shaped into a capital letter "G." His watch was gold, too; big and chunky, as if he'd strapped bullion to his wrist. He wore a trim mustache and a goatee, trying to give his pointed face some semblance of a chin, but the whiskers were blond and so closely cropped, I could barely see them.

He was about my age, late thirties, but he carried himself as if he were somehow older and more distinguished. Made me want to check my own posture.

"You're the detective?" he asked, and I recognized a trace of sneer.

I don't like the term "detective." I rarely "detect" anything. I prefer "private investigator," which offers fewer guarantees. An investigator asks questions; a detective is expected to come up with answers. Still, "detective" is better than "snoop" or "peeper" or other names I've been called, so I just said, "Yeah. Bubba Mabry. And you are?"

"Noah Gibbons. I work here."

Aha. Another one from Loretta's list. The number two man.

"Curator of mammals, right?"

I thought I'd surprise him with that one, but he nodded impatiently, as if everybody knew that.

"I'd like to talk with you," he said. "Come to my office."

He turned on his Italian heel and strutted back the way we'd come, confident that I'd follow. I almost ran for my car, just to spite him, but what the hell, I might learn something. I sauntered along, made him wait for me at the door.

We went back through the waiting room, and I figured the receptionist would report immediately to Carolyn Hoff that I'd returned. But she was busy doing her nails. Barely looked up as we passed.

We walked past the closed door of Hoff's office and went halfway down the main corridor. I waited while Gibbons unlocked his office.

As the door swung open, the office emitted a shriek that nearly scared me out of my socks.

"Relax," said Gibbons. "That's Mongo."

As if that explained anything. Gibbons went inside, but I hesitated. I wanted a look at this Mongo character before I entered. Anybody who'd scream like that as a form of greeting—

"Oh, come in and shut the door," Gibbons said. "Before he gets out."

I stepped through the door, but kept one hand on the knob, just in case. To my right, I found a monkey sitting on a forked perch that jutted up from a carpet-covered table in the corner. The pointy-eared simian wasn't leashed or caged. He squatted on the thick, leafless branch, staring at me. He was about the size of a house cat, covered with sparse, two-inch-long reddish fur. His face was pink as a newborn's. As I examined him, he yawned, showing a full set of yellow fangs.

I said, "Yikes," or something to that effect, and Gibbons said, "Christ, it's all right. He's harmless."

"Says you."

"I guess I should know. Primates are my specialty. And I've had Mongo for years."

The monkey reached a demanding hand out toward me. Those fuzzy little fingers, with their perfect black nails, made me shudder.

"He's hoping you have a grape," Gibbons said.

"No grapes here, pal," I said. "Juicy Fruit?"

Gibbons frowned. "Don't give him gum. He gets it in his hair."

I edged away from the monkey. Mongo had large brown eyes that watched me intently, as if he expected me to produce grapes out of thin air.

The guest chair faced Gibbons, but that meant I'd have the monkey behind me and I wouldn't go for that. I rearranged the chair and sat down, my back to the wall farthest from Mongo.

"Never seen a grown man so nervous around a monkey," Gibbons muttered.

"Bad history," I muttered right back.

"I understand you've been poking around the zoo today, asking questions about Jeff Simmons."

"Yeah. So?"

"Why are you snooping around?"

There's that "snoop" word. I wished he'd stuck with "detective."

"Simmons was killed yesterday," I said. "You might've heard something about that."

His face flushed with impatience. "Cute. But what does that have to do with you?"

"I've been retained to—"

"Retained by whom?"

That "whom" put me off. Wiseass.

"That's private," I said. "But my client believes Simmons was killed because he knew about something that was going on here at the zoo."

"Like what?"

"Well, I don't know that yet, do I? That's what I'm doing here."

He sat back, crossed his arms over his chest. The cufflinks glinted.

"I'm surprised Carolyn let you through the front door. If it had been up to me, I would've had Security throw you off the premises."

"And yet you chased me down in the parking lot and invited me back inside."

"Wanted to see what you were playing at," he said.

"I'm not 'playing' at anything. I'm trying to find a killer."

"That's a job for the police. I'm guessing there's some other reason for your interest. Maybe you think you can blackmail somebody, make some money off Jeff's death."

That got me sitting up straight.

"Look, I didn't seek this out. Simmons called me. He wanted help with an investigation. Before I could tell him to buzz off, some guy in an ape suit put two bullets in him. Now I've got a new client, who doesn't want anybody sweeping stuff under the rug. She wants to make sure Simmons didn't die in vain—"

"*She?*"

"What?"

"You said 'she.' So your client's a woman?"

"I said nothing of the kind. You must've misunderstood me."

Gibbons's face glowed as he smiled at me. His undersized teeth looked as if they'd been capped.

"You said it. You let it slip. You know you did."

"What are you, ten years old? I'm trying to talk about something serious here—"

"It's Loretta Gonzales, isn't it?"

Okay, that threw me. I didn't expect him to figure it out that quickly.

"Oh, I know all about Loretta," he said, still showing his expensive little teeth. "She and Jeff thought they were fooling people, acting like they weren't dating. But you can't hide something like that from your colleagues."

I said nothing, wishing I'd stopped talking about two minutes sooner. Wishing I'd run for my car when I had the chance.

Gibbons leaned forward, his hands clasped together on his desk, index fingers pointing at my chest.

"Let me tell you something, Mabry. If you besmirch the image of this zoo in any way, I'll make sure it all comes back on Loretta. She'll be fired so quick, she won't know what hit her."

"Hey, buddy. I never said my client was named Loretta."

"She's the logical one. She's got the family fortune. She can afford to waste money on some third-rate private eye—"

"Hey," I snapped. "I've had enough of the insults."

Gibbons gave me a smarmy smile. "When you're insulted, you'll take it and like it."

"I don't think so."

"Yeah? What are you going to do about it?"

I stood up quickly, thinking I'd loom over the little bastard and put a scare into him. But he didn't even blink. I jabbed a forefinger at him and said, "Keep pushing, boy, and you're gonna find out—"

A piercing scream filled the office, about made the hair leap right off my head. I wheeled to find the monkey pissed and red-faced. He leaned toward me, stretching forward from his perch, showing me his teeth.

"Careful," Gibbons smirked. "Mongo's very protective."

I gulped.

"You'd better go now."

I nodded and backed toward the door. The monkey hissed at me. It stabbed one hand in my direction and made grasping motions, like it was daring me to come within reach.

"Remember what I said, Mabry. Cause problems for this zoo and I'll make sure Loretta's fired. And I'll find a way to take care of you as well."

"You can't touch me," I said, but I was distracted, still watching the menacing monkey.

"We'll see about that. As soon as you go out that door, I'm calling Security. See if you can get off zoo property before they find you."

He reached for the phone. I stepped out into the hall and slammed the door behind me. Then I hurried down the corridor, headed for the parking lot, visions of Mongo yipping at my heels.

Chapter 11

The wind had picked up, and it sliced at my clothes like an icy machete. I trotted across the parking lot to where I'd left the Oldsmobile. It was cold inside the car, too, and I blew on my hands while I waited for the engine to warm up.

My ears still burned from Gibbons chewing on them, and from embarrassment over my obvious unease around his monkey. My distraction over Mongo was the reason I'd let too much slip in talking to his owner. At least that's what I told myself.

Now I worried that I'd put my client in jeopardy. I dug in my wallet and came up with Loretta's phone number and dialed her on my cell.

"Hello?"

"Loretta. It's Bubba Mabry. Can you talk?"

"Just for a minute. I've kinda got my hands full at the moment."

"Feeding Christians to the lions?"

"Close. Chunks of horsemeat to the tigers."

I pictured what a bloody mess that must be. In the background, I heard a rumbling that could've only been a tiger's purr.

"Need me to call you back?"

"No. Go ahead. Have you uncovered something?"

"Not exactly. I've been at the zoo all day."

"I know. I saw you a little while ago. Remember?"

"Right. Sorry. I'm not thinking clearly right now. I've got monkey fever."

"What?"

"Never mind. Look, the reason I called is I kinda got into it with that guy Noah Gibbons, and he figured out you were my client."

"Uh-oh."

"Sorry. I tried to deny it, but lying didn't seem to work on him. He's sort of a, um—"

"Prick."

"Well, yeah. Not the word I was looking for, but it will do. He kind of gloated over it and then he has this damned monkey—"

"Mongo."

"Yeah. It gave me the creeps, so I was distracted."

"It's okay, Mr. Mabry. Don't worry about it."

"But he said he could get you fired."

"I'd like to see him try."

"He seemed like a mean little bastard to me. I wouldn't want him for an enemy."

"He's not nearly as influential as he thinks," she said. "He's always trying to throw his weight around. Thinks he's next in line when Carolyn Hoff retires."

"Is he?"

"I doubt it. Besides, Carolyn's not going anywhere soon."

To me, Hoff looked as if she could keel over any second, but I didn't say so. It's not polite to speculate about others' impending demises.

"All right, then," I said, "I just wanted to warn you. This guy Gibbons—"

"He can't touch me. The truth is, Mr. Mabry, that my dad is a major contributor to the zoo. Did you notice that big plaque outside the entrance?"

"Sure," I lied.

"Our biggest donors. Daddy's name is at the top."

"Ah."

"Is that how I got my job? Probably. And I'm not above using him to keep it. I'm a hard worker. I do a good job for them.

But this is Albuquerque. Patronage goes a long way here. As long as Daddy's pouring money in ZIA's pot, I don't have anything to worry about."

"Any other way Gibbons can get at you?"

"He might get me assigned to some crappy work detail, hosing out cages or something, but even that would be short-term. There's nothing he can do that will make me back off."

I appreciated her resolve, but I said, "I was surprised to see you back at work so soon. You need time to grieve."

"I thought about taking a few days. But I'm better off staying busy. I need to get busy right now, in fact. The tigers are getting restless."

Another rumble in the background.

"One more thing," I said quickly. "Gibbons said lots of your co-workers knew about your romance with Jeff, but I was under the impression that you kept it quiet."

"We tried, but word got around. Especially once I started wearing an engagement ring. Perry Oswalt noticed that right away. I'm sure he blabbed to everybody."

I told her I'd seen Oswalt during my tour, but hadn't had a chance to speak with him. I didn't mention that he'd been making out with a boa constrictor at the time.

"Perry's got a little crush on me," she said. "But I've never done anything to encourage him. He's a little weird, to tell you the truth. We had coffee together once, and he acted like we were on a first date, all hot and bothered. I've tried to keep my distance since then, but I wouldn't be surprised if he figured out that Jeff was my fiancé. And he's tight with Gibbons. God, they've probably all been talking about Jeff and me."

This last she said almost to herself, sorting it out.

"Anyhow," I said, "I just thought you should know about Gibbons's threat. Watch your back."

"I will. You do the same."

I hung up, letting Loretta return to her tigers. No surprise that she was so fearless. Someone who's comfortable working around ferocious felines wouldn't let a little rat like Noah Gibbons worry her.

But he worried me.

Chapter 12

I turned the car's heater up to full blast and got out my notebook. I often make notes right after interviews. Pull out a notebook in front of a nervous subject like Carolyn Hoff, and she might clam right up. Make it feel like a more-or-less normal conversation, and she might forget she's talking to a private eye. Anyway, I had a few thoughts I wanted to jot down, including a note to myself to follow up with Perry Oswalt. If Oswalt nursed a crush on Loretta, then maybe—

Ba-bam! The sudden noise nearly made me jump through the roof. Someone rapping on my window, right by my ear, for shit's sake. I jerked around, expecting zoo guards or Gibbons or freaking Mongo, but what I found was a young blond woman in a business suit. She was bent over, smiling into my face with perfect teeth. Her hair was down, flipping about in the wind, so it took me a second to recognize her. Felicia's intern. Oh, hell.

I cracked the window an inch. "What?"

"Mr. Mabry, do you remember me? Julie Keen? We met yesterday outside the Flying Squirrel. After the homicide? I was with your wife? Intern at the Gazette?"

Christ, she talked faster than an auctioneer.

"Yeah, yeah. I remember. What are you doing here?"

"Chasing the story. I heard you were coming out here to the zoo today, so I thought I'd try to run into you out here, and here you are! I'm lucky that way. I tried to talk to people who work at the zoo, but they only wanted to let me—"

"Wait a minute."

"—talk to their spokeswoman. But I know there's a story here, and talking to the flack certainly isn't the way to get it—"

"Would you hold on a second?"

She finally paused. "What's wrong?"

"You said you heard I was coming to the zoo. Where did you hear that?"

She twinkled at me. "I've got my sources. A good reporter always cultivates—"

I rolled up the window. She kept talking, but it was muted by the layer of glass between us.

Only one person could've told her I was coming here today. Felicia. But why would my wife sic this intern on me? I told Felicia I'd give her the story first if I broke anything in my investigation. Usually, that's enough to get her to give me a little breathing room. Part of the crazy-quilt domestic truce that allows our marriage to work.

But it must've been her. Not like anyone at the zoo would've called this young journalist manqué and tipped her off. And nobody else knew my plans to spend the day at the zoo.

Julie still prattled on the other side of the glass. The smile was gone now, and she seemed a little steamed about being shut out in the cold. Tough.

I got out my cell phone again, hit the speed-dial to call my wife.

"Gazette city desk," she snapped. "Quattlebaum."

"Hey, it's me."

"Not now, Bubba. I'm in the middle of writing a story."

"Don't give me 'not now.' I'm sitting in my car, in front of the zoo, and your intern is outside my window, yapping like a terrier. And you're the only person who could've sicced her on me."

Felicia laughed.

"Sorry, Bubba, but I had to get rid of her. I'm on deadline here, and she was driving me crazy."

"So you told her to come after me?"

"I figured you could handle her. Tell her to get lost. Tell her to go interview a chimp. Something. Just don't send her back to the Gazette. I need more time to get this story wrapped up."

"Are you kidding me? You intentionally put this kid on my trail, and now I'm supposed to baby-sit her?"

"Tell her to go away. But give her a little morsel, something to chase after. As long as she's busy running down a story, she won't come back here to yak at me."

"Why should I play games with this little—"

"Come on, Bubba. She's just a kid. Surely you can outwit her."

That gave me pause. Felicia rarely admits that I have any wits at all, much less that I could use them to outsmart somebody else. Before I could come up with a retort that wouldn't refute what she'd just said, she beat me to the punch.

"Call coming on the other line. Gotta go."

"Hang on a second—"

Too late. I was talking to a dial tone.

Julie Keen had given up on talking to me through the window. She still stood next to the car, her fists on her hips, glaring at me in the cutest possible way.

I rolled the window down. She immediately started talking again, something about riding along with me and helping in my investigation, but I wasn't listening. I held up a forefinger and waited.

When she finally hushed, I said, "I talked to Felicia. She's terribly sorry that she misled you."

"Misled?"

"She apparently gave you the impression that I would be cooperative, when she knew darn well that wasn't the case."

"But I—"

"Felicia says she made a mistake. She says you should immediately go back to the Gazette and help her with her current story."

"But she told me—"

"Hey, I'm just repeating what she said. She clearly needs you back there right away."

If Felicia wanted to unload Miss Bushy-Tail on me, then turnabout was fair play. Let them duke it out in the newsroom. I wanted no part of it.

"Oh, my," the young woman said, looking at her watch. "I don't know what to do."

And then I made a mistake. I said, "What do you mean?"

"I took a taxi to get here. My car's in the shop. If Felicia needs me right away, then I'm stuck. No way I can get a cab back there before the afternoon budget meeting. That's where they decide what goes on the front page and—"

I cut her off with a loud, dramatic sigh. I said, "I've got to go now. Hope your problems work out."

I shifted the car into gear.

"Wait! Could you, um, give me a ride?"

"What?"

"I could freeze to death out here, waiting on a cab. You know how taxis are in Albuquerque."

True. If you're anywhere in town except the airport, good luck getting a cab. You can summon one by phone, but you'd better not be in any kind of hurry. It's a spread-out city, and there aren't many taxis to service it all. And the cab drivers are on perpetual lunch break, here in the Land of Mañana.

But give her a ride? All the way out to the Gazette? The newspaper office sits on the north end of town, amid office parks and chain restaurants and traffic jams. It could easily take twenty minutes to run her all the way up there. And if Felicia saw me dropping her off ...

"Please, Mr. Mabry. It would mean so much to me."

Either she had something in her eye, or she was batting her lashes at me. I didn't know how to tell her how little I'm affected by flirtatious behavior. I used to have a problem, falling for the wiles of beautiful young women, but I'm an old married man now and Felicia's pretty much beaten that out of me. I still suffer from a genetic gullibility—people in my family tend to fall for things; we're a used car salesman's wet dream—and I have to check every fact two or three times to make sure I'm not being tricked. But

I'm no longer blinded by every babe who crosses my path. It's backfired on me too many times.

I heard myself say, "Get in."

What was I doing? Why didn't I just floor the gas pedal and race away, leave her standing there in the parking lot? Because I'm too damned polite for my own good, that's why. I was raised a Southern gentleman, more or less, and a gentleman would never leave a member of the fairer sex stranded in a chilly parking lot. No matter how tempting it might be.

She hurried around the front end of the car. I fought off the urge to run her down. She popped open the passenger-side door and climbed in. She was wearing a tight skirt, and I did a pretty good job of not looking at her trim legs as she slid onto the bench seat.

Yes, good manners doomed me to twenty minutes of incessant chatter. Yes, I should know better than to let any reporter get into my car when I'm working on a case. And, yes, I'd probably piss off Felicia by delivering Julie to within earshot. But what kind of animal would I be if I'd just left her at the zoo?

Here's how I handled her: I didn't speak. Not a word. I didn't answer her questions and I didn't volunteer anything. I didn't comment on the weather or ask about her hometown or make any kind of chitchat at all. I just drove, my shoulders hunched up by my ears, hoping she would take a hint and shut the fuck up.

Such subtleties apparently didn't work on Julie Keen. She talked as we drove through downtown, she talked as we got on the freeway and she talked all the way out to the Gazette building. As near as I could tell, she never paused for breath. I started to wonder whether she had a blowhole under that blond hair that allowed her to talk nonstop without the occasional inhale. That got me to thinking about dolphins, which made me think how much her high-pitched voice sounded like Flipper. Pretty soon I had that TV theme song in my head: "We call him Flipper, Flipper, faster than li-i-i-ightning …"

I'll spare you the details, but let's say that Julie asked every conceivable question about my investigation, about Jeff Simmons, about the zoo, about Felicia, about Albuquerque in general and the Gazette in particular. I've never heard anyone fire questions so rapidly. She was the Uzi of interviewers, spraying questions in every direction. After a while, I'm not sure she even registered the fact that I wasn't answering. She was on a roll. She was asking for asking's sake, words filling the air around her pretty little head.

I pulled into the parking lot in front of the Gazette, and came to a stop. If she saw that we'd arrived, she didn't mention it. She kept firing questions.

"Are you denying that Simmons's death was related to some chicanery at the zoo?"

"Get out," I said.

"Do you know who was in that ape suit?"

"Get out."

"Was it someone who works at the zoo?"

"Get out."

"What are you planning to do next?"

I leaned across her, popped the door latch. The car was parked on a slight slope. The passenger door swung open wide.

"Do you deny that—"

"Get out now."

She huffed through her blowhole, unhappy. But she got out.

"Thanks for the ride," she said from the curb. "But I have to say, you weren't very helpful otherwise."

I had to stretch, but I managed to grab the passenger door and shut it. Then I sat up, put the car in gear, and got the hell out of there.

When I paused at the corner to check for oncoming traffic, I glanced at my mirror. Julie was still back there at the sidewalk, and her lips were still moving. She turned on a high heel and stalked off toward the arched entrance of the Gazette building.

I goosed the Olds into a gap in rush-hour traffic. My ears were tired and my head swam from all the chatter. The light was fading, and I was tempted to just go home and recover from my ordeal with Dolphin Girl.

But I had one more stop to make before I could justify calling it a day.

Chapter 13

I'm always grateful when people list themselves in the phone book. Like a lot of private eyes, I keep a spare phone directory in my car, and I can't tell you the time and energy it saves. These days, with computers and databases and the information glut, you can track down anybody if you've got the time and the know-how. But it sure is easier to let your fingers do the walking.

Perry Oswalt's home number and address were listed right where they should be, and that saved me having to go home and bloodhound him online. The address was in a neighborhood north of Lomas Boulevard, near the state fairgrounds.

The south side of the fairgrounds, along East Central Avenue, is iffy territory. Lots of hookers and crooks and seedy bars along that stretch, catering to the cowboys and the bikers and the methheads and the cigarette-puffing Asians who make East Central a volatile human stew. All very familiar to me, of course. For years, I lived in one of the cheap neon-lit motels that dot East Central—Old Route 66—before Felicia came along and made me act respectable.

But that's the south side. Lomas borders the fairgrounds to the north, and the older neighborhoods in that direction are quiet and middle-class and well-tended. The houses are smaller than the whoppers they're throwing up in the Northeast Heights these days, but it's a nice area, with level lawns and corner streetlights and kids playing outside.

Oswalt's house was the smallest on his block, a brown Pueblo-style stucco job that looked like a box of mud. The property's most outstanding feature was a huge, spooky cottonwood, barren of leaves this time of year, that reached long arms over the neighbors' homes on either side. Oswalt's lawn was patchy and dry, and I figured that the tree siphoned off every drop of water poured onto the grass.

I'd been parked along a curb half a block away for five minutes when an aging Honda Civic pulled into Oswalt's gravel driveway. I watched him haul his plump body out of the gray car. He pushed up his little round glasses and glanced around the neighborhood before waddling to the front door.

Lights came on behind the windows of his house. I waited a few minutes, giving him time to get settled.

A few other cars passed on the quiet street, people coming home from work, and I couldn't sit there much longer without attracting attention. I got out, locked the Olds, and sauntered down the sidewalk like I belonged in the neighborhood.

I went up Oswalt's front walk, watching my step because the concrete was bulged and cracked from tree roots. I rang the doorbell and stood on the stoop with my hands in my pockets, whistling the *Flipper* theme while I waited.

Oswalt threw open the door, and I got the distinct impression that I'd interrupted something. His face was flushed, and he looked exasperated. Light and warm air flowed out the open door.

"Perry Oswalt?"

"Yeah?" He glanced around warily, as if he expected a team of Jehovah's Witnesses to leap out of the bushes. Up close, I could see he was younger than I'd thought, maybe thirty. His rust-colored hair was cut short, and he dressed like a lumberjack, in a plaid shirt and boots and baggy jeans that dipped low under his belly.

I handed him one of my business cards. "Private investigator. We need to talk."

He looked at the card, then up at me, then read the card again, like he couldn't quite believe the gomer standing before him was really a private investigator. I get that a lot.

"Talk about what?"

"Jeff Simmons."

His doughy face paled, and I thought it would be easy to read this guy. Then he surprised me.

"I've got nothing to say to you."

He went to close the door. I was still on the stoop, down a step, so I couldn't stick my foot in the way. I threw out my hand, nearly got my fingers cut off as the door slammed shut. Goddamnit.

"Hey!" I banged on the door. "Open up. I only want to talk."

"Go away!"

"You can talk to me right now," I shouted, "or you can talk to the cops."

I don't know where I got that threat. Not like I could get the cops over here to interrogate Perry Oswalt for me. Not like I can get Steve Romero to do a damned thing. But Oswalt didn't know that. After a second, the latch rattled.

He opened the door a crack. "The police?"

"Did detectives talk to you already?"

"No," he said. "They were at the zoo, interviewing people. But they never got around to me. I was pretty busy in the reptile house—"

"I just need a few minutes of your time. Maybe I can save you the trouble of talking to the cops."

Some people can't differentiate between private eyes and real cops. You'd think, with all the TV shows about cops and detectives and crime scene investigators and forensic pathologists, people would know better. But I'm always willing to take advantage of ignorance. Plenty of folks have done the same to me.

Anyhow, he fell for it. He opened the door and meekly let me enter. I immediately wished he hadn't.

Snakes. Freaking snakes everywhere. Every horizontal surface—every table, every shelf, every countertop—held glass-front containers full of serpents. Rattlers and cottonmouths and coral snakes and rat snakes and exotic boas and I don't know what all. Must've been thirty of them. In the largest cage, a giant python lay piled up like a fire hose.

I nearly ran out of the place screaming. Snakes! God, I hate legless, poisonous, fanged, slithery, squirmy, sneaky snakes.

"Got a, um, few snakes here." I sounded pretty calm. A little gulp, but I don't think he noticed.

"My pets," he said. "Nothing to do with the zoo."

"Right. Everybody needs a hobby."

"I keep them separate. I've got the sales receipts for every one of these reptiles."

"Don't be so defensive. That's not why I'm here."

Oswalt fidgeted, didn't seem to know what to do with company. I wondered whether he ever had human visitors in his little house. I wondered whether his neighbors knew his place housed this collection of vipers. But I let all that go. I had a few questions about Jeff Simmons. The sooner I got answers, the sooner I could get the hell out of here.

He finally located his manners. "Would you like to sit down?" he asked, gesturing toward the sofa.

I'd been so busy freaking over the snakes, I hadn't noticed the two-foot-long iguana stretched along the back of the couch. The spiny-backed lizard was so still, so absolutely motionless, I thought for a moment it was stuffed. Then it winked at me. Yikes.

"That's Agatha," he said. "She'll move if you sit down next to her."

Exactly what I was afraid of.

"This is fine," I said. "I only need a few minutes."

He looked me up and down, apparently still sorting out whether he was required to speak with me. I didn't want him thinking too much about it. I said, "You knew Jeff Simmons, right?"

"Sure. We'd worked together for three years."

"Would you say you were friends?"

"We were friendly, if that's what you mean, but we didn't see each other outside of work."

I wondered whether Perry Oswalt had ever had a real, live, human friend. Guys who are fascinated with snakes tend to be reclusive types. At least that's been my (admittedly limited) experience. Maybe that's not their fault. Maybe it's because people like me are too busy shrieking and fleeing to get to know them better.

"Did Jeff ever confide in you? Talk about work?"

"Sometimes." Oswalt seemed uncomfortable, standing there, surrounded by his writhing buddies. Not nearly as nervous as I felt, but still. I stepped to one side, so he could reach the sofa if he wanted. He picked up his cue. Edged around a coffee table and lifted Agatha, sat down with the big lizard across his lap. Shudder.

"Had Jeff talked with you lately?"

He squinted at me through his round glasses. "About what?"

"Animals dying at the zoo. The numbers being a little high?"

He paused to swallow that, his plump hands massaging the motionless lizard, then shook his head.

"I don't know anything about animals dying. You always lose a few animals, especially when winter comes around, but that's natural. Cost of doing business."

"What about other people at the zoo? Anybody there who seemed to have a problem with Simmons? Anybody giving him trouble?"

He hesitated. Apparently, he took time to swallow each question before he could regurgitate an answer. "Not that I know of. Jeff was pretty well liked. He didn't get into conflicts with people. We all get along pretty well at the zoo."

I nodded. Getting nowhere fast.

"Somebody clearly wasn't happy with Simmons. Somebody dressed up in an ape suit and shot him."

Oswalt scowled. "You're stating the obvious."

"What about Loretta Gonzales?" I asked. "How well do you know her?"

No sense keeping Loretta's name out of it now. Once Noah Gibbons guessed her identity, there wasn't much chance my client would remain a secret.

Oswalt's eyes widened enough that I could see that they were robin's-egg blue, which surprised me. I would've expected black and beady. His face flushed, as if the mere mention of Loretta's name was enough to excite him.

"Well enough," he said. "She's real nice."

"You knew she was engaged to Jeff Simmons?"

His face shut down just as quickly as it had lit up. He said nothing.

"Let me rephrase the question. How many people, aside from you, knew about it?"

After a few seconds' pause, he said, "Lots of people. We've got a nepotism policy that's supposed to forbid all that, but zoo people tend to end up dating each other. We all work long hours, you know how it is."

I'd noticed it was the same among Felicia's co-workers at the newspaper. Yet another reason to work solo.

"Did anybody seem upset that they were seeing each other?"

I watched him carefully for a reaction, but he had himself under control now. He let nothing show. Just shook his head.

I caught movement out of the corner of my eye. Turned to find that a brown snake in one of the terrariums had caught a white mouse. The rodent's back legs and tail hung out of the snake's unhinged mouth. The little pink feet were still kicking.

A wave of nausea washed over me. I've got a weak stomach when it comes to shit like that. I can't even watch nature shows on TV. They always show some predator devouring some smaller creature, blood all over his snout. Yeah, yeah, it's the natural order and survival of the fittest and all that, but yecch.

Time to get out of here. I thanked Oswalt for his time, and said I'd show myself out.

He didn't say good-bye or ask me to keep in touch or even apologize for being such a fucking freak. Just sat on the sofa, stroking his lizard, watching me go.

After the door shut behind me, it was all I could do not to run up and down the block, shouting alarms: "Snakes! Poisonous snakes in this house! Right here among you!"

Instead, I sucked in the refreshing evening air and walked briskly to my car, watching my feet, tripping only once on the broken concrete.

Chapter 14

$\mathcal{I}$ could tell Felicia was home when I pulled up to our brick bungalow near UNM because lights blazed in every window. I've tried to talk to my wife about energy conservation and how much we'd save on our utility bills if she turned off a light once in a while, but the discussion never gets very far. She trots out the fact that she pays most of the bills around here, and I lose the argument.

That's a pretty good summation of Felicia: She's the kind of person who leaves the lights on. She's so busy, hurtling from one project to another, one idea to the next, that she doesn't heed such mundane details as burning lights or empty cupboards or oncoming traffic. She's secure in the knowledge that someone else will flip the switch or buy the groceries or get the hell out of her lane, goddammit.

She's a woman on a mission. She told me once that the Journalists' Creed is to "comfort the afflicted and afflict the comfortable." Felicia mostly does the latter. With her, everybody is guilty until proven innocent. And she's in a hurry to nail them all.

Tonight, I was glad she was wasting electricity. The lights warned me that she was home. I'd had enough surprises for one day.

No doubt she was pissed. I was perfectly within my rights when I returned the jabbering intern to the Gazette newsroom, but I didn't think Felicia would see it that way. I expected an earful.

I parked next to her dented Toyota and approached the front porch with trepidation. I could've sneaked into the house through the side door, the one with the sign that says, "Bubba Mabry Investigations." It leads straight into my office, which is where I'd likely end up sleeping if Felicia was still mad. I keep a lumpy sofa in there for just that reason; it gets used more often than I care to admit. But I bravely went through the front door, and jumped only a little when Felicia called from the kitchen, "There's no fucking food in this house!"

A fine greeting. And not that unusual. I typically do the shopping, but when I get busy with a case, we tend to run out of things. It apparently never occurs to Felicia to go to the supermarket herself.

"I ordered a pizza," she said as she came out of the kitchen, one of my green Heinekens in her hand.

I tried a smile. If she was bringing me a beer, then she couldn't be too mad.

She flopped onto the sofa, tipped up the bottle and drained half of it in a single swallow. Oh.

"Rough day?" I ventured.

She wiped her mouth with the back of her wrist. "What makes you say that?"

"Well, you're having a beer—"

"I'm thirsty."

"Right. I just thought—"

"You thought I might be exhausted from listening to my damned intern all day."

Ouch. I braced for the thunderclap that would signal a domestic storm. But Felicia caught me off-guard. She grinned.

"It's all right, Bubba. I finished my story before she got there. Soon as the city editor read through it, I split. Left Julie there, yakking at anybody who'd listen about her big day at the zoo."

"That girl does like to talk," I said.

"You, sir, are a master of understatement. I've never seen anything quite like it. We expect the interns to be eager beavers, all excited about working at a real newspaper. But somebody forgot to tell Julie that you learn by listening, not by flapping your lips."

"Have you tried to tell her?"

"You've seen how she is. I can't get a word in edgewise. And when I do, she's not listening. She's too busy thinking about what she'll say next."

Felicia put her sneakers up on the coffee table. Took another slug of beer.

"Is that why you sent her after me?" I put my hands on my hips, taking the offensive. "So I could see what you're up against?"

She let her head fall back onto the sofa cushion. Closed her eyes.

"It was her idea," she said to the ceiling. "She thinks you're onto something. Witness to a homicide, real-life private eye, blah, blah, blah. When I told her where to find you, she flew out of the newsroom, hot to chase down the story."

She swiveled her head and gave me a look. "Are you onto something?"

"Not so I can tell it."

Her eyes slammed shut again. "Good."

"Thanks."

"That's not what I meant. I'm too tired to worm it out of you right now. Wait until I get a slow day, later in the week. Then we can break a big story together."

Just what I wanted. I left her there on the sofa while I slumped off to the kitchen to get my own beer. While I was in there, I checked the answering machine, found that I had three messages. The first was from Marvin Pidgeon, the slip-and-fall attorney, demanding that I call him back immediately. He sounded pissed. I erased the message.

The second was from my Mama, calling from Mississippi.

"I was just praying over you, Bubba," the message began. Arrgh. My Mama's prayed so much on my behalf over the years, it's a wonder her knees still work. "I worry about you, son. I haven't heard from you in two weeks. Has something happened? Are you all right? I know you're very busy, bless your heart. But give me a call when you get a chance."

That's Mama. Spreading guilt and God's love with a shovel.

I erased that message, too. I try to be the good son and call my folks two or three times a month, but it's never enough. Mama worries. You'd think someone so devout would be an optimist, that she'd assume all was fine in God's green world unless she heard otherwise. But not Mama. She's got too good of an imagination. If I haven't called, it's because I'm in intensive care, at death's door. Or worse.

Of course, there have been times when I've gone incommunicado because something bad has happened. That's the nature of my business. And I am prone to physical clumsiness and the occasional boneheaded move that results in injury or violence or other life-threatening circumstance. Mama knows all this. She's known me all my life.

I couldn't deal with her tonight. I'd come home expecting Hurricane Felicia, and so far had dodged that potential disaster. No sense in pressing my luck.

The third message was the one worth saving. A woman's voice, identifying herself as Cristina Tapia. The zoo's "outreach director."

"I understand you were asking questions around the zoo today," she said. "You should've been referred directly to me, but I was out much of the day, dealing with the news media on the Simmons matter."

Spoken like a true flack. Not "Jeff's tragic death" or "surprising homicide," but "the Simmons matter," as if the murder was some niggling business item that needed to be cleared up.

"Please call me at your first opportunity," the message said, and concluded with her office number.

Another zoo official heard from, another from Loretta's list. I made a mental note to call her first thing in the morning.

I carried my beer into the living room. Felicia still sprawled on the sofa, her head tipped back, and I thought she might've dozed off.

"You were gone a long time," she muttered as I plopped down beside her.

"Checking my messages."

"Anything good?"

"Not unless you consider Mama's prayers a good thing."

"Oh, but I do. Your Mama's got a hotline to God. She might be all that's saving us from some gruesome end."

"If God really cared about us, He'd take away Mama's phone privileges."

"Don't be like that. She's a sweet lady."

I still can't get over the fact that Felicia and Mama have become such pals. We'd been married for more than a year before they finally met in person, and they hit it off right away. Spent all their time together giggling over what a doofus I can be. Which I didn't need.

Felicia set her empty bottle on the end table and cuddled up next to me. I put my arm around her shoulders and held her close, while using my free hand to guzzle beer.

As scary as Felicia is, she can be sweet sometimes, too. I kissed the top of her head. Her hair smelled of citrus. Her warm body stirred something in me, and I started having lascivious thoughts about the night ahead. It had been a while, and maybe Felicia would want to—

The doorbell rang.

"That," she said into my chest, "would be the pizza."

"Dinner is served," I said, as I untangled myself from her. "Damn it."

Chapter 15

I overslept the next morning. Dinner with Felicia had given us both some energy, and one thing led to another, and we'd gone to bed early and gone to sleep late. Must've been something in the pizza. By the time I awoke from my sex-sapped slumber, the sun was high in the sky and Felicia had already left for work.

She'd left some coffee in the pot. It was bitter from sitting on the warmer for hours, but I drank it anyway, standing in the kitchen in my old flannel bathrobe, scratching and yawning and trying to get ambitious about the day ahead.

I remembered that Cristina Tapia had called the day before. I didn't expect her to be any help. If anything, she'd try to freeze me out to keep me from tainting the zoo's public image. But she was one person at ZIA who hadn't already told me to take a hike and, since she was on the administrative side, she wasn't likely to have an office full of shrieking monkeys or hissing serpents.

I dialed her number, and she answered immediately.

"Good morning. This is Cristina."

I wasn't ready. I'd expected a secretary or a receptionist or something. When officials answer their own phones, it's always a little startling.

"Hi, um, Ms. Tapia. My name's Bubba Mabry. You left a mess—"

"The private investigator!"

"That's right."

"I was wondering whether you'd call back."

I didn't mention that I'd only gotten out of bed a few minutes earlier.

"We need to talk," she said. "Right away."

"So talk."

"I'd rather do it in person. I feel that this is a serious matter and—"

"When?"

"Sooner the better," she said. "I'm concerned that you might have been given the wrong impression here at ZIA. I wouldn't want word to get out that—"

Yeah, yeah. She kept talking, but I wasn't listening. As I suspected, she was busy flacking for the zoo. The spin doctor, trying to put some distance between Simmons's murder and his job. No, the homicide couldn't possibly be connected to the fact that Jeff was ready to blow the whistle on somebody at the zoo. No way. It must've been something else. Blah, blah, blah. Finally, I couldn't stand it anymore and I interrupted her again.

"Do you want me to come there?"

"That would be fine. But, um, most of us are going to the funeral in a little over an hour, so unless you could come here immediately—"

I looked down at my bathrobe and my naked feet. That wasn't happening.

"—it might need to wait until this afternoon."

I hate funerals. Hate formal occasions of any kind, but especially funerals. What kind of weird party is it, where the guest of honor is a stiff? Still, it might be interesting to see who showed up for Jeff's sendoff and, better yet, who didn't show up.

"When's the funeral start?" I asked her.

"It's at eleven. Graveside service at Sunset Memorial Park. A bunch of us are riding over there together."

"How about this," I said. "I'll meet you there."

"At the funeral?"

"I don't mean we'll talk there. But I could give you a ride back to the zoo afterward, and we can talk on the way."

She hesitated, but only for a moment.

"All right. But I might need to hang around for a few minutes after the service, in case the media's there—"

"Fine. Whatever. I'll find you."

We hung up. Once again, I'd doomed myself to a car ride with a talkative stranger. But I'd be asking the questions this time. Maybe I'd get some useful information out of Cristina Tapia. Maybe I'd learn something from the funeral service itself.

I trudged off to the bedroom. Time to break out my one suit, which was, appropriately, black. Time to hunt through the pile of shoes in the closet, find some that don't say "Reebok" on them. Time to locate—gulp—a necktie.

God, I hate funerals.

Chapter 16

In my black suit, white shirt, and narrow thrift-store tie, I looked like a character from that movie *Reservoir Dogs*. Blues Brothers sunglasses added to the effect, but they were absolutely necessary. Simmons's service was to be conducted under cloudless blue skies, and the sun was fiercely bright, if not particularly warm.

I was running late. By the time I found a place to park and hiked halfway across Sunset Memorial Park to the correct grave, a crowd of maybe seventy people had gathered around the hole in the ground. Their breaths fogged the air above the closed casket and the wreaths of flowers that surrounded the grave.

A green canopy had been erected over rows of folding chairs on the far side of the grave, and I could see Loretta there, sitting in the middle of the front row. The widow's seat. She was dressed all in black, her hair pinned up behind her head. She dabbed at her eyes with a lacy hanky. A handsome middle-aged Hispanic couple, looked like they could be her parents, sat beside her. On the other side was a gray-haired Anglo couple, both with red-rimmed eyes behind thick eyeglasses, who I took to be Simmons's shocked parents. A family resemblance told me the others under the canopy were also Simmons relatives. Several of the men wore cowboy boots with Western-cut suits and had Stetsons resting on their knees. I'd taken Simmons to be an Easterner, but clearly the family was from somewhere out in these parts.

The other bystanders had segregated into clumps around the grave. One bunch was around Jeff's age, and I assumed they were friends or old college chums. Another group consisted of colleagues from the zoo. I spotted cadaverous Carolyn Hoff with Noah Gibbons close by her side. Towering Jungle Jim Johansen, who looked uncomfortable in a suit not made of khaki. The receptionist was there, though she'd left her chewing gum at home. A few others, including a striking raven-haired woman whom I guessed might be Cristina Tapia. She wore a pinstriped suit and teetery high heels, which appeared to sink into the soft earth around the grave.

No sign of Perry Oswalt, which was just as well. If he'd been there, he probably would've been turning over gravestones in search of slithering snakes.

So far, no surprises. The one person I hadn't expected to see was Lieutenant Steve Romero, who slipped up beside me without me noticing.

"Whadaya say there, Mr. Pink?" he said.

"Jesus, don't do that. I nearly jumped into the grave."

"That wouldn't be seemly."

"What are you doing here?"

"I was gonna ask you the same question."

"Well, um, I felt like I should come," I stammered. "You know, since I was with him when he died and all."

I was glad I was wearing dark glasses. Maybe Romero wouldn't notice my eyes darting around. He gave me the hard squint but didn't get a chance to follow up because the service started.

The minister was a pink-cheeked, white-haired hamster of a man, as wide as he was tall. He stepped up to one end of the grave, cleared his throat and opened a black Bible. All the whispering and mumbling fizzled, and his high tenor echoed across the cemetery.

"My friends," he began. "We welcome you today to the final resting place of Jeffery Joshua Simmons, a fine young man whose life was cut tragically short."

Sniffles, sobs, et cetera, as the minister continued. Behind the safety of my dark glasses, I let my gaze flit from one mourner to the next, looking for anybody who seemed smug or shame-faced. Beside me, Romero was doing the same, I felt sure, though you couldn't tell it to look at him. He stood as still as a statue, his hands clasped in front of his overcoat, a model of respect. Next to him, I felt fidgety as a schoolboy. I suppose Romero gets a lot of practice, attending funerals. More than me anyway. That's the problem with avoiding these rituals. When I finally do attend one, I no longer know how to act.

I tried to pay attention to the minister's poetic eulogy and the mourners' tearful farewells to Simmons. But all I could think the whole time was: One of these people could very well be the murderer. I mentally tried ape suits on several of them, but that shaggy costume had been so baggy, it could've fit most anyone except the most petite and frail. I couldn't see Carolyn Hoff loping around in a gorilla suit, for instance. Her brittle bones couldn't bear the weight. But Noah Gibbons would look good in fur. Jungle Jim was half ape already. And probably two-thirds of the friends and acquaintances standing around the grave were of a physical type that could've fit the disguise.

That got me to thinking about the ape costume itself. Gorilla suits aren't exactly rare. You can pick one up at any theatrical shop or costume store, or order one online, have it delivered to your door. Plus, plenty of people probably have ape outfits in their closets at home. Not the sort of Halloween get-up you'd throw away once the holiday passed. Probably expensive, for one thing. For another, it might come in handy in the future. Once you had one, you'd store it someplace—basement, garage, back of a closet—for the next time you needed a costume.

I glanced over at Romero, wondering whether his investigators had met any success in tracing the gorilla suit. Surely it had labels in it, or some other indication of where it was purchased. I was dying—so to speak—to ask him about it, but this wasn't the proper time or place.

I'd been so busy chasing around, trying to interview people, I hadn't given full consideration until now to the whole idea of the gorilla suit. It wasn't your typical disguise. It indicated a certain amount of advance preparation.

The killer must've known Simmons was going to meet me at the Flying Squirrel, far enough ahead that he had time to gather up his gorilla outfit and his gun and drive downtown. Who knew Jeff Simmons was coming to see me? Who needed to keep him quiet?

The crowd rustled and shifted, and everyone bowed heads for the closing prayer. The minister's sparse white hair lifted in the breeze as he talked to the Lord. I'd missed the whole service, so busy thinking about ape suits and opportunity.

I glanced over at Romero, saw that his head was unbowed. His hawk eyes roamed the mourners. I looked, too, wondering what I was missing.

Then everybody said "Amen," and there was a general clearing of throats and sniffling of sinuses and shuffling of feet. The mourners closed ranks around the grave, and I heard clumps of dirt thump onto the casket, a sound that always makes me vote for cremation.

I turned to Romero and opened my mouth to ask about the gorilla suit, but he gave me a shushing look. Fine. I'd ask him later.

Since I was here, I decided I should at least go comfort Loretta Gonzales, show her I cared enough to come. Show her she was getting something for her money. I edged away from Romero, trying to make my way around the crowd that encircled the grave.

"Where you going, Bubba?"

I mumbled something about paying my respects and kept moving. Romero stayed right behind me, practically breathing down my neck.

The mourners nearest the canopy hugged and wept and consoled one another. The cowboys had clamped their hats on their heads, so they stood taller than the rest. Somewhere in that morass of black and gray was my client. I didn't particularly want Romero to see me talking to her, but I figured I'd lose him as I elbowed my way through the grieving multitudes.

I hadn't gotten far when Noah Gibbons suddenly squeezed between people, coming the other direction.

"You," he said, stabbing an index finger into my chest. "What are you doing here?"

I tried the "paying my respects" bit on him, but he wasn't buying it.

"You dirtbag," he growled. "If you disturb these people, I'll have you arrested. I'll take you to court and make so much noise that—"

He stopped flapping his gums, distracted by something behind me. I glanced over my shoulder, found Romero looming there.

"Lieutenant," Gibbons said, his tone suddenly formal and polite. He tugged at his jacket and adjusted his cuffs so that his gold cufflinks shot reflected light into my eyes. "Do you know this man?"

I figured Romero would deny it, but apparently he nodded because Gibbons flushed and scowled.

"Do you know he was at the zoo yesterday, poking around, asking questions?"

"Is that right?" Romero clapped a big hand down on my shoulder. Meant to look friendly, but I was pretty sure it left a bruise. "What's that about, Bubba?"

I stuttered and stammered and generally acted like a retard, wincing as the lieutenant massaged my shoulder with his powerful fingers.

"He wouldn't tell us who he's working for," Noah Gibbons said. "But I'm pretty sure his client is Loretta Gonzales. She works at the zoo and she and Simmons were—"

"I know who she is," Romero said. Of course he knew her. Romero knows everything. He is all-seeing, all-knowing, always able to anticipate what will happen next. He's like God. My Mama should be praying to him.

I was about ready to say some prayers of my own. Now that Romero knew I was working the Simmons murder, he'd likely drag me downtown. We could have a little chat about interference in police investigations and homicide being a serious matter and me being a moron. We've had that chat before, but he never seems to tire of the topic.

Romero let loose of my shoulder, but I wasn't going any-where. I was trapped, the turkey in a sandwich formed by Noah Gibbons's well-dressed form and the lieutenant's looming bulk.

Then the murmuring crowd parted and Loretta emerged from between black suits. I don't know whether she'd heard Gibbons toss-ing her name around or if she was just making her way through the mourners to go home, but her appearance felt like a rescue to me.

"Mr. Mabry," she said. "Is that you?"

I lifted my dark glasses and gave her a pained smile.

"So good of you to come."

Noah Gibbons shifted to the side so she could reach me and shake my hand. We had no choice but to stand close. The herd was starting to disperse, but we were still rounded up pretty tight on this side of the grave.

"Is Noah bothering you?" Loretta asked, and it was all I could do not to squeal and point fingers. Again, not the time or the place.

"Not at all," I said. "We were just, um, talking."

"Noah's upset that I hired you." She gave him a sidelong look, one with some heat to it. "He called me into his office yesterday and chewed me out."

"Is that right?" I felt like punching the pugnacious little monkey-lover, but I reminded myself that Romero stood close behind me.

"Like I told him," she said, "it's a free country. I can mount an investigation if I want."

"Right." I cringed a little, figuring Romero was taking notes, preparing for his coming lecture on the idiocy of interfering pri-vate eyes.

"Loretta!" A sharp-dressed man with streaks of gray in his shiny hair stepped out of the crowd behind her. He was about my size, but handsome, with broad shoulders and an Errol Flynn mus-tache. I recognized him as the man who'd sat beside her during the service, the guy I'd pegged as her father.

"Daddy," she said, and I almost smiled, so pleased over my correct deduction. "This is Bubba Mabry. The man I was telling you about. Mr. Mabry, my father, Armando Gonzales."

A cloud passed over his face and his jaw jutted.

"You," he said. He stepped up to me, body-checking Loretta out of the way, and stood so close I could smell peppermint on his breath. "I want to talk to you."

The dude looked angry. But it couldn't go too badly, not while I had Romero shadowing me.

"Are you some kind of scam artist?" Gonzales demanded.

"Huh?"

"You say you're a private eye, but what proof do we have?"

"I've got a license—"

"If I find out you're taking my daughter's money and doing nothing, I'll fuckin' kill you."

Hey, hey, I'm thinking, you shouldn't threaten somebody with murder when the star of the APD Homicide Division is standing right there. I turned to say as much to Romero, only to find that he'd disappeared. I whipped my head around, but I couldn't see him anywhere. What a time for him to vanish! Just when a murder's about to be committed.

Armando Gonzales jabbed my chest with a finger. Which hurt. Loretta grabbed his arm.

"Daddy," she hissed. "Stop it. You're making a scene."

"I don't care. I didn't work hard all my life, provide you with a fortune, so that some con man could steal from you."

Loretta's mother appeared beside her husband, grasped his other arm.

"Come on, 'Mando," she murmured. "Let's go home."

"I'm not done with this guy—"

"Yes, you are," she said firmly. "Let's go."

She steered him away. He glared at me until mourners closed ranks between us and I couldn't see him anymore.

"Sorry, Mr. Mabry," Loretta said. "Daddy's always like that. He thinks everybody's after our money. He even thought Jeff was some kind of gold-digger at first, until he got to know him."

She patted my arm and turned away, following her parents through the diminishing crowd.

A few of the mourners glared at me, like it was my fault that Armando Gonzales was an asshole. Tired of playing the goat, I glared right back at them until they turned away.

I looked around once more for Romero, but he was gone. Whew. Maybe he wasn't planning to haul me downtown after all. Noah Gibbons had disappeared, too. The little shit.

The crowd thinned until only a dozen or so people still mingled around the grave. Most walked to freshly washed cars and pickups parked on a gravel drive a hundred yards away. I spotted the attractive woman I'd mentally identified as Cristina Tapia standing halfway between the grave and the row of shiny vehicles. She looked around, checking faces, apparently trying to determine which of the mourners was the private snoop.

Sighing, I went to fetch her. I wasn't looking forward to our conversation, but it beat the third-degree with Romero or a few rounds with Armando Gonzales.

Chapter 17

Cristina Tapia was not happy to hear that my car was parked the other direction, across three acres of lawn. Her spike heels sank in the irrigated sod, forcing her to hang onto my elbow as we hiked across the cemetery.

She was about forty, but well preserved, as they say, with no wrinkles or sags, no gray allowed in her sleek hair. Trimly built, and her black suit looked tailored to show off her curves. She wore sheer black hose with her ridiculous shoes, and the dark maroon polish on her fingernails matched her lipstick. No wedding ring, which meant she probably paid for all this expensive personal maintenance herself.

How much were they paying people down at the zoo these days? Cristina seemed expensively decked-out. Noah Gibbons, with his Gucci suit and his chunky wristwatch and his imperious manner, sure seemed to have money. I expected zoo people to be safari types like Jungle Jim Johansen or rumpled nerds like Perry Oswalt and, let's face it, Jeff Simmons. Funny how the ones most concerned with personal appearance also seemed to be the ones most worried about the zoo's image. Some people operate only skin deep, I guess.

Cristina Tapia certainly tried to keep up the good front, smiling her ass off while she spiked her way across the sodden cemetery.

"Such a nice service," she said as we struggled along. "Jeff would've been pleased."

That always strikes me as a goddamned stupid thing to say. Jeff would've much rather been alive. Once that was no longer an option, I doubt that he gave two shits about the color of the flowers at his funeral. People always talk about the newly dead like they're sitting on a cloud right above us, looking down, nodding in satisfied approval. Which is happy horseshit. It's like the way they always say, "He looks so natural. Just like he's asleep." You mean, when this guy was still alive, he slept fully dressed in a suit and tie, with his hair lacquered into place and makeup smeared on his face? Jeez, that gives me a whole different take on the dearly departed.

Of course, I didn't say any of that. I just nodded grimly and kept trekking toward the car. Cristina, teetering along beside me, seemed truly relieved when we reached pavement. Then she got a look at the Olds.

"This is your car?" she blurted, as if she couldn't be expected to ride in such a piece of junk. I said nothing. Just popped open the passenger door and gathered up the fast-food trash, the phone book, my city map, and my thermos and chucked it all into the back seat. I brushed the crumbs off the seat the best I could, and stepped out of the way. She climbed in, her smile winking off and on like a neon sign.

I went around to the driver's side and got behind the wheel. Took three tries to get the car started—naturally—and I could feel my cheeks burning as I slammed it into gear.

We bounced onto Yale Boulevard, headed north toward UNM. Coal and Lead Avenues, the three-lane streets known locally as "the One-ways," were up ahead. I could take Lead westward, downhill into downtown, and beyond to the zoo.

Traffic was light, which was good because I needed to focus on my conversation with Cristina. I know how wily flacks can be; Felicia bitches about their stonewalling tactics all the time.

"Thanks for the ride, Mr. Mabry. Frankly, I'm glad to be away from the others. Everyone's so upset about Jeff's death. It's really taken a toll on all of us. Emotionally."

I nodded, not believing a word. She'd try to spin Simmons's murder some way, I just knew it. If she started telling me how Jeff Simmons was her close personal friend, how much she'd miss him, I might gag.

"It's important to me that we have a chance to talk privately," she said.

Here it comes.

"I know it must seem sort of heartless, all of us so worried about how Jeff's death makes the zoo look. But we're a publicly funded institution, and image is everything."

"Uh-huh."

"We rely on volunteers a lot, too. If they thought a killer was roaming the zoo—well, you can see our problem."

"Right."

"And we owe so much to our employees as well. There's no sense in frightening people, when there may be nothing—"

"What about Simmons? He was an employee."

I glanced over, saw her smile go frosty.

"Yes, of course. And, believe me, we want whoever killed him to be caught. But there's no evidence that the murder is connected to his work at the zoo."

"No evidence that it isn't."

She shifted on the seat, and tugged at her hemline.

"True. But what I'm saying is there's no sense in sullying ZIA until we have some proof that there's a link."

"Nobody's sullying the zoo," I said. "It's not like I've gone around, blaming you folks in public. All I did was show up and ask some questions. Took a look around."

"Believe me, that was enough to alarm our employees. We're like a big family at ZIA, and you know how word spreads through families."

"If you're all so tight, seems to me you'd want to do anything to find the killer."

Again with the squirming. I'd expected this conversation to make me uncomfortable, but so far it seemed to work the other way. Cristina, for all her spin-doctor intentions, was the one getting spun. It made me smile.

"You're enjoying this, aren't you?" she said. "Torturing me this way."

"Hey, I'm just discussing the situation. Not my intention to make you uncomfortable."

Heh-heh.

"Look, Mr. Mabry, this isn't easy for me. I really did like Jeff. We all did. Nobody's happy about his death."

"Somebody is. Whoever killed him is tickled to pieces. Because, so far, he's gotten away with it."

"Yes, I suppose that's right. In a twisted sort of way. But there's no reason to think that person is connected to the zoo."

"But what if he is? What if a killer's on the loose down there? If we all act like that's impossible, then the killer gets off. And who's to say he won't do it again?"

She rode in silence for a minute. We were in stop-and-go traffic through downtown, and she stared out the window at the passing nightclubs and office towers. Her hair screened her face from view, but her hands were busy, fiddling with the hem of her skirt. Clearly, I'd gotten to her.

"Look," I said when I stopped at the next red light. "I'm not trying to cause a scandal. Loretta Gonzales wants whoever killed her fiancé brought to justice. The cops are working on that. It's their show, and they'll do their best. In the meantime, if I can provide some comfort to her, show her that no stone's being left unturned, then that's worth the money she's paying me."

She gave me a long look.

"You don't think you'll solve it yourself?"

Ouch, she'd hit the nail on the head there. I didn't expect to solve anything. I never do. I just stir things up, and hope somebody makes a mistake. I had a lot more faith in Romero than I did in myself. But I didn't want to admit all that out loud. I shrugged.

"Isn't there something to what her father said then?" she said. "Aren't you taking her money under false pretenses?"

"You heard all that?"

"I didn't hear it, but Noah Gibbons did. He told me about it on his way to his car."

Ouch again. Now everybody at the zoo will think I'm a scam artist. Be a wonder if anyone else talks to me.

"Loretta's father caught me off-guard," I said. "I wasn't expecting that. I was just trying to express my condolences."

"Uh-huh."

"To tell the truth, I was thinking about something else as I was making my way over to see Loretta. So Gibbons caught me off-guard, too."

"For a private eye, you seem to be 'off-guard' a lot."

"You don't know the half of it," I said glumly.

Another silence while we both chewed on that.

"Here's what I was thinking about at the funeral," I said finally. "Where did the killer get the gorilla suit?"

We'd driven into a residential area west of downtown, and I pulled the Olds to a halt at an intersection with four-way stop signs and looked over at her.

"Do you guys have ape costumes down at the zoo?"

Ha! That caught her off-guard. Her face flushed and her eyes cut to the side as she tried to evade the question.

"I … I don't know—"

"You do, too. Look at you. It's written all over your face."

She blushed brighter. Apparently, even a flack can be embarrassed when caught in an outright lie.

"We used to have one," she said. "A few years ago. Jungle Jim used it in a couple of promotions. With school kids, you know? I don't know if the costume's still around anywhere."

"I'm guessing it's not," I said. "I'm guessing it's in police custody. They recovered it after the murder."

"You have no way of knowing if that costume was the same one—"

"Maybe not. But the police will have ways to prove it. Have you even told them yours is missing?"

"I don't know that it is," she protested. "For all I know, Jungle Jim's got it stored somewhere. Or he might've sold it, or given it to charity or—"

"Assuming it was stored at the zoo someplace, who all would know about it?"

She flustered and blustered some more, but finally admitted that lots of people could know about the gorilla costume.

"And I'm guessing that nobody reported that to the homicide investigators," I said.

"I don't know—"

"You're all so worried about your public image. You might very well be covering for a murderer."

"Not intentionally."

"Right."

We'd been sitting at the intersection all this time, with no other cars around. Now somebody honked. I looked in the rear-view to see a red-faced guy gesturing angrily in a pickup truck behind us. I spun the wheel and gunned the Olds toward the zoo.

"One way to prove your gorilla suit isn't the right one," I said.

"What's that?"

"Go find it. The cops have the one used in the murder. If you can produce the costume the zoo owns, it would go a long way toward convincing me that there's no connection."

"But I don't have any idea where it might be."

"Ask around. Maybe you can turn it up."

"But—"

"And do it right away," I said. "Otherwise, I'm gonna have to call the cops and inform them that you've been holding out on them."

"You wouldn't do that."

"The homicide lieutenant is a friend of mine. He was at the funeral today, checking out everybody who showed up. Looked particularly suspicious of your group from the zoo. I make one phone call to him, and he's all over you, trying to prove that our killer gorilla came from ZIA."

She paled. We'd reached the parking lot in front of the zoo and I pulled up to the main gate. I fished a business card out of my pocket and handed it to her.

"There's my cell number. Soon as you find that costume, give me a call."

"And if I can't find it?"

"If it's missing, then we'll need to go to the cops."

She looked at my card, then back up at me, deciding. Finally, she nodded.

"I'll go look," she said. "Right now."

"You do that."

Chapter 18

I sat in the car, my motor running, and watched the quick twitch of Cristina's behind as she hurried on her high heels to the administrative entrance.

Could I trust her? Would she really search for the gorilla suit? Would she instead call Romero and inform him that the zoo owned one? If she did that, I'd lose my leverage with her. But I thought she'd play ball. She wanted to keep it hushed up.

The heavy door barely swung shut behind her before it was flung open again, and Noah Gibbons scurried out. At first, I thought he was headed my way, ready with a fresh load of malice and manure. But he turned the other way, hurried down a sidewalk toward the rear of the administration building.

He was still in his black suit, and a breeze blew his necktie back over his shoulder, where it flapped like the wing of a bird. He didn't bother to fix it. Hmm. If Gibbons was in too big a rush to care how he looked, then something must be eating at him. Maybe I should follow him and find out what.

I eased the Olds out of the visitors lot and around the corner to where he'd disappeared. I caught sight of him as he climbed into a low-slung sports car. One of the newer models, a Solstice or a Miata or a Miasma or a Siesta; I can't tell them apart anymore. It was a convertible, but the black canvas top was up this time of year. The silver body was dusty, the wheel wells spattered with wintertime grime. Surprising for someone as prissy as Noah Gibbons. But then, I suppose he'd been too busy lately—chewing me out and going to funerals and covering his ass—to keep his car meticulously clean.

Gibbons slammed through gears and the little car whirred away. I barely kept up with him as he sped through downtown traffic and up a ramp onto Interstate 25, headed north. Once on the freeway, he really let it unwind. Fortunately, there wasn't a lot of traffic, and I could keep him in sight.

Albuquerque freeways are pretty dreamy these days. We suffered two years of construction and chaos when they rebuilt the "Big I," the giant junction in the center of town where Interstates 25 and 40 cross. Highway engineers added lanes and ramps, increasing the freeway's capacity, building with an eye toward the city's future growth. We who live here now get the benefit of a few years of not-so-crowded roads. It won't last, and there still are times when a wreck or some other interruption will snarl traffic in every direction. But sometimes, like today, you can zip along unimpeded for miles. Sweet.

The concrete guardrails of the ramps and flyovers at the new, improved "Big I" are painted the color of Tang with racing stripes of crisp turquoise blue, part of the city's beautification effort, and they always make me smile. I followed Gibbons up a curving ramp onto eastbound I-40, headed toward the sun-blushed Sandia Mountains.

He exited the freeway at Wyoming Boulevard, then went north past gas stations and strip malls and the blank back walls of residential subdivisions. The Heights, where it's all made out of ticky-tacky and it all looks the same.

We passed the fragrant barbecue joint called Quarters, and my stomach growled, reminding me I still hadn't eaten anything today. I had to ask myself what the hell I was doing, following Gibbons halfway across town. So he left his workplace in a hurry and zoomed up to the Northeast Heights. So what? Maybe he was meeting someone for a late lunch. Maybe he was headed to an afternoon tryst. Maybe he'd shop for more cufflinks. Nothing suggested that tailing him would result in anything more than the burning of overpriced gasoline.

Finally, he steered into a modest neighborhood off Wyoming. I followed, keeping a couple of blocks between us so he wouldn't spot my anonymous gray car. Almost lost him when he turned, but I caught a glimpse of the silver car's butt as it wheeled around a corner beyond a spreading elm tree.

Gibbons's car stopped two blocks later, and I saw his brake lights in time and turned onto a side street. The winter sun glinted on his fair hair as he got out of the car. I let the Olds creep forward some, out of his sightline, then parked at the curb. I leaped out of the car and hurried back to the corner to see which house he visited.

Gibbons crossed the street and went up the front sidewalk of a yellow brick house with a scrubby front lawn. He banged on the door so loudly, I could hear it where I stood, half a block away behind the thick trunk of another elm.

The door opened after a few seconds and a fiftyish guy stepped outside. He was a few inches taller than Gibbons, and dressed in jeans and sneakers and a collarless green shirt like doctors wear, what they call "scrubs." Lots of folks wear those shirts for casual wear or pajamas, but this guy looked like he could be a doctor. Lean and clean-cut, with horn-rimmed eyeglasses and what I imagined to be a kindly manner. The image was betrayed somewhat by the tall-boy can of Bud in his hand.

They kept their voices low, and I couldn't make out what they were saying, but I got the feeling the words were harsh. Gibbons's face glowed and his hands jerked around as he chewed on the other guy. The doc didn't seem overly fazed. He took another slug of beer, then another, as Gibbons talked. When the can was empty, he crushed it in his hands. I heard the aluminum crunkle all the way down the block.

The homeowner shook his head as Gibbons continued railing. When he turned to go back inside, Gibbons grabbed his arm. The taller man yanked his arm free, his own face flushing now. He wagged a finger an inch from Gibbons's nose, apparently telling him off, but keeping it to a whisper.

God, I could hardly stand it. I so wanted to hear what they were saying. I couldn't move closer without being spotted, and I didn't want to risk another encounter with Noah Gibbons, not when he clearly was riled up. But I was dying to know: Why were they arguing? Did it have anything to do with Jeff Simmons's death?

The taller man turned on his heel and went back inside. Slammed the door in Gibbons's face. Ooh, that must've been satisfying. I'd like to slam something into his face myself.

Gibbons stormed back to his car. The engine roared and the tires shrieked as he shot off down the street like a bottle rocket. I let him go. I figured he was going back to work, and the way he sped off, I wouldn't have been able to catch him anyway. I was more interested now in finding out who lived in the yellow brick house.

I stepped out from behind the tree, and sauntered down the sidewalk. Just another neighbor, strolling along on a sunny Wednesday afternoon, dressed like an undertaker.

When I reached the spot where Gibbons had parked, I glanced across the street to the doc's house. Curtains were drawn over the windows. A Buick was parked alongside the house, the only indication anyone was home. I made a mental note of the address, then walked around the block, muttering the address over and over so I wouldn't forget it before I got back to my car.

Once inside the slightly warmer confines of the Olds, where I'd left my cell phone recharging, I dialed Felicia's office.

"Gazette city desk. Quattlebaum."

"Hi, hon, it's me. Got a second?"

"Not really."

"I've got an address here, and I was wondering—"

"What am I, the public library? Google? Do you think you can just call up here any time and I'll go running to look up some address for you?"

"Might be important," I interjected.

That slowed her up. "The Simmons case?"

"Yup."

She sighed, stalling, but I knew she couldn't resist. "All right. What's the address?"

I told her.

"You want to call me back in a minute?"

"I'll hold."

She growled and dropped the receiver onto her desktop with a loud thunk. Didn't bother me. I'd expected it, and was holding my phone away from my ear.

Lots of private eyes use reverse directories, which list addresses and the people who live at them. The "reverse" part is because the directories are arranged by address rather than by residents' names. You can go down a street, checking the numbers to find out who's hidden behind each closed door. The directories cost a bundle, and have to be updated every year, so I don't own one. Similar services online are making them obsolete anyway. But I always know where to turn in an emergency. The Gazette keeps a set of reverse directories right in the newsroom.

Felicia came back on the line two minutes later.

"Okay, I got it. But this has got to stop, Bubba. I can't drop everything and go look up an address every time you get a bug up your butt."

"Yes, dear."

"I mean it. In case you haven't noticed, we're busy down here and—"

"Yes, dear."

"Grrrr."

I waited.

"The directory lists one person living at that address," she said. "A Charles Tedeski. Name mean anything to you?"

Yes, it did! Whoo-hoo! So, naturally, I said, "Never heard of him."

"Then this is no help?"

"Guess not. Sorry I bothered you."

"Look, I meant it when I said—"

I hissed into the cell phone receiver, then shouted, "What? You're breaking up. I can't hear you."

"Come on, Bubba, don't give me that—"

"I'm losing you!" I made a crackling noise in my throat. "Talk later."

I thumbed the button that cuts off the call. Felicia might phone me back to finish yelling at me. But she said she was busy. Maybe she'd let it go. I needed to think.

Charles Tedeski. Also known as "Buck," I'd bet. The zoo vet Loretta had mentioned, the one in charge of the necropsies on the mysteriously perishing animals. What's he doing home in the middle of a workday, drinking beer? Why hadn't I seen him at Simmons's funeral? And why was Gibbons so pissed at him?

I thought about knocking on Tedeski's door and putting these questions to him directly. But before I could decide whether I wanted to go face-to-face with him, my cell phone rang.

I figured it was Felicia, which meant it would go unanswered, but I checked the little readout window, saw that the call was coming from the Zoo In Albuquerque.

Now what?

Chapter 19

"**Mr.** Mabry." Her voice came rushed and hushed. "This is Cristina Tapia."

"Yeah?"

"I'm calling about the costume."

That was quick. I had expected her to stall me for hours, if not days, by claiming she was searching for the ape suit. But here it was, less than an hour after I'd dropped her off at the zoo, and she was already calling.

"I asked a few people if they'd seen it, and everybody said it was kept in the same place. I'm there now, and, um, well, it's not here."

"Where are you?"

"Behind the amphitheater where Jungle Jim does his show in the summer. Do you know where I mean?"

"Vaguely." I'd seen that open-air show, or part of it, years ago. It involved birds flying loose above the audience, doing tricks, plucking people's hats off, crap like that. And Jungle Jim brought other animals onto the wooden stage to show off—a cheetah tame enough to walk on a leash and a koala Jim carried like a teddy bear. When Jungle Jim came onto the stage with a python draped over his shoulders, that had been enough for me, and I'd repaired to the concession stand for another funnel cake.

"There's a backstage area, just like at a regular theater," she said. "Supposedly, that gorilla costume's been gathering dust in the workshop here the past couple of years. So I got the keys and came back here and looked around, but I can't find it anywhere."

"No?"

"I see a place where it might've been. It's pretty dusty in here, but there's this one place where the shelf is empty and there's no dust."

I was starting to think Cristina Tapia would make a pretty good detective herself. Would I have noticed the dust quotient if I'd been the one looking? Of course, she was wearing all black and probably trying like hell not to get dust on herself. I could just picture her, in those wobbly heels, tripping around among—

She gasped on the other end of line.

"What's wrong?"

"Somebody's at the door!"

My heart tried to climb up into my throat. I choked it back and attempted to calm her.

"It's probably somebody you talked to, coming to see whether you found the ape suit," I said. "It's probably—"

She shushed me. Something crashed on the other end of the line. I wondered if she'd fallen.

"Cristina?"

"Oh, my God," she said.

"What? What?"

"No!" she shouted. "Don't! Please!"

A loud crack. Hard to tell over a cell phone, but I was pretty sure it was a gunshot. Oh, shit. A thump and a clatter, loud in my ear, as if her phone had hit the floor.

"Cristina!"

Another clatter. I sensed that someone had picked up the receiver, was listening, waiting for me to say something. I heard heavy breathing. I said nothing, scared shitless.

Clunk. Then a dial tone, loud as a police siren in my ear.

Chapter 20

Not every private investigator has the police Homicide Division on his speed-dial. But like I've said, Romero is a friend, more or less, and I sometimes have reason to call him at work. I stumble over the occasional corpse. Might as well save looking up the number each time.

Soon as I recovered from my initial shock—which took a minute—I hit the speed-dial for Romero. I also hit the gas in the Olds, steering back to Wyoming to trek across town to the zoo. Buck Tedeski would have to wait.

Naturally, Homicide put me on hold. Yeah, yeah, they're very busy and the victims aren't in any hurry and all that, but I might've just overheard the shooting of Cristina Tapia and I wanted a cop right now. Not Muzak.

When I finally reached a real live human, he told me Romero wasn't available. Aaugh. I tried to explain what had happened, but the languid detective on the line wasn't buying.

"Sounds like an emergency situation," he said.

"Exactly!"

"Then you should talk to 911."

"But I think somebody got shot!"

"Not good enough," he said. "We only respond after we have proof of a homicide. You need Patrol Division. Call 911."

"But—"

"If somebody's been killed, the patrol officers will call us."

"But—"

"That's the way it works."

"But—"

"Unless you can see a murder victim with your very own eyes."

"No, I just heard it on the phone—"

"Maybe it wasn't a gunshot. Maybe somebody dropped something. Maybe it was static on the line. Did you try to call back?"

"No, I—"

"Star 6-9?"

"I didn't think to—"

"Try not to panic, sir."

"I'm not panicking—"

"Call 911. They're used to dealing with panicky people."

"I'm not panicking."

"Then, as I said, if there appears to be a homicide, they'll call us."

"But—"

"You have a nice day, sir."

Click.

Ooh, that son of a bitch. I'd report him to Romero. Put his ass in a vise. Of course I hadn't caught the detective's name. But Romero would know what kind of smug jerk—

An oversized pickup truck turned across my lane, cutting me off, and I had to stand on the brakes and drop my phone and yank the steering wheel with both hands to keep from plowing into his tailgate. The truck swerved onto a side street, and it took all my will power not to chase after it so I could give the driver a piece of my mind.

My heart pounding, I reined to a stop at a red light and looked around the Olds for my cell phone. It wasn't in the seat, and I couldn't see it on the floorboard anywhere. I felt around with my feet, trying to turn it up. I needed to dial 911, get a patrol car over to the zoo, see what had happened to Cristina Tapia.

If she'd been killed or wounded, it would be all my fault. I'm the one who sent her looking for that goddamned monkey suit. If it weren't for me, she never would've gone to that workshop—

My sneaker bumped something. Had to be my phone. I bent over, reaching under my seat, feeling around for it.

A horn honked behind me. I ignored it, still fumbling under my seat. Got it. I sat up straight just as my fellow motorists really laid down on the horns. The light was green, and cars were stuck behind me while I fiddled with my phone. I glanced in the rear-view, saw an irate woman wagging her finger and flapping her lips. I looked back to the light. Just as it switched to red, I gunned the Olds through the intersection and left her and the others trapped where they sat. Teach 'em to honk at me.

I dialed 911 as I rocketed along. A dispatcher came on the line. She was terse and efficient and methodical, everything you'd want in a police operator, and it only took two minutes to report what I'd heard.

"You're sure it was a gunshot?" the dispatcher asked.

"Not a hundred percent sure, but that's what it sounded like. And it fits. She said, 'Oh, my God,' and like that. Then there's the shot. Then nobody's there."

"Right. And this was at the zoo?"

She seemed to have a little trouble with that part, like she thought I might be a crazy person phoning in my latest hallucination. I imagine they get a lot of that. I did what I could to persuade her I was sane, which isn't as easy as it sounds, particularly in a time of stress.

"All right, sir," she said. "We'll get someone there immediately."

Surely, I thought, someone at the zoo heard that shot, too. Surely someone was on the phone right now with another 911 operator, confirming that a shooting had happened over there. Did the 911 operators talk to each other? Cross-reference their reports? I didn't know. Never had any reason to explore how that works.

I set the phone on the seat beside me. I needed to focus on my driving now. I was flying down a ramp onto I-40.

Noah Gibbons most likely had taken this same route back to work. Had enough time passed for him to get to the zoo? I wasn't sure. He'd roared away, then I ambled around the block, then I called Felicia, and she put me on hold for a couple of minutes, and then Cristina called. Hmm. Gibbons might've reached the zoo, if he really hauled ass, but he probably hadn't had time to track down Cristina. Too bad. I didn't like Gibbons, with his gold cufflinks and his shellacked hair and his menacing attitude. Be sweet if he was our killer. Instead, I'd probably end up being his alibi. Damn.

As I changed lanes, cutting off a Volvo, I recognized that I was assuming that someone shot Cristina Tapia. Indeed, I was assuming she was dead. I prayed that wasn't the case, that somehow what I'd heard didn't add up to another murder. But I didn't have much faith my prayers would be answered.

I had a few more near-misses during my fifteen-minute zoom to the zoo, but I arrived intact. Two Albuquerque Police Department squad cars were parked at angles near the front entrance, their light bars flashing.

I parked some distance away and leaped out of the Olds and hurried to the main gate. Only one of the glassed-in ticket booths was open for business. A bald, elderly man, wearing the green vest of a ZIA volunteer, sat inside, peering out through thick eyeglasses.

"I need to get inside," I yelled through the little speaker that was set into the window.

"Police say we can't let anybody in or out," he shouted back.

"I'm the one who called the police. They're waiting on me."

"Nope. They said nobody in or out, and we're sticking with that."

"But I'm the one who called them! I was talking on the phone to the woman who got shot!"

"What woman?"

"Didn't a woman get shot here?"

He scratched his naked scalp. "I wouldn't know anything about that. I'm just working the gate. They said tell everybody that the police said nobody in or out."

This guy was making me nuts.

I reached for my wallet. "I'll pay you," I shouted. "How much do you want to let me in?"

He gave me a sour, who-farted-in-church kind of look.

"You can't buy me, young fella. I'm following orders here."

The turnstile was only waist-high. I could vault over it, sprint into the zoo. What could this geezer do about it?

He must've seen me looking.

"I wouldn't, if I were you," he said. "I'm expecting Security to come and spell me any second. They're sealing off all the exits."

"But—"

He shook his head. Had a twinkle in his eye, like he was enjoying being in charge, if only for a few minutes. Arrgh. If it hadn't been for that thick glass, I would've wrapped my fingers around his scrawny old throat and—

"What's up, Bubba?"

Romero. I turned to find the lieutenant hurrying up the sidewalk from the parking lot.

"I think somebody got shot in there, and this guy won't let me in. I'm the one who called—"

"I know."

"I think Cristina Tapia—"

"I know."

"Somebody shot her?"

"Sure did."

"Aw, hell." Guilt and grief washed over me. "Is she dead?"

"That's the report I got over the radio. One bullet through the chest."

"Oh, man." My knees felt suddenly weak, and I wobbled where I stood. The news was exactly what I'd feared, but it still took the wind out of me. Some part of me had continued to hope it would turn out to be a big mistake, that what I'd heard hadn't been gunfire. But no. What a lousy time to be right.

Romero grabbed my elbow and steadied me. He still wore his funeral suit and his tan overcoat, and he sort of stepped sideways, out of range in case I yarked. I did feel queasy, but it had been too long since I'd last eaten anything. I was too empty to hurl.

"You all right?" he asked.

"I don't know."

Romero slipped past me and pushed against the turnstile, but it wouldn't budge. He told the old man in the booth to let us through.

"Can't do it," he said. "Orders from the police. Nobody in or out—"

Crack! Romero slapped his gold badge against the glass, right in front of the volunteer's nose.

The geezer flinched, then peered at Romero's badge. Satisfied, he pushed a button that unlocked the turnstile with a buzz.

Romero jerked me along by the arm.

"He's with me," he said as he went through the turnstile.

The old guy was a little slow with the button, so the turnstile didn't turn again as Romero tried to drag me through it. One of the chrome arms goosed me in the groin. Ooooch. Then the buzz again and the arm rotated and I was inside. Hurrying to the murder scene. In the grasp of a homicide lieutenant.

Not the best circumstances for a visit to the zoo.

Chapter 21

Romero dragged me halfway across the zoo, taking me ever closer to the scene of the crime. He badged a couple of security guards who were headed toward the front gate, and they deferentially waved us past.

We hustled past pens full of birds and bears and butt-ugly baboons, but Romero paid them no mind. He quizzed me about what I'd heard over the phone.

"I was talking to Cristina and then she said somebody's at the door, and I'm like, whoa, who could that be, but she shushes me, and then she starts screaming, 'Don't! Please!' and then there's a big noise and it sounded like she dropped the phone—"

"This noise," he said, "how did you know it was a gunshot?"

"I know what a gun sounds like."

"Over the phone? How did you know it wasn't a hammer or a firecracker or something?"

"I just knew."

"Did it sound like the gun at the Flying Squirrel? A thirty-eight?"

Okay, that connection I hadn't exactly made yet. I guess the algebra was out there, floating around the edges of my mind: Simmons slain by guy in ape suit + Cristina shot when she goes to look for said costume = the same killer. But I hadn't worked it out yet. I'd been busy rushing to the scene. If it were the same killer, it certainly would make sense that he'd used the same gun—

"Hey, Bubba," Romero said. "Are you in there?"

"Huh?"

"You drifted off. I asked you, did it sound like the same gun?"

"Could be. Sounded different over the phone, of course. And I wasn't expecting it—"

"You expected the first killing?"

"Huh? No! But I saw the gun. There was a split second between the time the ape pulled the gun out of his bag and when he fired it. I was expecting to hear a gunshot, see? But this time, on the phone, I wasn't expecting anything like that."

"What were you expecting?"

"Huh?"

"Can you stop saying 'huh'? It's getting on my nerves."

He gripped my arm a little tighter. Ow.

"Sorry," I said. "I think I'm in shock."

"Yeah, right."

We passed the small lake that's in the middle of zoo. A few swans skimmed its surface, which reflected the blue sky. Pigeons bobbed along the footpath, gurgling and purring. I felt like kicking them out of the way.

We veered left at the zoo's café, and I got a whiff of grilling hamburgers. My stomach growled loudly, practically howling at the scent. I'm sure Romero noticed, but he didn't mention it.

"What were you expecting when she called?" he repeated.

"Oh, right. She'd told me after the funeral that she'd go look for the gorilla suit and—"

Romero stopped cold. I took another step or two before he yanked me to a halt.

"Say what?" he demanded.

"The gorilla suit. Didn't I mention that? That's what this is all about."

"She went to look for the gorilla costume? The one the shooter wore when Simmons got hit?"

"Right."

"But we've got the costume downtown."

"Right."

"Then what the hell are you talking about?"

"I asked her if the zoo ever owned a gorilla costume, and she said they did."

His eyebrows shot up, making me feel a little superior. It's so rare that I surprise him. With Romero, raised eyebrows are the equivalent of somebody else turning backflips.

"Why didn't you call me immediately?"

Damned good question. Boy, I sure wished that I had called him. But I didn't tell him that. Instead, I said, "She wanted it kept quiet. If she could've found the zoo's gorilla suit, then that would've cleared everybody here and the zoo's image wouldn't have been sullied."

I know. I sounded just like Cristina Tapia. Occasionally, in times of stress, I turn into a parrot. It's not pretty.

"Bullshit," Romero said. "Finding the costume wouldn't have cleared anybody. There's more than one gorilla suit in the world."

"But if the zoo's ape suit was missing, then it might be the same one you've got locked up as evidence."

Romero started walking again, dragging me along beside him. "And that's what happened."

"Right again. She found out where the gorilla suit was kept, and she went to look for it, and it was gone."

The walls of the amphitheater were made of rough-hewn, pointy logs standing on end, what I think they call a "stockade." Like the cavalry forts in Westerns. Or that giant wall in *King Kong*. The gate stood open. We went down a ramp past twenty rows of aluminum bleachers. A few zoo security types in khaki uniforms milled around outside a door by the stage. Romero flashed his badge and marched me right past them.

It was dark in there, especially compared to the bright sunshine outdoors, and it took a second for my eyes to adjust. Not that it mattered. Romero dragged me into the darkness, and I trusted that he could see where he was going.

We turned a corner and saw a light up ahead. Two uniformed APD patrolmen stood under the light, and several dark figures filled the hallway beyond them. One cop was stringing yellow "Crime Scene" tape across a doorway to our right, making an X.

"Hey, Lieutenant," the other patrolman said as we approached. "Your people are inside already."

Romero finally let go of my arm, which tingled all the way to my fingertips as blood surged into it again.

"Wait here," he said to me. As he ducked under the yellow tape, he told the patrolmen, "Watch him."

The cops put their hands on their pistol butts and glared at me, as if I might sprint away. That wouldn't make any sense. I was the one responsible for calling them to the scene. But of course they didn't know that. For all they knew, I was a suspect.

I edged closer to the cops, getting fully into the pool of light, so they could see I wasn't armed or dangerous. Didn't seem to do any good, but it put me closer to the door of the workshop.

I didn't really want to see Cristina Tapia dead. I knew her corpse would be one of those sights that would haunt my dreams for years to come. But I couldn't help myself. I glanced through the door, past the yellow tape.

The workshop was brightly lit by two bulbs suspended from the ceiling in wire cages. Three police detectives dressed in jeans and jackets were in there with Romero. They wore rubber gloves and paper booties as they secured evidence and took photographs. Romero snapped gloves on, too.

The workshop was larger than I'd expected, nearly thirty feet wide, lined with wooden shelves full of props and a rack of hanging safari suits and pieces of plywood "scenery" leaning against concrete-block walls. A workbench fit against one wall, dusty and cluttered with a jumble of saws and hammers and other tools. An old-fashioned black telephone squatted on the concrete floor, and I guessed from its long cord that the phone probably sat on the workbench most of the time. Next to the phone lay Cristina's body.

She still wore her funeral clothes. She lay on her side, her arms in front of her, reaching toward the phone, her legs bent as if running. The skirt of her black pin-striped suit was hitched up around her thighs, and she still wore those ridiculous spike heels. Her black hair covered her face and haloed around her head. A round red puddle had spread onto the cement floor, blood that leaked from the hole in her ribcage.

My eyes felt hot and sawdust filled my throat. My fault. All my fault. If only I hadn't sent her in here to look for that ape suit—

"Hey!" A deep voice called from the shadows beyond the cops. "You're that private investigator!"

Not now. I didn't need more attention. Not until I could pull myself together anyway.

Jungle Jim Johansen elbowed his way past the officers. He grabbed my hand and pumped it several times, as if we were old friends. The cops looked annoyed, but they clearly recognized Johansen from TV.

"Still on the case, huh?" he said loudly.

I made a shushing face. Romero had yet to fully explore what I was doing, meddling in his murders, and I didn't need some loudmouth reminding him.

"I thought you were gonna call me!" Johansen said. "I've got some ideas about these killings."

Couldn't he take a hint? Couldn't he shut the hell up before he got us both thrown behind bars?

"Well, okay," I stammered. "Sure."

"So you got here in a hurry," he said. "Police give you a call? I didn't think they cooperated with private eyes. Or is that just in the movies?"

That got the patrolmen glowering at me again. Johansen still had my hand gripped in his paw, and I gave him a tug and turned away from the police. He followed—finally, finally understanding my situation—and we put out heads together, as nearly as we could with the wide brim of his Aussie hat in the way.

"Stuff a sock in it, Jungle Jim," I muttered. "These cops are mad at me already."

"Really? How come?"

"Because they don't like me messing around in their business," I said tightly. "And because I was the one who called in the shooting."

He drew back and squinted at me. "No, you weren't."

"Yes, I was."

"Don't kid me, buster."

"It's 'Bubba.'"

"Whatever. I guess I know who reported the shooting. Because I was it."

"Huh?"

"I'm the one who called the cops," he said. "I heard the shot as I was crossing the meadow. Thought it sounded like it came from back here, so I came to investigate."

"And you found her body?"

"That's right. And I immediately called the police."

"Okay, but I called them, too. I was on the phone with her when she got shot."

"Really?" His eyes widened. "That must've been weird."

"You have no idea."

"What was she doing in here anyway?" he asked. "Hardly anybody comes back here except me."

I opened my mouth to answer, but a thought flashed through my mind: I might be talking to the murderer right now. This workshop was Johansen's turf. Which made him a pretty good suspect.

"Where were you when you heard the shot?" I asked.

"Crossing the meadow. Over by the lake? I'd just finished a meeting with Carolyn Hoff, and I was coming here."

"For what?"

He grinned. "Tell you the truth, I was looking for a hideout."

"What?"

"Carolyn has a way of getting under my skin. I was all pissed, so instead of going to my office, I decided to take a walk. Get some air. When I need a place to cool off, I come back here to my workshop."

So Jungle Jim's headed this way. He's already angry. He finds Cristina snooping through his stuff …

"Hey," Romero said right behind me. I jumped into the air six or eight feet. "You two having a nice chat?"

"Um, uh, sure."

"Don't you know it's dangerous to talk to him?" Romero asked Johansen. "Everybody who talks to this guy ends up dead."

I made a face at Romero. Jungle Jim looked back and forth between us, confused, his smile fading.

The lieutenant stripped off his tight rubber gloves. He was nearly as tall as Jungle Jim and easily as wide. I was wedged between them, and it felt as if they were looming over me.

"Um, turns out that we both reported the shooting," I said.

"Isn't that something?" Jungle Jim chimed in.

"Then Bubba started questioning you about what you found?"

"Sort of," Johansen said. "Just comparing notes, you know."

Ouch. Wrong thing to say. But Johansen didn't seem to understand that he was pissing off the lieutenant. He blundered ahead.

"I was telling him how I was coming over here to chill out for a while. A little goldbricking session."

"You do that a lot?" Romero wasn't even looking at me now. His attention was on Johansen. I wrung my hands anyway. My turn was coming.

"Now and then." Johansen grinned. "I'm like those cops you see sometimes, sitting in the shade in their cars, grabbing a siesta."

The uniformed cops shifted and grumbled. Johansen seemed to have a real knack for saying the wrong thing. How had he lasted so long on TV? Probably everything he said in front of a camera was scripted, but damn—

"Were you surprised to find her here?"

"Hell, yeah. I would've been surprised to find anyone in here, to tell the truth. Like I was telling Buster here, I'm about the only one who uses this workshop."

The corner of Romero's mouth twitched when Jungle Jim called me by the wrong name, but he remained otherwise impassive. As usual.

"What did you do then?"

"I called 911."

"On that phone?" Romero gestured with his thumb back over his shoulder, toward the workshop door.

"No, I didn't touch that phone. I used my cell." He pulled a folded silver phone out of one of the pockets of his safari jacket and showed it to us.

Romero nodded.

"What was she doing in here anyway?" Johansen said. "We were just getting to that—"

I shushed him again, waving both hands at him, like he was on fire and I was trying to put him out. Romero cocked an eyebrow, which froze me in place.

"Looking for an ape suit, I understand," he said. "You know anything about that?"

"An ape suit?" Took Jungle Jim a second to put it together. "Oh, the one we used in the school programs! Why did she need that?"

There was no shutting him up. I might as well cut to the chase. "She was trying to see whether it was missing."

"Missing? How come? Oh! You think it was the same one that was used when Simmons was killed—"

Johansen finally got the situation through his thick head. His golden face paled a little.

"Is it?" he asked.

"What?"

"Missing?"

Romero cut in. "You don't know?"

"Nooo. I haven't used it in a couple of years. It should be on one of those shelves in there. Along the back wall."

He stepped past Romero, toward the crime scene tape. The lieutenant grasped his arm before he could burst into the workshop. But apparently, Johansen had sharp eyes.

"It's not there," he said. "I can see that from here. It used to be on that shelf over there. Third one down. See that empty space?"

Romero leaned closer to the big man. "You didn't know it was missing?"

"Hell, no."

"But this is your work space."

"I hardly ever use it during the winter. During the summer, when we're doing the amphitheater show, I'm back here every day. But this time of year, I mostly work out of my office. It's way over there by the other offices and—"

He caught himself and his eyes went wide.

"You don't think I had something to do with this?"

The lieutenant shrugged.

"Hey, now," Johansen said. "I just called 911 after I heard the shot. I didn't see anybody. I don't know anything."

"We'll see about that," Romero said. "Let's go outside and talk some more."

Johansen looked suddenly miserable and afraid. Nice to see Romero make somebody else squirm for a change. But then he said, "You too, Bubba."

I followed the big men around the corner, toward the glaring sunshine in the distance.

Strange to find it was still sunny outside, that for most people it was just another bright February day in Albuquerque. Felt gloomy as hell to me.

Chapter 22

Romero kept me fidgeting on the chilly aluminum bleachers in the amphitheater for a couple of hours. He came over a few times, asking questions to clarify details, but mostly he just made me wait.

I watched as Romero sat on the edge of the stage and quietly interviewed a stream of bundled-up zoo employees—Jungle Jim and Carolyn Hoff, smirking Noah Gibbons and twitchy Perry Oswalt, an assortment of security guards and zookeepers and others I didn't recognize. Most didn't seem to have much to offer. Lots of head-shaking and terse answers and a little weeping over poor Cristina, but nobody acted particularly guilty or suspect, at least not from where I sat.

Cops came and went. Crime scene technicians hauled out bags of evidence. I looked away when two paramedics wheeled Cristina's body bag out of the amphitheater on a gurney.

At times, I could divorce myself from the moment, as if I were watching a cop show on TV rather than a real-life tragedy. Then the truth of it would hit me with an emotional wallop and I'd feel rotten all over again.

Finally, as the sun was setting and it was starting to get pretty damned cold sitting on that metal bench in my funeral suit, Romero looked up, acted surprised that I was still there in the cheap seats. He walked up to me, moving slowly, looking fatigued.

"You think of anything else?" he asked me.

I shook my head.

"Then go home, Bubba."

"Really?"

He frowned, like he couldn't believe I didn't sprint for the exit. A good point. I sprang to my feet.

"Bubba?"

I froze. I'd been waiting all afternoon for Romero to explode at me. Was this it?

"Just go home," he said. "Stay out of trouble. For a change."

I nodded and hurried away, intent on obeying. I'd had enough of this case for one day. Maybe forever. Maybe I'd give Loretta Gonzales her money back—most of it, anyway—and tell her I wanted nothing more to do with this. Quit before I got somebody else killed.

I crossed the shadowy meadow and passed the dark lake and the flamingo-free pool. By the time I reached the front gate, I felt bleary and weary and blue.

Beyond the turnstiles, a mob of news media clustered around their satellite trucks. Spotlights glared as the TV types got ready for their live-at-five reports. Technicians and reporters swam in and out of pools of light. My spirits sank.

I slipped through the gate and veered left toward the parking lot. I was dressed all in black. Maybe if I stuck to the shadows—

"Mister Mabry!"

Oh, no. That chirp could only belong to Felicia's chatterbox intern, Julie Keen.

She hurried out of the crowd, her heels clacking on the concrete. She was dressed in a different suit, but still in that narrow retro style, and her blonde hair flipped up at her shoulders. As she ran toward me, her bouncy hair flapped like wings.

I trotted away. Not easy to run in my black dress loafers, but I could outdistance a pair of high heels.

I looked back over my shoulder. She wasn't giving up. She had her pen upraised, as if it were a totem, a badge of honor. As if it were mighty enough to make me stop. Not even close. I ran faster.

Other media types noticed her chasing after me. A couple of cameramen jogged in my direction, minicams on their shoulders. No idea who I was, of course, but they didn't want to miss anything. If the Gazette intern thought I was worth pursuing, then maybe they should be baying behind me, too.

I reached the Olds, which was locked. I fumbled with my keys, trying to get the door open, as the journalists hounded closer.

"Mister Mabry! Wait!"

No way, sister. The door clicked open and I dived inside. Locked the doors. Keyed the ignition.

Julie reached the car and peered through my window, calling my name. I shook my head at her. A blast of light poured past her into the car. One of the cameramen had turned on his minicam, recording my flight.

I nearly ran over the other cameraman as I roared out of the parking slot. They scattered as my tires squealed and the Olds shot away.

I checked my mirror when I reached the street in front of the zoo. The cameramen had already turned away, getting back to work now that their prey had fled. Julie stared after me, looking disappointed.

Tough.

Chapter 23

When I got home, I was relieved to find that Felicia wasn't there. Not the proper matrimonial thing to say, I know, but I'd narrowly escaped one pack of reporters. I didn't need one woofing at me in my own living room.

I left the lights off as I padded to the kitchen, desperate for a beer and some food and a little peace. The red light on the answering machine threw its glow over the kitchen, but I ignored it. Nothing but bad news waiting there, and I'd had enough bad news for one day.

I squinted against the light in the refrigerator when I opened its door. Only two Heinekens left, which I'd classify as an emergency situation. They'd have to do for now. I opened one and drank deeply of the magic elixir. Aah. I sat down at the table, leaning forward on my elbows, my head drooping. At rest. Finally.

Naturally, the goddamned phone rang. I jerked upright, but made no move to answer it. After four jangling rings, the answering machine came on. I heard my recorded voice saying "Bubba Mabry Investigations" and asking the caller to leave a number.

"Mabry?" Not a voice I recognized.

"This is Armando Gonzales. I saw you at the funeral today."

Ah, Loretta's father.

"I told you then to stay away from my daughter."

The asshole.

"I just heard what happened to this Tapia woman down at the zoo."

Uh-oh.

"And let me tell you right now. If anything happens to my daughter, if any trouble should come her way because of you, I'll ruin you. I mean it, buster."

Why do people keep calling me that?

"If anyone harms a single hair on her head, I'll make you wish you'd never been born."

I was beginning to wish that already.

"I know people in this town, people who'll do whatever I need. Don't make me use them."

Don't worry.

"Stay away from her."

The machine clicked as he hung up.

I sat motionless, wondering whether I should save that tape in case Gonzales really did send some goons around. Maybe I ought to hand it over to Romero. Second time the jerk had threatened me. Maybe the cops should know about him.

I drained the beer, and wearily got up to fetch the last one from the fridge. I should eat something. Take my shoes off. Get out of my funeral suit and into something comfy. Get some rest. Instead, I'm sitting in the dark in my own kitchen, listening to Armando Gonzales menace me.

I pulled off the necktie that had rubbed at my throat all afternoon. Christ, what a day. Long and emotional and wearing. Bad as mine was, though, it was worse for Cristina Tapia. The image of her limp body, lying in that pool of blood, flooded my mind. I wondered about her family, her friends, what they must be going through. A vibrant woman, in the prime of her life, snuffed out by the quick exhalation of a pistol. Who knew how many people were affected, how many lives had been wounded today? All because I sent her to check out a monkey suit. Damn.

Only one thing would make me feel better: Justice. Whoever killed Cristina must get what's coming to him, one way or the other. It wouldn't bring her back, wouldn't fill the empty space she'd left behind, but it would settle accounts for society. I understood at that moment how Romero must feel about his job, how he represents the victim on society's behalf, how he avenges our loss and sets things right. Maybe I could help. If only for my own peace of mind.

You just don't get to go around killing. Of all of the Commandments, I'd put that one at Numero Uno. Someone had decided differently, had decided he could solve a problem by eliminating people. Such arrogance. What kind of person ignores thousands of years of taboos? What kind of sociopath sees murder as a solution?

Which brought me back to Armando Gonzales. Clearly, he considered himself above the law. So confident of his own social standing that he'd leave a threatening message and not worry that I'd run to the cops with it.

Could he be behind these murders? Loretta said he wasn't happy about her engagement, that he suspected Jeff Simmons was only after her fortune. Could he have been so worked up about their betrothal that he'd actually had Simmons killed? Didn't seem likely. For all his bluster, a fat cat like Gonzales would be more likely to try to buy off a suitor. And, surely, his daughter's own happiness was more important than all his worries about gold-digging. Even an asshole like Armando wouldn't send his own daughter spiraling into mourning, would he?

I shook my head, trying to clear such crazy thoughts. The murders clearly were tied to the zoo, not to Armando Gonzales. The timing of Simmons's murder, the gorilla suit, Cristina's death, all indicated the murderer was someone at the zoo. But who?

I wanted the killer to be Noah Gibbons, the little prick, but the timing was all wrong. I'd seen him leave Buck Tedeski's house shortly before Cristina was shot. He just didn't have time to make it back to the zoo and kill her. And Tedeski was out. He'd still been at home.

Who else? Not brittle Carolyn Hoff, surely. And I couldn't see weirdo Perry Oswalt wielding a weapon either. He wouldn't have the guts.

Jungle Jim Johansen, for all his offers of help, had to be considered a suspect. He had easiest access to the ape suit. Cristina was killed in his workshop. Granted, he'd called the cops about the shooting, but wouldn't a wily killer do that to divert suspicion?

The pool of potential suspects was much bigger than the people I'd met, of course. Dozens of other people worked at the zoo, and any of them could have a motive for murder.

I thought again of the suspicious animal deaths. Maybe it was time to consult Jeff Simmons's spreadsheets again. Now that I knew more of the players, maybe the numbers would add up to something meaningful. I got up and turned on the lights and unfolded the papers I still carried in my pocket. I stared at them like they were a Ouija board, as if the numbers would suddenly arrange themselves into something I'd understand, but no such luck.

All I succeeded in doing was giving myself a headache. I sighed and pushed the papers away. My beer bottle was empty. I needed to eat something. Maybe go to bed early. If I was asleep when Felicia came home, I could avoid all her questions and demands.

Then the doorbell rang.

Chapter 24

I made the mistake of turning on lights as I went to the front door. Once I'd done that, I couldn't pretend I wasn't home. Which is what I wanted to do when I peered out the peephole. Julie Keen stood on the front porch, shifting from one high-heeled foot to the other like a twitchy pony.

I sighed and opened the door. She beamed when she saw me. "You're home! Great!"

Given her chirpy voice and excitable manner and floodlight smile, I would've chosen to be most anyplace else. I thought about slamming the door, but she'd just ring the bell again. And again. She seemed determined to drive me crazy.

"After the way you ran off at the zoo, I thought you were trying to avoid me," she cheeped. "But then I realize you were just trying to get away from those TV cameras and who can blame you? I probably would've done the same if I were you, though that's never come up before in my life. I mean, why would they ever try to put me on TV? I haven't done anything. It's not like I'm a famous private eye, like some people we know. Besides, I like being behind the scenes, not in front of the cameras. That's one reason I want to be a newspaper reporter. It's like an eye on history. You see things happen without being directly involved in them, you know? You stand in the background and stuff unfolds right before your very eyes. How cool is that? Anyway, I didn't come here to talk about me. May I come in?"

She paused, her perfectly plucked eyebrows arched. I was so surprised by the sudden silence, I nearly fell over. I stammered before finally spitting out: "What do you want?"

"Why, to talk about this latest murder, of course. It's all connected, isn't it? The gorilla killing, and now this Tapia woman at the zoo. I mean, Jeff Simmons worked at the zoo, and now there's a new murder there. Got to be a connection, right? And you were right there, on the inside, so you must know all about it and I could—"

I held up a hand to stop her. It felt like stepping in front of a runaway train, but, surprisingly, it worked.

"I'm not talking," I said. "You want information, go to the cops."

"But everybody's doing that. I want something different from the pack. I know you're investigating the whole thing. I want to help. Let me do legwork for you. Let me brainstorm with you. I'm full of ideas—"

I'll bet.

"—and you might find that they're helpful. I mean, you're probably way ahead of me. I wouldn't be a bit surprised if you solved the whole thing before the police do—"

Boy, that would surprise the hell out of me.

"—but maybe you could use an extra set of eyes, you know? Tailing people or something. I think that would be very exciting. I think I might be good at it, too. I can be, like, really stealthy. When I was kid, I used to sneak up on my brother all the time, and he never caught me. I remember one time—"

"Stop!"

The shout froze her in place. Her mouth hung open. Its accustomed position.

"Just stop talking for a second. I've got a headache."

"Oh, I'm sorry. I didn't know. Have you taken something—"

"Stop. Now." There was an edge of menace in my voice. I couldn't help it. To her credit, she picked up on it. The quiet was a balm to my ears. I could see she was ready to crank it back up again, though, so I talked before she could.

"You want to help?"

She nodded. Started to say something, but caught herself and stuck with nodding.

"If I give you something to do, will you stop following me around?"

"Well, sure. I mean, if we're a team and all—"

My scowl silenced her this time. She was catching on.

"Okay, fine. Let me think a second. There's bound to be some way you can help."

"Great! Can I come in?"

"No. Just give me a second."

She didn't seem at all taken aback by the fact that I made her stay on the porch like a pooch. She produced a pen and pad and stood poised to write down my instructions.

Of course, I had nothing. I couldn't think what I should do next on this case, much less what I might assign to a newfound assistant. But I had to come up with something if I wanted to get rid of her.

"I know," I said. "You can do background checks."

"Background checks? Oh, I could do a great job of that! Who do you—"

I held up a hand. She got the message.

"Write down these names," I commanded. "Carolyn Hoff. Noah Gibbons. Charles Tedeski, goes by Buck. Jim Johansen. Perry Oswalt."

She furiously scribbled down their names. I was running out of suspects. Was that enough to keep her busy?

"All those people work at the zoo," I said. "Also, see what you can find on Armando Gonzales of ArGon Foods."

She opened her mouth to question that, but I kept talking.

"While you're at it, see what you can find out about the two victims. And Loretta Gonzales. She's Armando's daughter and was engaged to Simmons."

Julie Keen wrote down those names, too. When she looked up again, her eyes shined with excitement. She was a beagle on a scent.

"I'll get right on it," she said.

"Okay. Give me a call when you've got something."

"I'll bring you all the information in person."

"A phone call would be fine. Really."

"I'll run them through Google and see what I can turn up. And the newspaper's electronic library. Then I'll—"

"Stop." She did. "Don't tell me how you're going to do it. Just bring me some results."

"Yes, sir!"

She shut her notebook and stuffed it in her handbag.

"Thanks for this opportunity, Mr. Mabry. I really appreciate it and I guarantee you that I'll—"

I slammed the door.

Chapter 25

I avoided the Felicia Inquisition that night by feigning sleep, but I awoke the next morning braced for the full grilling. To my surprise, she wasn't interested. Somebody else at the newspaper had been assigned to the zoo murders, she said. She was already on some other scoop, one that would be much more exciting and interesting than a couple of killings. Her terse manner told me there was more to the story, but I didn't pursue it. Pressing her is like poking a stick at a pit bull.

She went off chasing her new story, and I had the house to myself. The sudden peace and quiet led my brain back to the questions that had plagued me during the long, restless night: Who killed Jeff Simmons? Was it the same person who shot Cristina Tapia? And why?

I felt no better sense of direction by the time I was shaved and showered and spruced up. I shambled back into the kitchen for the last of the coffee, and saw that the answering machine had taken a message while I was in the shower. I hit the buttons to make it play.

"Bubba! Where the hell are you!" Marvin Pidgeon, the attorney who'd been my regular client before all this zoo crap erupted. "I need you right away! Grave injustices are being done—"

Sorry, but that's the way Marvin talks.

"—and I can't get them investigated properly. Why aren't you returning my calls? I've got accident cases coming out my ears, but I need photos and interviews. Evidence, damn it, I need evidence! If I don't hear from you, and I mean right away, I will have to take my business elsewhere."

I erased the message. I needed to keep Marvin happy—he was the source of most of my income lately—but I couldn't focus on his troubles right now. Sidewalk cracks and slippery floors couldn't hold a candle to murder.

I stared at the floor, my arms crossed over my chest, my head bowed under the strain of strategizing.

Should I badger Carolyn Hoff again? She'd barely consented to talk to me the first time. Now that Cristina had been killed, right at the zoo, Hoff was probably apoplectic. Nothing like headlines of homicide to put off donors and volunteers and visitors. If I showed up at the zoo offices, she'd probably have her guards toss me off the premises.

Should I quiz my client? Could I face another round of Loretta's fresh grief? And what could she tell me that was new? I'd pursued the only suspects she'd given me and gotten nowhere with them.

My gaze wandered the cluttered countertop until it snagged on a silver camera near the spot where Felicia usually dumps her purse and keys and notebooks and other day-to-day detritus.

It was a spanking new digital camera, no bigger than a pack of cigarettes, and it belonged to the Gazette. The newspaper recently equipped all its top reporters with such cameras. The idea was that reporters would start taking some of their own photos, now that the technology was so easy to use. I wondered how the photographers felt about this plan.

Felicia hadn't seemed interested in the shiny camera, but it was all I could do to keep my hands off it. Guys love gizmos. This camera was so much more compact than the old Nikon I use to photograph sidewalk cracks, it was like a gumball-machine toy. Now, with Felicia not around, I was sorely tempted to play with it. The way things had gone lately, I'd probably find some way to break it. Who needed that grief?

I paced around the kitchen, telling myself to concentrate. The shootings. Simmons. The zoo. Tapia. The ape.

I kept coming back to that gorilla suit. Was it indeed the one missing from the zoo? If it was, then the killer almost certainly was someone who worked at ZIA. Who else would know it even existed, back there on that dusty shelf?

On impulse, I picked up the phone and dialed Steve Romero. By now, he might've identified the gorilla outfit that he had in custody as the one missing from the zoo. Maybe he'd tell me about it. Maybe he'd collected other information from the crime scenes that, once he shared it with me, would generate sudden insights that would help us solve the case together. Yes, and maybe monkeys would fly out of my butt, too, but I didn't know what else to do.

I almost hung up while holding for Romero. Wasn't this like walking into the lion's den? I'd gotten away clean the day before, after clearly being the responsible party in Cristina's untimely demise. Romero had warned me to keep my nose out of this case. What was I doing, calling him up, giving him another crack at me? I was as bad as Felicia's intern, yapping and squirming and begging to be included. Pitiful.

"Romero." Too late. He was on the line.

"Hey, Steve, it's Bubba."

"What the hell do you want?" A fine greeting.

"I, uh, I was thinking about the zoo murders some more, and I was, um, wondering whether you had arrested anybody yet."

A long silence.

"No, huh?"

Still, he said nothing. I hate when he does that. The silent treatment makes me blither.

"What about the gorilla suit? Did it turn out to be a match? Because if it was, I have some, uh, ideas about who at the zoo might've, you know—"

"Bubba." Finally, something back.

"Yeah?"

"Didn't I tell you to go home and forget about all this?"

"I did. I was beat anyway, and I thought a good night's sleep might—"

"Bubba."

"Yeah?"

"What about the forgetting part? Did you work on that?"

"I can't put it out of my mind. I feel like it's my fault that woman got killed yesterday."

Nothing. Guess he felt like it was my fault, too.

"I keep thinking," I said, "that maybe I could do something to help."

"You want to help, then keep out of it. We'll take it from here."

"Well, sure, but maybe I could—"

"No, Bubba. I guarantee you that Loretta Gonzales isn't paying you enough to face an obstruction of justice rap."

"Come on, you wouldn't charge me with—"

"Like hell. You mess up my case against this killer, and see how quickly you're in the DA's office."

"I'm just trying to help."

"No, you're not. You're trying to make yourself feel better."

Ouch. That hurt as only the truth can.

"Is that so bad?" I whined.

Another long silence. Was he softening toward me and my pain?

"Look," he said finally, "we've got it, okay? Just sit tight. Won't be long before we nail this son of a bitch, and everybody can forget any of this ever happened."

"I won't forget. How can I? Two people dead, just because they talked to me?"

"If that's the reason. Might have nothing to do with you."

"I think it's my fault. Somehow."

"You're such a mope," he said. "You believe you're responsible for every bad thing that happens."

"Isn't that usually the case?"

"Well, yeah. But we don't know for sure this time. Let me do my job. Maybe it's not about you at all."

"It's about the zoo, though, that much is certain."

Guilt hammered me. I should've told Romero from the outset about Simmons's suspicions and the animal deaths. Instead, I'd concealed the spreadsheets from him, and kept mum about what little I knew. I had a sudden urge to tell all, but I couldn't now, could I? I had, by God, obstructed justice by keeping my little secrets. Romero wouldn't be able to overlook that, no matter how many years we'd known each other.

"Look," he said, "I'll tell you this much just to settle you down. The labels on the gorilla suit check out. Manufactured by a company in New Jersey. It almost certainly was the one missing from that backstage workshop."

Aha! I knew it. Before I could gloat, he said, "That's the only connection we've found so far, other than the fact that both victims worked at ZIA. But it would seem to narrow down the list of suspects."

"What about the bullets? Same gun kill both people?"

"We don't have the ballistics tests back yet. I assume they were killed by the same person, and probably by the same gun. Ballistics won't be much help beyond confirming that."

"Unless you recover the gun."

"My guess is that gun is at the bottom of that lake at the zoo," he said. "That's what I would've done if I shot somebody there. Short walk across that meadow and—splash—problem solved."

"You gonna drain the lake?"

"Oh, yeah, based on nothing more than my suspicions. The city fathers would love that. You know how much it would cost? And how much duck shit and dead fish we'd find at the bottom? The stink would force 'em to close the zoo for weeks."

"Really?"

"I'm sending divers in today, but I don't expect them to find anything. I'm told it's pretty murky down there."

"Duck shit, huh?"

"They're prolific poopers, those ducks."

I tried to come up with anything else I might worm out of him.

"Bubba?"

"Yeah?"

"I want you to think carefully about that lake. If you feel you must go sticking your nose in my case some more? You're gonna be just like the bottom of that lake."

"Murky?"

"In deep shit, Bubba. Deep shit. Got me?"

"Okay, okay. You've made your point."

We talked for another minute or so, but I didn't get anything out of him other than another warning. After I hung up, I sat wringing my hands, trying to figure out some way to uncover the killer. I couldn't leave it alone.

Deep shit or no.

Chapter 26

One thing was certain: I wouldn't make any progress sitting around the house, fretting. I decided to go to the zoo and rattle some cages.

The New Mexico weather was doing its usual glorious sunshine deal, with just enough of a bite to the breeze to make me happy to be wearing my leather jacket. I climbed into the Olds and the engine cranked right up, which I took as a good omen. I backed out of the driveway and turned toward Central Avenue.

While I waited for a break in the traffic on Central, I hunted up my sunglasses and fiddled with the radio and tried to get the heater to work. A Jeep Cherokee with oversized tires loomed in my mirror, putting the pressure on me to stop screwing around and jump out onto the busy boulevard. I couldn't see who was behind the wheel, but I know Albuquerque drivers. If I kept him waiting long, that Jeep would start honking like a crazed goose.

I caught a gap in the traffic flow and turned right onto Central. I figured I'd cruise past UNM—never passing up a chance to ogle the milling coeds—then cut over to the One-ways before I got snarled in downtown traffic.

A red light froze traffic at the intersection where Central, Girard, and Monte Vista come together at odd angles. I gave up on the radio, and snapped it off. Checked my mirror out of habit. The Jeep with the big tires was right behind me. Hmm.

Once the light changed and I got through the dangerous intersection unscathed, I changed lanes, figuring to get out of the jacked-up Jeep's way, but he swerved into my lane and tucked in behind me again, right on my ass.

Okay, you could say I'm paranoid. But the last time a vehicle rode my tail, I ended up losing my Dodge pickup, rolling it several times in a snow-covered field. This Jeep wasn't trying to ram me, but it was following too close and that made me nervous.

At Cornell, I got into the left-turn lane. What the hell, I was too busy watching my mirror to admire the college girls anyway. Might as well go on over to the One-ways and—son of a bitch, the Jeep stayed right with me.

I turned onto Cornell and gunned the Olds up the block to the next stop sign. Checked my mirror. Still back there, closing fast. I blasted across the intersection, went a block and—miracle of miracles this close to UNM—saw an empty parking space at the curb. I wedged the Olds right into it, threw the shifter into Park, and watched my side mirror, my heart thumping. Come on, Jeep, drive on past. Prove me wrong. Please.

Bad move. The big Jeep stopped beside me. I was hemmed in. I was unarmed. If that was the killer behind those tinted windows, he had me cold.

The Jeep's passenger-side window hummed down. Mother of God, here it comes. It wouldn't even do any good to duck. The Jeep was so much taller than my car, the shooter would still have the angle on me—

Jungle Jim Johansen sat behind the wheel, dressed in his usual safari duds, minus the Aussie hat. Only thing he aimed at me was his big handsome grin.

"Hey there," he called. "I finally caught you."

At least I think that's what he said. My pulse pounded so loudly in my ears, I couldn't really hear.

"Hey," I said weakly. "Um, you want something from me?"

"Wanted to follow up on our earlier conversations. You never called me. I was on my way to your house when I saw your car pulling out of the driveway. Took me this far to get your attention."

I took a deep breath as my racing heart slowed. Jungle Jim wasn't here to kill me. He was just a blabbermouth. I reminded myself he was still a suspect, though. A pretty damned good one at that. Wasn't it suspicious, the way he kept wanting to chat me up? I spend my whole life getting snubbed and shunned, doors slammed in my face. How come this guy wants to be my new pal?

"Okay," I said warily. "Where do you want to have this conversation?"

Thinking: You'd better make it a very public place. No way I'm going somewhere alone with you. Just in case.

"How about the Frontier? I'll buy you a cinnamon roll."

My stomach instantly growled at the mention of the Frontier Restaurant's giant pastries. I already had a parking place within two blocks of the restaurant. How could I resist?

I nodded, and he said, "Let me just find a place to park this rig. I'll meet you in there."

The Jeep roared away, turned at the next corner. I waited until it was out of sight before courageously getting out of the Olds. Then I hurried along the street, past a post office and a bookstore and an overdecorated pizza joint, until I reached Central, across the street from the adobe Legos of UNM. I crossed Cornell and ducked into the noisy bustle of the Frontier.

The Frontier has stood for generations on this corner directly across from the university. The restaurant expanded over the years, gobbling up neighboring storefronts, and now its red-and-white façade takes up half the block. Inside, the walls are covered in Wild West décor: wagon wheels and branding irons and Navajo rugs and innumerable paintings of the owner's idol, John Wayne, the perfect hero for the Duke City, as Albuquerque's known. (We're named after the Duke of Albuquerque in Spain, not the actor, but what the hell.)

As usual, the Frontier teemed with sleep-deprived students and verbose faculty members and hungover revelers and a sprinkling of gawking tourists. Two raw-boned cowboys in creased Wranglers and new Resistol hats stood by the door, and I wondered if they were on their once-a-year visit to the big city, or if the owner of the Frontier had hired them as local color.

I spotted an empty booth near the front door and threw myself into it. It was in the busiest section of the restaurant, squarely in front of giant windows that faced the tumult and traffic of Central Avenue. You couldn't get much more public.

Jungle Jim came in a few minutes later, smiling and nodding at people who recognized him. Big-shot celebrity, swooping down among us commoners. He spotted me in the booth and cocked his hand into a gun, gave me a little forefinger shot. Then he got in the serving line.

I sat biting my nails until he arrived at the booth a few minutes later, carrying a tray with two steaming mugs of coffee and two aromatic, turban-sized cinnamon buns. Yum. I dug in immediately, but Johansen just sipped his coffee. His thick forearms rested on the table, and the white mug looked small in his tanned hands.

"Boy, I need this," he said. "I was awake all night, thinking about Cristina and all."

I grunted, my mouth full of sweet, buttery dough.

"I kept thinking how it must look to the cops—and to you—that she got killed in my workshop."

I was too busy chewing to answer, so I cocked an eyebrow at him.

"I'm about the only one who uses that workshop," he said, "and I'm the one who dressed up in that monkey suit in the past. That's got to make people wonder."

I swallowed mightily and said, "It hadn't occurred to you earlier to check whether that costume was missing?"

"No!" he said, so loudly that people in neighboring booths whipped their heads around. "I knew that whoever killed Jeff wore a gorilla suit. Everyone knew that. It was in the newspaper and all. But I honestly never thought it might be that old costume from the zoo."

He must've read skepticism on my face because he said, "Really! You have to understand, it had been weeks since I'd even been backstage there."

"So you said. But you were headed there when you heard the gunshot yesterday."

"Yeah. I was kinda pissed, like I told you, so I was going there to cool off."

"You've got a temper, huh?"

He glanced around the restaurant, then leaned closer before he said, "I don't always get along with the people at work. I blow up sometimes. But I wouldn't hurt a fly. Everybody knows that."

"Do they?"

"Who you been talking to?" His brow creased with worry. "Are people carping about me? They tell the cops I'm a hothead?"

I had no idea what anyone was telling the cops, of course, but I frowned thoughtfully.

"Son of a bitch, I knew it," he said. "That's why I couldn't sleep all night. I had a feeling people were talking about me. Sure, I can be crabby sometimes. And, yes, I didn't always get along with Cristina Tapia—"

Whoa. That was something I hadn't known.

"—But that doesn't mean I'd ever harm her. I liked her, to tell you the truth, though we didn't always see eye to eye."

"You had a lot of disagreements?"

"A few. Mostly over her volunteers. She wanted me to work with them, train them, like that. I didn't want to bother. Not in my job description, you know?"

He lowered his voice.

"They pay me to be a celebrity. That's the truth. You saw how it was when I came in here just now. People recognize me from TV. They wave and smile and ask for my autograph. I'm not really famous, but I go anywhere in town and people recognize me."

Which, I thought, would be a good reason to wear a disguise if he were planning to, oh, shoot somebody in a busy coffeehouse.

"I get a little full of myself sometimes," he said. "I know that. Anybody in my position would. Sometimes, the brass asks me to do things—like train volunteers—and I feel like it's, you know, beneath me. I make a lot of noise, but I would never, ever hurt somebody over it."

I nodded along. If his policy about injuring others suddenly changed, I didn't want to be the first victim.

"Anyhow," he said, "I kept thinking about it, and I thought I'd talk to you, see if I could help in some way. I know the zoo inside and out. I've worked there twenty years. If somebody there is a killer, I could help you figure out who it is."

What was it about this case? Everybody wants to be my assistant. Town's suddenly crawling with Junior Detectives. Maybe it was obvious that I needed help. But Jungle Jim Johansen? I still wasn't convinced he was innocent. I could be taking a big chance, revealing too much.

He finally carved off a chunk of cinnamon roll—I guess he'd caught me eyeballing it; mine was all gone and seconds were tempting—and he chewed manfully, waiting for me to take up the conversation. I took a deep breath, and let the cat out of the bag.

"You know anything about the death rate among the zoo animals?"

He leaned back in the booth, looked at me from beneath beetled brows.

"Deaths?"

I watched him carefully as I said, "That's why Jeff Simmons originally approached me. He thought too many animals were dying off."

"Really?" Johansen seemed truly surprised, which I took as a good sign.

"He showed me some numbers, comparing the deaths here to those at other zoos, and ZIA's rate looks bad for its size."

"I'll be damned," he said. "I had no idea. I mean, every zoo has a certain amount of turnover in its exhibits. Lots of animals have short lifespans, even in captivity. But I never realized ours was out of whack."

"That's what Simmons said anyway," I said. "He seemed to think something fishy was going on."

"Like what?"

"I don't know. That's what we need to find out."

He grinned at that "we." Here we go. Junior Detectives Unite!

"Any ideas?"

He thought about it for a few seconds, then shook his head. "Don't see how it would benefit anybody for animals to die. Covering up the deaths, that's another matter. If somebody's screwing up, then they could get fired."

"But would that be reason enough to bump somebody off?"

He shrugged. "Doesn't seem like it, but we're clearly not talking about somebody normal here. Some sick bastard who could commit murder, well, who knows?"

I had to agree with that.

"I have to tell you, Mabry, I don't think much of humans most of the time. We're an evil species, if you ask me. But other animals mean everything to me. If somebody's hurting or killing them for some reason, then we've got to stop 'em."

"Okay, but how?"

Johansen stroked his chin. "We need information. We need to see the numbers Jeff was talking about."

I could feel the folded-up spreadsheets in my hip pocket, but I wasn't ready to share those with Johansen or anybody else. Not yet.

"What we need is probably in Buck Tedeski's lab," he said. "That's where they do the necropsies. You know about those?"

I nodded.

"I like ole Buck. I doubt that he'd be involved with anything screwy. But if someone's covering something up, it would have to be with his cooperation. Everything goes through that lab. Maybe there are records or something in there that would tell us what's going on."

"Could you get in there and look around?" I asked.

"Too many people coming and going. If I started snooping around the lab, people would snap to it right away."

"What about after hours? Is there a way you could get me into the lab? Could you get a key?"

His smile spread wide.

"Not a key," he said. "But I've got an idea."

Chapter 27

The day crawled past like a wounded snake. I made phone calls and ate a late lunch at home and buzzed around town, checking a couple of worthless leads, but my mind was occupied with plans for the evening ahead.

Shortly before 4 PM, I went to the zoo and bought a ticket and went inside. I'd agreed to meet Jungle Jim by the giraffe enclosure at 4:30, and I didn't want to be late. I strolled over there, pausing to look at llamas and elephants and antelope. Acting like a regular zoo visitor, in case someone noticed me.

It was a sunny afternoon, and the place would've been crowded if it had been a Saturday. But not many people were enjoying the exhibits on a Thursday afternoon. No crowds to use for cover, so I tried not to do anything obvious.

Jungle Jim was late to our rendezvous. I loitered in front of the giraffes, watching them gracefully amble around their large, dusty pen, reaching out for forage with long, black tongues. I wished I'd brought Felicia's new camera with me. I could've gotten some dandy snapshots of the long-necked beasts. And a camera would've given me something to do, so it didn't look like I was waiting for somebody.

I heard a hiss of escaping air, and I crinkled my nose, thinking that one of the giraffes had farted. Damn, was I downwind? I didn't want any part of—

The hiss again. Behind me. I turned and spotted Jungle Jim Johansen peeping out a door fifteen feet away. I hadn't even noticed the blank door, sunk into fake rocks painted the same shade of desert brown.

"Mabry!" he whispered. "Hurry up!"

Nobody was looking my way, and I scurried across the concrete walkway and slipped through the door.

We were in a narrow service corridor, dimly lit, and it got all the darker when he shut the door behind me. I had a momentary panic, remembering that Johansen was still a suspect and I'd possibly just shut myself up with a killer. But he said, "Follow me," and set off down the tunnel like he knew where he was going. What could I do? I followed.

Small doors were cut into the left-hand wall every so often, covered by wire screens, and I realized we were walking behind the exhibits, under the piles of fake boulders that separated the naturalistic enclosures. The waist-high doors were used to shove animals in and out of pens, or to shovel in food for the larger animals. We were truly backstage at the zoo now, right where I wanted to be, but it made me uneasy that unseen beasts paced just the other side of those steel doors.

We went down some dimly lit steps, and the tunnel made a ninety-degree turn to the right. Suddenly we were in a wider hallway, one with fluorescent lights overhead, and I felt better.

Johansen put on the brakes and I almost walked up his back before I realized he'd stopped. He stood close as he whispered, "We're underground now. This tunnel ties into the main corridor. You know which one I mean? By the offices?"

I nodded. He meant the hallway by Jeff Simmons's computer lab. If I walked past Simmons's office, crossed the main corridor that led to the administrative offices, and kept going to—

Voices! Someone was coming our way. Johansen held a thick finger to his lips to tell me to be quiet, as if I couldn't have figured that out for myself.

His head whipped around, checking for hidey-holes, and he settled on the nearest human-sized door, which was about ten feet away. He sprang over to the door, grabbed the knob and twisted. Thankfully, it was unlocked. We ducked inside.

Darkness. I kicked something, and nearly screamed when a club whacked me in the chin. I caught myself in time, realizing that it was a mop handle. The mop was standing in a bucket. I'd kicked the bucket, so to speak, and the mop had swung around and nailed me.

We were in a janitor's closet. It stank of ammonia and dust and solvents. I stood very still, afraid that other buckets and brooms lurked in the darkness.

Johansen and I were jammed close together, and I could feel the heat coming off him. He'd kept the door cracked half an inch and I bent over a little, so we could both peek out.

The voices got louder—a man and a woman, chatting—then two khaki-clad zookeepers passed, their rubber boots squeaking on the floor. The man carried a wooden baton, which I assumed he used to poke stubborn animals. I didn't want him using it on me.

We stood still until we could no longer hear them talking, then Johansen opened the door, stuck out his head and peered up and down the corridor.

"Okay," he said. "Let's hurry."

I was careful to quietly close the door behind me, and Jungle Jim was thirty feet away by the time I looked up again. I ran to catch up.

"Come on," he hissed over his shoulder, like that wasn't exactly what I was doing. "If you get caught down here, it could cost me my job."

I panted for breath, trying to keep up with the long-legged TV star. The tunnel angled upward, and I guessed we were above ground again. We passed another section of animal-sized doors. A deep rumble made the steel doors vibrate.

"What's that?" I squeaked.

"Lion," Jungle Jim said. "We're right behind the big cats."

I walked faster.

Granted, it was late in the day, nearly closing time, but I was surprised we didn't encounter more zoo workers. Not exactly a beehive of activity, behind the scenes at the zoo.

Up ahead, I recognized Simmons's office and the junction with the main hallway beyond. A lot closer than I'd thought. I held my breath, tensed for someone to pop out of the administrative wing and catch us.

But we'd reached our destination. Johansen opened a plain wooden door, and we entered a storeroom. One high, dingy window covered in chicken wire admitted enough late-afternoon light to see old furniture and dusty shelving and stacks of cardboard boxes.

"Okay," he whispered. "This is it."

"This is what?"

"Your hiding place. Just stay here for two hours. Give everybody time to go home."

I nodded.

"When the coast is clear, slip out into the hall and continue the direction we were going."

"Right."

"No. Left."

"Right. That's what I meant. Left."

He rolled his eyes.

"Just follow the hall. When you pass the main corridor, start counting doors. The lab's four doors down, on the left."

"Right."

"Don't start that again."

"Sorry. I meant, okay."

"Right. I've got to get out of here now before somebody comes along. You'll be okay?"

"Sure you don't want to tag along?" I tried not to whimper. "I mean, you know your way around and all—"

"We covered this already. I've got an appearance tonight at Bandelier Elementary School. I can't miss that."

"Go ahead. I'll make do."

"Call me later, let me know what you find."

Fluorescent light angled into the storeroom as he opened the door. He slipped through, stealthy as a jungle cat. The door clicked shut behind him.

I moved an empty box out of the seat of an old swivel chair. The upholstery was split, but the chair looked solid enough. I eased myself onto it and tried to relax. Tried not to think about trespassing charges. Tried not to wonder whether Jungle Jim Johansen had locked me in this room. Tried not to wonder whether a killer waited for me outside the door.

It made for a long wait.

Chapter 28

Night fell while I sat waiting. I anxiously checked the luminous dial of my wristwatch every few minutes, and finally was rewarded by the passing of two hours. Time to get moving.

The zoo was more dangerous now. If Johansen and I had been caught earlier, we might've been able to bluff our way out of trouble. But after hours, the only people I'd encounter likely would be security guards. And they'd assume I was a burglar or, at minimum, a trespasser. I could get my ass shot off before I had a chance to explain.

I eased over to the door of the storeroom, one foot asleep and tingling. In the half-light, I managed to wham my hip against the sharp corner of a desk. Damn it.

The doorknob turned, which was a relief. I opened the door an inch and peeked out, ears on high alert. Nothing.

The corridor's overhead lights had been extinguished, leaving only the occasional low-wattage emergency light burning. The shadowy hallway made me nervous. I might literally stumble onto a guard. I stuck close to the wall as I crept along the corridor, fearing the sudden flare of a flashlight, the quick bark of gunshots.

I tiptoed past Jeff Simmons's office, with its blinking computers and whirring air-conditioning, then hurried past the hallway intersection without seeing anyone. So far, so good.

I counted doors until I reached the correct one. Amber emergency light illuminated a sign that said "Medical Lab" with Tedeski's name underneath. Bingo.

As expected, the door was locked. I'd come prepared, though. I had a short pry bar in the inside pocket of my leather jacket. I braced it against the door jamb right at the lock. A little pressure and—nothing. Okay, a little more pressure. The lock wouldn't budge.

I glanced around once more, took a deep breath and, wincing against the expected noise, really put my weight into it. The door gave way with a loud crack, and a long sliver of wood splintered away from the jamb. Oops. The door was open now, but it would be clear to anyone passing in the hall that the lock had been jimmied. Damn. I'd need to hurry.

I shut the door behind me and flicked on the lights. Some light probably spilled out under the closed door, but since I'd already butchered the jamb, it didn't seem to matter much.

The lab was about what I expected. Two stainless steel examination tables, gray desk, gray file cabinets, white supply cabinets, a counter holding a microscope and assorted science stuff, a wall of wire cages of various sizes to hold sick and injured animals. I approached the cages carefully. No telling what kind of wild critters might be inside. But only one cage was occupied. Some kind of spotted cat, not much bigger than your average Siamese. An ocelot? Whatever, it seemed in no mood to screw around with me. It lay curled up, and it opened its yellow eyes just long enough to give me a disdainful look before turning over the other way. Fine.

Nothing much in the lab to tell me what I needed to know. No dead animals. No obvious clues. The white medical cabinets were locked. My only hope of doing any good was in the file cabinets that lined the wall opposite the cages.

The file cabinets were unlocked, which was great news. As much trouble as I'd had with the door, imagine how much noise I would've made whanging open the hollow steel cabinets. The drawers were labeled in alphabetical order, and I let my fingers run down the fronts, wondering where incriminating information might be stored. Finally, I settled on "N" for necropsies, hoping one file would cover all the post-mortems. The "N" drawer was at the bottom. I squatted and started rifling through the folders, pulling out any that looked promising.

I guess the dry rustle of the papers covered any other noise in the lab. Did the door click when it opened? Was there a rush of air? I don't know. But I suddenly sensed someone else was in the room. Right behind me. Oh, shit.

I tried to spring up and turn around at the same time, to take some sort of defensive posture. But I was too late.

Something hard and swift and painful—a baseball bat? a nightstick?—cracked against my head, just above the ear.

Unconsciousness dropped over me like a heavy black tarp. I must've fallen, but I didn't feel myself hit the concrete floor.

Chapter 29

$\mathcal{I}$ awoke slowly. Sensations flooded my brain: Intense pain in my head. My heart pounding in my chest. Grit against my cheek and the prickle of dry grass against my neck. Chilly night air. A musty, musky, unfamiliar smell. Strangest of all, the feeling of a damp, fat finger wiggling around in my ear. Someone was giving me a Wet Willy, which seemed an unusual way to wake the near-dead.

I parted my eyelids the slightest bit, afraid of what I might find. What I saw frightened me so, it took every ounce of will-power to stay still.

I was outdoors, just as I'd thought. Dim light came from somewhere, because I could see through my eyelashes that a black shape crouched near my face. Looked like a small child, squatting there, and I prayed that was the case, that I'd been discovered unconscious by a curious child. One who happened to be wearing a shaggy fur coat.

But no. The child shifted on his haunches, bent down closer to me, so close that I could feel its hot breath on my face. Light glinted off its rubbery lips, its white teeth. A fucking gorilla, right in my face, jabbing me in the ear with its hairy black finger. A small ape, granted, not much more than a baby. But still.

Add it up: I've been left outdoors. At the zoo. A baby gorilla is now mooshing my face with his hairy hands. Only one place where such a thing could happen. In the gorilla enclosure. Which meant this ape here, this inquisitive child, was the least of my worries.

As if to confirm my deductions, a deep-throated grunt came from behind me. Oh, Jesus. I closed my eyes tight.

A giant hand landed on my back.

Oh, please, Jesus. Oh, please. I'll be good. I'll stop lying. I'll stop cussing. I'll stop drinking. I'll stop ogling coeds. Oh, please.

The hand roughly grabbed my leather jacket and gave me a good shaking. I tried to stay limp, though every fiber of my being wanted to scream and run away.

Feet shuffled in the sandy soil around me. More gorillas. I couldn't tell how many. Probably the whole tribe. How many was that? I wished now I'd paid more attention when I passed this way a couple of days earlier. Like it mattered. One big old silverback could tear me limb from limb by himself. The rest would just help him strew the parts. And there wasn't a damned thing I could do about it. Usually, when I find myself stuck in terrible situations (it happens, though this one was a first), I try to talk myself out of trouble. It rarely works. I'm not that persuasive. Even if I overcame my terror enough to make sense, the gorillas wouldn't understand what I was saying. I was no match physically for these apes, and I couldn't outsmart them with rapid patter. What was left?

More hands on me. Something yanked at my shoes. The one who'd been pawing my back grabbed my jacket with both hands and shook me some more. I bounced around like a Samsonite bag. Another hand was tangled in my hair. Which hurt. I can't really spare any more lost hair, but impending baldness wasn't the top concern at the moment.

The baby gorilla shrieked in my face. The others hooted and grunted and harrumphed. Oh, please, Jesus, get me out of here.

Then the one that had been yanking on my back brought both giant hands down on me, whamming the breath right out of me. Felt like my ribs caved in under his sudden weight.

I couldn't help it. I gasped for air. And everybody let go. They must've all jumped back, alarmed that I'd finally made a noise, that I wasn't dead after all. I knew it wouldn't last. Now that they knew I was awake, the fun and games were just beginning.

I took a deep breath and let out the loudest shriek I could muster. The noise filled the night. I struggled to my feet, shouting, flailing my arms around, trying to produce as much noise and movement and menace as possible.

I whirled, dizzy and terrified, my eyes taking in my surroundings. It was just as I'd feared. A half-dozen gorillas surrounded me, though they recoiled from my noisy display. The baby scampered out of harm's way.

The enclosure's wall of fake rocks was right behind me, and the steel door was shut tight. Somebody had carried me here unconscious from the lab. They'd shoved me through that door, leaving me to the apes.

Across the pen, thirty feet away, yawned the empty moat that separated the gorillas from their daily audience. On the far side, across fourteen feet of thin air, wire fencing with a metal rail leaned out over the moat. Beyond that was the landscaped patio where humans belonged. A couple of halogen lamps glowed pinkly atop poles there, illuminating the scene.

Three adult gorillas howled and hooted at me. A couple of smaller ones that I took to be adolescents shrieked and jumped up and down and threw dirt and generally acted like teen-agers.

But my biggest worry was the alpha male, the one who'd been pounding on me. He'd backed off a little when I jumped up, but he clearly was unafraid of this puny, hairless human. He stood on all fours, only ten feet away, his pointed, furry head sitting squarely on top of his wide shoulders. His face was in shadow, but I didn't need to see his expression to know he felt threatened and angry. A growl rumbled from his throat and he sat up. He thumped his chest with his fists, just like you see in the movies, and the sound was like thunder. Then he dropped back to all fours and charged me.

I dodged sideways, but he swatted out with a long arm and caught my knee, sent me tumbling. I hit the ground rolling, dust in my eyes and up my nose, and I kept rolling until I slammed up against the fake-rock wall, where it curved toward the moat.

The silverback turned and galloped toward me. My life passed before my eyes, and it was a short, sad movie with a terrible, bloody ending. Aaugh. I curled into a fetal position as the gorilla reached me. He cuffed me with either hand, sending me rolling in the dirt some more, bouncing around like a soccer ball.

The other apes hooted happily, rooting on their champion. I rolled away from him, up onto my feet, the wall still tight behind me.

The big male bounced from side to side, ready to charge again. I could see his face now, scowling and black, his yellow fangs dripping. Oh, sweet Lord.

I feinted to my left. The big ape went for the fake, jumping sideways to cut me off, and I sprinted the other direction, faster than I've ever run in my life.

The gorilla was right behind me, all roar and hot breath and flying saliva. The moat gaped before me. No way I could jump across it. I mean, if that were possible, these apes would've figured it out long ago and made their escape. That was the whole reason for the moat. But I had no choice but to try. My feet hit the concrete rim and I leaped forward, the gorilla just brushing my back as he made a last grab for me.

I stretched as far as I could, flying through the air like Tarzan, and my hands hit the steel rail at the top of the fence. Oh, thank you, Lord. I grasped the metal with all my might. My feet swung down behind me, and slammed against the concrete wall of the moat, almost made me lose my grip.

I dangled there, my feet scrabbling at the smooth concrete, all my weight on my arms, the sharp edge of the rail cutting into my palms.

Behind me, the simians shrieked and screamed and somersaulted in frustration. Their new plaything was escaping, and they couldn't stand it. A leafy branch bounced off my head, and other missiles quickly followed, pelting me. Most seemed to consist of feces. I tried not to think about that. I tried to chin myself up onto the rail, my arms trembling against the strain, my feet slipping against the concrete.

It was no good. I couldn't do it. I wasn't strong enough to pull up the dead weight of my dangling body. My arms were tiring and my hands burned.

I looked down, trying to see how deep the moat was, but it was all shadows down there. Twelve feet? Fifteen? Twenty? A long fucking way, that much was certain. Would the fall kill me? Would I be trapped down there? Would the gorillas pounce on me?

Shit, here we go.

I lost my grip. Fell straight down into the moat, limp as a sack of manure. My feet hit first, and my right ankle twisted and pain shot up my leg. But I remembered to bend my knees, and that cushioned the fall. I threw my hands out before me to keep from toppling over onto my face, but I fell the other way. Fortunately, I've got some padding on my backside—all those hours of sitting in surveillance cars.

One second I'm dangling on the rail. The next I'm sitting at the bottom of the concrete moat, in a shallow puddle of water that soaked through my jeans. Dizzy and banged-up, but alive. Son of a bitch, I couldn't believe it.

The gorillas gathered above me. They pelted me with shit and leaves and dirt, but made no move to come down into the moat and kill me. I covered my head with my hands and yelled for help. The apes shrieked louder. Maybe, with all of us making a racket, somebody would come to check.

And that's exactly what happened. After the longest fifteen minutes of my life, I heard a man yelling at the gorillas to pipe down. A flashlight beam sliced through the night, hitting black fur and clouds of dust and the weedy lip of the moat.

"Down here!" I shouted. "Help! I'm down here!"

The flashlight beam shortened up as the man came closer. It was a security guard, dressed in khakis and a dark jacket, a baseball cap on his head. Looked like he had his hand on a gun at his belt.

The beam of light hit me square in the face. I squinted up at the guard, who said, "What the fuck?"

I responded, "My thoughts exactly."

Chapter 30

$\mathcal{I}t$ took an hour to persuade the security guards and the responding APD patrolmen to call Lt. Steve Romero.

First, the guard used a walkie-talkie to summon several of his peers to the gorilla pen. They pointed guns and flashlights at me and made a big fuss, yelling at the howling apes. Finally, somebody opened a door in the back of the enclosure and lured the gorillas away from their entertaining game of Throw-Shit-at-the-Private-Eye, and we could all hear ourselves think.

The guards snaked a ladder down to me so I could creakily climb out of the moat. I was in a great deal of pain and I was filthy and I reeked of ape shit, but that didn't stop them from cuffing my hands behind my back and frog-marching me to the security office.

Once the real cops arrived, they crowded around me and harshly questioned me about how I ended up in the gorilla pen. They didn't like my answers, and I figured I was on my way to jail and a whole different group of hooting inmates. The only thing that seemed to stop the police was that they didn't want Stinky Poop Boy in their patrol cars.

Finally, after I insisted about twenty times, a lardass patrolman with a walrus mustache telephoned headquarters and asked to be patched through to Romero.

"Sorry to bother you at home, Lieutenant," he said into the phone. "But I've got a burglar down here at the zoo."

He paused.

"That's right, at the zoo. Security found him inside the gorilla pen. Down in one of those moats? The apes were throwing shit at him."

The cop listened for a few seconds, then said, "He says he was down here because of a homicide you're working."

"Two homicides," I said.

"Two homicides. The ones in the newspaper?"

Officer Walrus listened for a minute, looking me up and down. "Yeah, that's him," he said finally. "How did you know?"

A grin spread across his face. I could only imagine what unflattering things Romero was saying.

"Okay, Lieutenant," he said. "You want him downtown or here at the zoo?"

Another pause.

"Well, to tell you the truth, he, um, doesn't smell so good. Know what I mean?"

The cop chuckled at something Romero said. Bastards.

"Okay, we'll wait here for you."

He hung up and turned to the other smirking cops and security guys.

"What do you know? Apparently, this perp is telling the truth."

"I'm not a perp."

"Shut up."

I crossed my dirty arms over my filthy chest and clammed up.

"The lieutenant's on his way. He suggested we lock this guy in a room until he gets here, since we're all tired of smelling him."

I was sitting at a desk in an otherwise empty office when Romero arrived fifteen minutes later. I'd taken off my sneaker and sock and was examining my twisted ankle, which was swollen and purple.

"Damn, Bubba, what happened to you?"

I started to explain, but the aroma hit him about then and he was too busy flinching to listen.

"Yeah, yeah, I know. I stink. You try rolling around in gorilla shit sometime, see if you come out smelling like a rose."

Though his nose looked as if it was trying to curl up within itself, a smile creased his face.

"The fixes you get yourself into," he said. "It's amazing."

"Tell me."

"You want to explain what you were doing, burglarizing the zoo?"

"I wasn't 'burglarizing.' I was snooping around."

"In the gorilla cage?"

"No." I sighed. "Somebody dumped me there."

"In with the gorillas."

"That's right."

"Why?"

"Beats the shit out of me. They could've just shot me or stabbed me or something. Instead, they tried to scare me to death, putting me in there with those fucking apes."

"You're lucky those gorillas didn't rip you to pieces."

"They tried! The only thing that saved me was that the big one went for a feint."

"What?"

"And I threw myself into that moat. The gorillas wouldn't come down there after me."

"They're too smart for that."

He grinned again. Why does everybody get such a kick out of my misfortunes? No wonder I hate authority figures.

"Go back to the beginning," he said. "What were you doing at the zoo?"

No sense evading him. I was completely in the wrong here—trespassing, burglary, you name it—and he could put me under arrest. So I told him the whole thing, including Jeff Simmons's original conspiracy theories about the animal deaths and why I'd thought breaking into the zoo's veterinary lab was a good idea.

I omitted a couple of things. One, I didn't mention the spread-sheets. It's one thing that I kept Simmons's suspicions from him, but it would be something else if he knew I concealed hard evidence. Two, I didn't mention that Jungle Jim Johansen was the one who smuggled me into the office area. The guy did me a favor—though it hadn't turned out so great—and there was no reason to drag him into this if I could avoid it.

"So," Romero said when I was done, "you've been operating under the notion that these dead animals are the reason somebody's now killing humans?"

"I haven't found any other reason somebody might've wanted to bump off Simmons. The gorilla suit and the Tapia killing all seem to point to some kind of zoo cover-up. Don't you think?"

He pondered that, scratching his chin and staring at the ceiling. I imagined the gears turning in his Holmesian brain as he sorted through the clues and facts and suspects. God, I wish I were as smart as Romero. My whole life would be different. I wouldn't fall for every stupid—

"I don't think so," he said.

"Huh?"

"This motive. The dead animals. I don't buy it."

"Why not?"

"Think, Bubba. Somebody wants to cover something up, they're not going to make more noise by committing a couple of homicides, including one very public murder in a Flying Squirrel café. It doesn't make any sense. If they wanted to get rid of Simmons, if that was the only way to keep the secret, they would've found some stealthier way to go about it."

Same argument that Felicia made, but I couldn't turn it loose.

"Simmons came to the café to talk to me. Maybe they figured it would all come out once an investigator was involved."

He narrowed his eyes. "You think your reputation as an investigator is so good, it would scare somebody into committing murder?"

Okay, he had a point, but he didn't have to take that tone.

"What else could it be?" I insisted. "Why would somebody kill Simmons and Tapia, if not to cover up shenanigans at the zoo?"

"'Shenanigans?'"

"You know what I mean."

He didn't answer my questions. Instead, he said, "You didn't really expect to learn anything by breaking into that lab, did you?"

"I thought I might find something. Some record—"

"Bubba. When people commit crimes, when they plot conspiracies, they don't usually keep good records."

"Well, sure, but—"

"Especially if they're planning a couple of homicides. Most murderers find it's not a good idea to leave a paper trail."

I gave him a look. He gave me one right back.

"You're incredible," he said. "A killer's on the loose, probably connected to the zoo. So what do you do? Break into the zoo and go prowling around in the dark. You're lucky to be alive. Whoever hit you on the head could've just hit you some more. Left a nice pudding where your skull used to be."

"Bad enough that they handed me over to the gorillas."

Romero rubbed at his nose, as if mention of the apes reminded him of how I smelled.

"It's pretty clever, when you think about it. Say you hadn't escaped. The guards might not have found you until morning, long after the gorillas had torn you apart and chewed up the pieces."

I cringed.

"Investigators probably would've figured you for a thrill-seeker," he said. "A nut. Some guy who busted into the zoo and climbed into the gorilla pen to see what would happen. Maybe nobody would've guessed that you got bopped on the head and put there intentionally."

"You would've figured it out. You know me. You know I'm no thrill-seeker."

"The thrills seem to find you, though."

What could I say? He was right. I try to conduct my investigations as quietly as possible. I try to avoid trouble. I certainly try to avoid violence. Yet trouble and violence keep finding me. Not to mention bad publicity. I wondered whether the newshounds would sniff out my adventure among the apes. I could just imagine the headlines.

"So," I ventured, "am I charged with something?"

"The zoo guys want to charge you with trespassing. They're worried about the precedent. They don't want every loser in town trying to sneak into the zoo."

That term "loser" rankled, but I let it go.

"I'll try to persuade them you've suffered enough," Romero said. "I mean, look at you."

I pointed at my purple foot.

"And that smell."

"I think I'm getting used to it," I said.

"You've probably got a concussion. You want a hospital?"

"No. I just want to go home."

He nodded. "All right. Go home."

"Really?"

"Yeah. I'll smooth things over with the security guys. I'm not saying they won't press charges. I would, if I were them. But there's no sense locking you up tonight. We know where to find you."

"Thanks, Steve." I gingerly pulled my sock onto my foot, not wanting to give him time to change his mind.

"I'll ask around, see if I can find out who conked you," he said. "But you need to stay out of this mess. If you insist on poking your nose into this, it's liable to get cut off."

"Don't worry," I said. "I've learned my lesson. I just want to go home and go to bed."

"You might want a shower first." He grinned. "Felicia will probably insist on it."

Chapter 31

Romero was right about Felicia.

"Holy mackerel!" she bellowed when I limped through our front door. "What happened to you? Never mind that. What's that fucking stench?"

"Monkey poop."

"What?"

"It's a long story."

She clasped her nose in one hand, and shooed me back outside with the other.

"Take off your clothes," she demanded.

"I can't take off my clothes out here on the porch. The neighbors—"

"Nobody's looking."

"But—"

"You're not coming in my house smelling like that," she said. "Strip. Now."

"Don't you even care that I'm injured?"

"We'll address that next. First, we've got to burn those filthy clothes."

"You're not burning these clothes. We can wash them."

"Whatever. Take 'em off."

"Okay, okay."

It was cold out on the porch, and I felt conspicuous as I stripped down to my boxers, but I obeyed.

"Damn, Bubba. Look at your ankle."

"I know."

"And you've got bruises all over your back."

"You should see the knot on my head."

"What happened to you?"

"Somebody at the zoo hit me on the head. Then, while I was out cold, they locked me in the gorilla pen, where apes beat me up and pelted me with filth."

"You're shitting me."

"Would I make up something like that?"

"Good point. Come in now. But go straight to the shower."

"What about my clothes?"

"Leave 'em there. We'll tend to them later."

I didn't like that. I took my wallet and keys from the pockets of my jeans, just in case, then shuffled into the house.

"God," she said once I was in better light, "you're absolutely covered in dirt."

"I know."

"What's that in your hair?"

"I'm afraid to look. Just let me get a shower."

Hot water seemed to help. I stood under the shower a long time, as if the streaming water could wash away pain and humiliation as well as dirt. I knew it was time to get out—and that Felicia had put my clothes in the washer—when the shower suddenly went ice-cold.

Damn.

By the time I emerged from the steamy bathroom in my robe, Felicia had calmed down, and curiosity had gotten the better of her. She plopped me down at the kitchen table, put a bag of frozen vegetables on my aching head and another on my aching ankle, then asked me to explain in detail what had happened at the zoo. While I told her, she interrupted with, oh, a thousand questions. It's tough sometimes, living with a reporter.

Finally, after I was all talked out, and she was done shaking her head at my foolhardiness, she remembered something.

"Hey," she said. "Julie Keen sent a package home for you."

"A package?"

"Stuff you asked her to look up?"

"She's finished already? I thought that would keep her out of our hair for days."

"She's a go-getter, that girl," Felicia said.

"No kidding."

She went into the living room and came back with a thick manila envelope. She slid it across the table to me, and I opened the flap and pulled out photocopies of newspaper stories and printouts of computer files and God-only-knows what else. The stack of papers was nearly an inch thick.

"I can't look at all of this now. My head hurts too much."

"Give me some of it," Felicia said. "I'll help."

So that's what we did. Just another old married couple, sitting around the kitchen table, sifting through other people's lives.

For all her electronic legwork, Julie hadn't turned up much of substance. A ton of newspaper stories mentioned Jungle Jim Johansen, for instance, but nothing cast any suspicion on him. Mostly, they were brief articles about his performances at schools or his TV appearances or his press conferences to introduce new zoo babies. Julie hadn't sorted the stories or shown any sense of prioritizing them. She'd just provided a glut of information and left the rest to us. Kind of like the way she talked.

Several articles mentioned Carolyn Hoff, but they mostly dealt with zoo finances, and I couldn't see anything squirrelly there. Background material on Jeff Simmons and Perry Oswalt and the rest at the zoo was sparse and uninteresting, mostly just short articles when they were hired or brief mentions in feature stories about various programs at the zoo.

Julie found lots of coverage of Armando Gonzales, but the clippings mostly were fluff stories about his civic work and charitable donations. Funny that a guy so concerned about someone stealing his fortune would be so willing to give it away for the public good.

I was ready to give up when Felicia said, "Wait a minute."

"What?"

"Did you see this one?"

She passed a printout across the table to me. It was a nine-year-old article from a newspaper in Iowa, which Julie had Googled up during her search for information on curator of mammals Noah Gibbons. It went like this:

ANIMAL PARK OWNER ARRESTED

Elkhart, Iowa—The owner of a wild animal park has been arrested and charged with illegally procuring exotic animals, authorities said Friday.

Isaac Gibbons, 37, was arrested at his business, a theme park called America Wild. Deputies with the Polk County Sheriff's Department also searched the park's administrative offices and seized several boxes of records.

America Wild is a 1,000-acre facility outside Des Moines that features animals roaming in pastures and prairies. Visitors are driven through the park in buses to observe the animals up close.

Sheriff Floyd Weejum said Gibbons was unable to account for purchases of several animals from Africa and Asia, including gazelles, a zebra, two cheetahs and an ibex, which is a type of goat.

"These parks are required to keep careful records," the sheriff said. "If they can't prove where they got a particular animal, then we have to assume it was stolen or smuggled into the country illegally."

Sheriff Weejum said his department was working with federal authorities in investigating the matter.

"We suspect these animals might've been stolen from zoos around the country," he said. "The feds told us there's quite a lucrative business in stolen animals."

He said Gibbons's brother, Noah Gibbons, 26, works at the famed St. Louis Zoo, but wouldn't confirm that some of the animals were believed to be missing from that facility. The younger Gibbons is cooperating with authorities, the sheriff said.

"That's it?" I asked Felicia. "There's no follow-up?"

"Nothing else here," she said, sorting through the papers. "Probably wouldn't have gotten that one if Noah's name hadn't appeared in the last paragraph. Computer spit it out, so Julie put it in with the rest with no follow-up. God, she's dense."

"It says Noah cooperated," I said. "You think he sold out his own brother?"

"That's what it sounds like. We'll know more once I contact the authorities in Iowa. I'll call them tomorrow. We don't even know whether this Isaac Gibbons was convicted of anything. Maybe it was all a big mistake. Maybe it was poor record-keeping."

"But what if it's true? What if this guy was getting hot animals from zoos? How would that work? I mean, the zoo would know immediately when a zebra turns up missing."

"Yeah. So?"

"And then the same animal shows up in a private collection or at a wild animal park like this one. Somebody's bound to notice."

"Somebody did. The authorities."

"In this instance. But I'll bet this goes on all the time."

Felicia shrugged.

"Say you're working at a zoo," I said, "and you want to make some extra money. You sneak a few animals out and sell them on the black market."

"And get fired in the process. Doesn't seem very cost-effective."

"But what if you covered it up?"

"The animals are still missing—"

"Not if they're dead," I said. "Jeff Simmons believed animals were dying off at ZIA at an unusual rate. That's why he wanted to talk to me, right?"

Felicia frowned.

"But what if they're really stolen? To cover his tracks, the thief could dummy up some paperwork that showed the animals died. Fake necropsy report, like that. They cremate all the dead animals."

"So there are no remains to prove whether the animals really died or were sold off."

"Right." I held up the printout. "Looks to me like Noah Gibbons has some experience in this area."

"Hmm. That might explain why he left the St. Louis Zoo, one of the biggest in the country, and ended up in little old Albuquerque."

"He dresses like he's got money. Drives a sports car. Maybe he's dealing in exotic animals to pay for his expensive lifestyle. Might explain that pet monkey of his, too. I mean, what kind of a zookeeper has a pet monkey? One named Mongo? That doesn't seem right."

Felicia wasn't listening. Her eyes glittered. "This could be a big story."

"If Noah thought Simmons was onto him, he might be behind these murders."

"An even bigger story," she said. "We need to find a way to pin it on him."

"We probably should take all this to Romero. Let him sort it out."

"Be a better story if we did it."

"But it's clearly dangerous. Look at what happened to me tonight."

"Think Noah Gibbons was the one who conked you on the head?"

"Maybe."

"Wouldn't that be all the more reason to go after him ourselves? Wouldn't you like to be the one to nail him?"

"I don't know, Felicia—"

"If he's the one who threw you to the gorillas?"

My cheeks warmed. "That cufflink-wearing son of a bitch. If I could prove that, then I'd happily slap him around a little before handing him over to the cops."

"Don't get yourself all worked up." She started collecting Julie's papers from the tabletop, stacking them up. She left the Iowa clipping sitting out. "You need to rest. You're banged up. A good night's sleep will make you feel better."

"I don't want to sleep. I want to get even."

She smiled. "I love it when you talk payback."

Chapter 32

I awoke Friday morning to the telephone ringing. I reached for the extension on the bedside table, and screamed a little at the soreness in my muscles. Felicia's side of the bed was empty. No help there. I managed to reach the phone, and gasped, "Hello?"

"Mr. Mabry? It's Loretta Gonzales. Sorry to call so early, but I've got some news, and I'm upset and—"

"Slow down," I croaked. "Take a deep breath, then tell me what happened."

"Two more animals died overnight," she said. "Two ocelots, a mated pair we've had for several years."

I remembered the cat I'd seen in the vet's lab the night before. I described it to her.

"Yes, that's one of them. The male, Jojo. He'd been sick for a few days, but I thought it was just a virus. He didn't seem near death."

He hadn't seemed that way to me, either. Sleepy, but not dying.

"And I was keeping a close eye on Margie," she said.

"Who?"

"His mate. She didn't show any symptoms. It seems really strange that they should both die the same night."

Seemed strange to me, too. Especially since it was the same night I'd gotten knocked out in the lab. My theory from the night before came rushing back into my head: Maybe Jojo and Margie weren't dead at all. Maybe they were being sold away. Maybe whoever was getting rid of the ocelots was the same one who caught me the night before in the lab.

I told Loretta the *Reader's Digest* version of what had happened to me at the zoo.

"That's so weird," she said when I was done. "Why would the gorillas attack you like that? They're used to having people around. Mostly, they're gentle as they can be."

"I don't know, but something had 'em stirred up. I tend to bring that sort of reaction out in people. Maybe it's the same with apes."

"Hmm." She didn't argue the point.

I told her my theory about the "dead" animals. Asked her whether it seemed possible that someone could be smuggling exotic animals out of the zoo for money.

"Gee, I guess so," she said. "But it seems really risky. Most of those animals wouldn't even bring that much on the open market. I mean, an ocelot? You could probably buy one for a few thousand dollars."

"A mated pair?"

"Okay, that would cost more, but still …"

She clearly wasn't convinced. But there had to be some way to check it out.

"These ocelots," I said, "where are they now?"

"You mean their bodies?"

"If they're really dead."

"They'd be in the vet's lab," she said. "That's where he'll do the necropsies. We'll need to find out what killed them. We don't want some kind of disease spreading to the other cats."

"I'm telling you," I said, "I think they're still alive."

"God, I wish that were true. I've worked with Jojo and Margie a long time. They're like family to me."

"We need to get into that lab and check it out," I said.

"I'll go there right now," she said. "Buck's probably not even at work yet. And you said you broke the lock on the door—"

Armando Gonzales' threats flashed through my mind. I didn't want Loretta doing anything dangerous. If something happened to her, he'd blame me, and that could go a lot worse for me than what had happened so far.

"Sit tight," I said. "I'll be there as soon as I can get dressed."

"But you're hurt—"

"Not that bad. I don't want you going to the lab alone."

"I'm not afraid of Buck Tedeski," she snorted.

"Maybe he's not the one you need to worry about." I thought about Noah Gibbons and the newspaper story from Iowa. But I didn't want to explain it all now.

"Just hang on," I said. "I'll be there in twenty minutes. Meet me at the entrance to the administrative offices and we'll go back there together."

She hesitated. I insisted. She agreed. Then we hung up and I forced myself up out of the bed.

My ankle was purple and black, but the swelling had gone down some overnight. The knot on my head was smaller, too. The gorilla-inflicted bruises up and down my ribcage had darkened and blurred, and my muscles were creaky and sore, but I managed to dress myself. I didn't take time to shower or shave or even comb my hair. Just a lick and a promise with a toothbrush, some clean clothes and a faded denim jacket and black sneakers, laced up tight to support my injured ankle.

Oh, and one more thing: My revolver. I checked that it was fully loaded, then shoved it into my waistband at the back.

Loretta and I might be onto something here. We might confront a killer. At minimum, we'd be accusing people of illegal acts that could cost them their jobs. I wasn't taking any chances on getting ambushed again.

This time, if things got ugly, I'd be the one doling out the hurt.

Chapter 33

$\mathcal{A}s$ I left the house, I found a scrawled note tacked to the inside of the front door:

"Went in early to call Iowa. XOXO. F."

I knew I should phone Felicia and fill her in on the latest. But she'd zoom down to the zoo and insist on accompanying Loretta and me as we barged into the veterinary lab, and I didn't need that. Besides, I might be completely off-base. We might charge in there only to find a couple of dead ocelots and an innocent vet. If I was wrong, I didn't need Felicia there to witness me making mistakes. She sees enough of that.

It was a little after nine when I pulled into the parking lot outside the zoo. Only a handful of cars and two yellow school buses were in the lot, and I found a parking space not far from the entrance. I limped across the blacktop, my gun a reassuring weight at my back.

My client waited just inside the door to the administrative wing, as requested. No sign of anyone else. Too early in the day, I guess, for the gum-smacking receptionist.

Loretta looked as if she'd been weeping again. Last thing she needed, on top of her fiancé's murder, was to have a couple of her favorite felines die during the night. The thought that someone had inflicted further grief on Loretta pissed me off.

"Is Tedeski here yet?" I growled.

"He's in the lab. I saw him arrive a few minutes ago, but I didn't talk to him."

"Good. Leave him to me."

We marched down the long main corridor, hurrying toward the lab. Well, she hurried. I limped along behind her, losing ground, my ankle twinging with every step. She had the good sense (or good manners) to wait for me in the hall when she reached the lab. The door was closed against its splintered jamb.

"Should I knock?" she asked.

I pushed the door open and bulled right past her.

Buck Tedeski was alone in the lab, standing near the wire cages. He looked just as he had when I saw him outside his house—doctorly and clean-cut, horn-rimmed glasses and scrubs—and he held a limp ocelot in his hands.

I whipped out my gun and said, "Drop that kitty."

"What?" He blinked at me. Took him a second to focus on the gun, but when he did, his face lost all color.

"That cat," I said. "Put it down."

He gently laid the ocelot on a steel examination table. The cat's eyes were closed. It sure looked dead to me. Damn.

Loretta hurried past me—right through my line of fire, thank you very much—and stood opposite Tedeski at the examination table. She placed her hand on the limp cat, right behind its foreleg.

"What are you doing?" he demanded. "Get away from there."

"Shut up," I said. "Don't move."

"What do you mean, busting in here—"

I waved the gun at him. "I said shut up."

He got the message.

Loretta's spaniel eyes had gone wide. She pulled her hair back on one side, bent over, and pressed her ear to the ocelot.

"A heartbeat!" she exclaimed. "Jojo's still alive!"

"Aha!" I shouted.

"Bullshit," Tedeski said. "That cat's deader than Nixon."

"Back away," I said, a menacing edge in my voice. "Move over to your desk. That's right. Sit your ass down."

Loretta hurried to the cages. The other ocelot was laid out in one, and she opened the door and did the heartbeat thing with Margie, too, and came away smiling.

"They're both alive," she said. "Heavily drugged, I think, but alive."

I stepped closer to the veterinarian, and pointed my gun at his head.

"All right, Buck," I said. "You've got some explaining to do."

His mouth pressed into a thin line. "I've got nothing to say to you."

"Wrong." I cocked back the hammer. "You'll talk to me right now, or you'll talk to the cops."

He crossed his arms over his chest and smirked at me. Unafraid. Red anger welled up within me. This son of bitch clearly was involved in the black-market conspiracy. He might even be the killer. Odds were very good that he was the one who brained me and tossed me into the gorilla pen. And he thinks he can just sit there, smiling at me like he's gonna walk away from it all—

Blam! My gun jumped in my hand. Loretta shrieked in surprise. Tedeski recoiled, throwing his hands up before his face. Gunsmoke filled the room. A perfectly round hole was punctured through the front of a filing cabinet behind Tedeski. The bullet had missed his ear by an inch.

"Holy shit!" he screamed. "You nearly shot me!"

"The next one goes between your eyes," I said. "I've had enough! You almost killed me last night. I shoot you, and any jury would let me walk. You'll either talk to me, or I'll pop you right now."

Okay, let's get a couple of things straight here. I wasn't really going to kill him. I didn't believe I could get away with it, even if it would've given me a certain amount of pleasure. I hadn't even meant to fire my gun. I was as shocked as anyone when it went off. I got mad, and my finger was on the trigger, and blam. But Tedeski didn't know that. Now that the gun had fired, I needed to make the most of it. The noise of that shot would have security guards and others swarming here any minute. I needed Tedeski to start talking, pronto.

I tried not to let my misgivings show on my face. I could feel that my lips were curled back, exposing my teeth, and my brow was furrowed into a scowl. I probably looked like one of those gorillas from the night before.

"Okay, okay!" he shouted. He stuck his hands up in air, though I hadn't asked for that. "It's Gibbons! It's all Noah Gibbons. He made me do it!"

"He's selling off animals, isn't he?"

"Yes! I didn't want to do it, but he forced me to help him. He wanted the money!"

"You got a cut."

"Well, yeah, but I didn't want it. He made me, I tell you. He, um, he knows something about me. He said he'd tell everyone—"

"What is it?"

Tedeski shook his head and clamped his lips together. He might be ready to blurt out his accusations against his partner, but he wouldn't give up his own secrets. I remembered his midday Budweiser, and guessed his secret had something to do with his drinking habits, but I didn't care. Romero would get to the bottom of it eventually.

"Is Gibbons the one who whacked me on the head last night?"

Tedeski blushed. "Okay, no. That was me. But I didn't know who you were, or what you were doing here. I just reacted and—"

"And then you dumped me in with the gorillas."

"That was Noah's idea! I called him after I found you here, and—"

"You must've helped," I said. "He couldn't have carried me halfway across the zoo by himself."

Tedeski flushed further. Caught.

"Get up," I said.

He started to shake his head, but I jerked the gun at him, and he remembered who was in charge here.

"Loretta," I said, "you stay here. Call the cops and tell them to get over here. Then take care of your cats."

She said, "Where are you going?"

"We're going to see Gibbons."

I looked out into the hallway, expecting it to be filled with security guards, but there was no one in either direction. Weird. Hadn't anyone heard the gunshot?

Tedeski had come around his desk. I stepped behind him, got a fistful of his loose shirt, stuck the barrel of the revolver in his kidney, and said, "March."

He marched.

Chapter 34

We turned the corner into the main corridor, headed back into the administrative wing. I jabbed Tedeski with the gun whenever he slowed. I still limped, but adrenaline blotted out most of my pains now. I was close to solving this thing. If I could get to Noah Gibbons before the cops arrived, I could—

A door opened up ahead on my left, and Perry Oswalt, the reptile guy, stepped into the hallway. His eyes widened when he saw us coming toward him.

"Get back!" I yelled past Tedeski's ear. The vet flinched.

Oswalt hesitated, staring at us, clearly not a fucking clue what's going on here. I helped him out by raising my gun, pointing it at him over Tedeski's shoulder.

"Go back into your office and shut the door. Now."

He leaped backward through the doorway, nimbler than I would've thought possible for someone built like a hippo, and the door slammed shut.

Tedeski muttered under his breath. I poked him with the pistol again and we marched on, until we reached the door labeled, "Noah Gibbons, Curator of Mammals."

I yanked Tedeski to a halt and said, "Open it."

"He's probably not even in there—"

"I said open it."

He did as he was told, and we stepped through the door, me tight behind the veterinarian.

Noah Gibbons sat behind his desk. He had a round mirror propped on the desktop and a set of tiny scissors in his hand, trimming his blond goatee. When we barged in, he jumped to his feet.

"Freeze," I said, showing him the gun.

He froze.

I closed the door, pushed Tedeski away from me, and said, "Stand against that wall."

From my right came a screech, and I whirled around and nearly put a bullet through Mongo the monkey, who was on his usual perch. He opened his mouth and showed me his fangs. Evil little fucker.

I quickly returned my attention to the humans in the room. The vet had his back against the far wall, as ordered, but Gibbons looked to be calculating a move. I pointed the gun at him.

"Drop those scissors and sit down," I said. "Keep your hands on top of the desk where I can see them."

Mongo growled deep in his throat.

"Tell your monkey to shut up," I ordered.

Gibbons sat, his mouth curled into a little smile, but he said nothing. Okay, screw it. If the monkey kept bugging me, I could always shoot it. Then see how Gibbons felt about being a smartass. I pointed the pistol at his face and said, "You and I need to talk."

Gibbons casually shook his well-groomed head.

"He's not kidding, Noah," Tedeski said. "He nearly shot me in the lab. Bullet went right past my ear."

"Was that what that noise was? I thought it was a door slamming. Never occurred to me that some crazy man was shooting a gun."

Maybe that's why the whole world hadn't come running at the noise. I wondered if they had a lot of door-slamming here at the zoo, but that thought was interrupted by a sound in the hall, the slap-slap of running feet on concrete.

"That would be Security," Gibbons said. "Soon as they find out you're in here, you'll be arrested."

"I don't think so," I said. "I think you're the one they're gonna lock up."

Gibbons leaned back in his chair and steepled his fingers. One cool customer. "I don't know what you mean."

"I'm talking about running a scam. Selling off zoo animals and pretending they're dead. Knocking me unconscious last night and throwing me into the gorilla cage."

He looked amused, the bastard, like it was all he could do to keep from laughing in my face.

"I suppose you have proof?" he said, in a tone that said I didn't.

"We've got two ocelots in the lab right now that aren't quite dead," I said. "That's a good start. I know about your brother back in Iowa, the one who bought black-market animals. The family business, eh? Won't be too hard for the cops to put it all together."

He said nothing, but some of the amusement had evaporated from his expression.

"You made two mistakes," I said. "You got greedy, and tried to slip those ocelots past while everyone was scrutinizing the zoo. The other mistake was trying to kill me. I don't take kindly to that."

He studied me for a moment, but didn't seem the least bit afraid of my vengeance or even of the revolver I kept pointed his way.

"You can't prove anything," he said. "And neither can anyone else."

"Buck's already talking," I said. "The cops will have him singing like a bird."

Gibbons snorted. "He's a drunk. Who would believe him over me?"

Tedeski said, "Hey now—" But he couldn't seem to come up with any further objection.

"You don't get it, do you?" I snarled. "The zoo animals are just the beginning. We're talking homicide here. You killed Jeff Simmons because he'd found you out. Then you killed Cristina Tapia when she tried to finger you."

"Horseshit," Gibbons said. "I didn't kill anyone."

"It's all part of the cover-up," I continued. "You knew people were onto you, so you eliminated the problem by killing them."

"You're wrong."

"Let's see what the police have to say about it."

"Yes, let's," he said smugly. "Once they hear how you came in here, threatening people with a gun, you'll be the one who's under arrest, not me."

Mongo shifted on his perch and growled. I could see the red-haired little beast out of the corner of my eye. I didn't need the distraction.

"Tell your monkey to stand down," I said.

"Mongo," Gibbons said, but his voice held no scold in it. He spoke matter-of-factly, as if it were normal to chat with a freaking monkey. "Jump."

The beast leaped at me. *Wham*, against the side of my head. Its hands and feet clawed at my cheeks and ears, tore at my hair. I shrieked and spun around, swatting at the monkey with my free hand.

Mongo writhed against me, clutched to the back of my head, his legs wrapped around my neck. His hairy little hands dug into my eyes. I was blinded and terrified. I got hold of one of his arms and pulled it loose from my face, just enough to get a glimpse of Noah Gibbons springing up from his chair and lunging around his desk. Tedeski still stood against the wall, his mouth hanging open.

Teeth raked the back of my hand, and I yanked it away, and Mongo's hands closed over my eyes again.

I still held the pistol, but I couldn't aim it to shoot. I wanted to reach up behind me, shove the gun up Mongo's red ass, and pull the trigger. But there was no way to accomplish that without possibly blowing off my own head.

Then a fist sank deep into my stomach, and all the air rushed out of me. I doubled over, and Mongo leaped off my head. My eyes were filled with tears and I bent over, facing a blurry floor. Another fist came down on the back of my neck, and knocked me flat.

Hands grabbed at my pistol. I couldn't have that. Bad enough that Gibbons was armed with a monkey. I rolled over, so the pistol was under me, pinned between my body and the floor. Blinking and cursing and spitting, I tried to see well enough to kick somebody, but by the time I could focus, Tedeski and Gibbons and Mongo were gone.

I clambered to my feet and stumbled out into the hallway. Tedeski was running toward the front office. I whipped my head around and saw Gibbons sprinting the opposite way, Mongo clinging to his shoulder.

"Halt!" I cried, but Gibbons disappeared around a corner.

I took off after him, running as best as I could on my gimpy ankle. I turned left at the T intersection and ran past the vet's lab and several closed doors. I was sweaty and bloody and madder than hell. My neck throbbed. My collar was wet, which made me believe that Mongo had peed on me while we were wrestling around. Something smelled foul, and I had to assume it was monkey piss. It says something about my mental state that I hoped it was pee, and not something worse.

Anger spurred me on, and I hobbled faster. I saw Gibbons up ahead, going through a doorway.

Shouts came from behind me. I glanced back, and saw two khaki-covered security guards coming out of Tedeski's lab. They ran in my direction, but neither had a gun in his hand. Not yet.

Before the guards could catch up to me, I ducked through the door where Gibbons had gone.

Heat and humidity hit me in the face, nearly bowled me over. Trees towered around me and something squawked up among their limbs. An overhanging banana leaf slapped damply against my shoulder.

I'd entered another world. A jungle. What the hell?

Chapter 35

$\mathcal{I}$'d followed Gibbons through a service door into the Tropical Rain Forest exhibit, the jungle room I'd bypassed on my zoo tour a few days earlier. Loose birds flapped among full-grown trees and hopped among the giant elephant ear plants. Skittering noises in the underbrush. The gurgle and slurp of water, water everywhere.

Of all the places in the world I might want to visit, a jungle would be last on the list. Venomous snakes and howling monkeys and growling cats, all hiding among twisted tree trunks and gnarly vines and damp ferns, add up to my idea of a scary hell-on-Earth. I often have nightmares in which I'm stranded in a jungle, the trees closing in on me, the glowing eyes of vicious animals glaring from the shadows.

The Tropical Rain Forest exhibit felt exactly that way, made even more claustrophobic because impenetrable concrete walls surrounded it. Only a few high windows let beams of sunlight slice down through the dripping trees.

A wheelchair-accessible boardwalk set atop pilings meandered through the exhibit. Here and there were placards with pictures of birds and plants so you could identify them while you stood on the wooden walkway, sweating and gawking.

The exhibit gave me a bad case of the willies on a good day, so you can imagine how I felt with Noah Gibbons and Mongo very likely hiding somewhere nearby, braced to pounce on me. I jerked from side to side, looking for something to shoot. Every time a bird screeched, I nearly climbed a tree.

No sign of Gibbons or his mangy monkey. The public entrances were on the far sides of the building, at either end of the forking walkway. I didn't think there'd been time for Gibbons to run through the jungle and escape out either door before I came bursting through the service entrance. Which meant he was still in here somewhere.

If I'd just hang on, keeping an eye on the place, the security guards would arrive. Together, we could flush Gibbons out of the underbrush and hand him over to the cops, who should be arriving any minute now. I could just hold this position, wait for the cavalry to arrive—

Then I spotted a flash of movement up in the trees. A glimpse of red fur. Mongo. He leaped from one limb to another, right above me, loosing a weird cackle.

Screw the cavalry. I was tired of being assaulted by primates. I aimed and fired twice. The bullets clipped leaves off the branch where Mongo squatted, but missed him. He scampered away, shrieking.

As the shots finished echoing around the room, I heard a rustle in the underbrush, right at my feet. I spun around, just in time to see a muddy Noah Gibbons rise up from his hiding place beneath the boardwalk. The plank floor was waist-high to him, perfect for what he had in mind. His hands shot out and snatched at my ankles, yanked me clean off my feet.

First thing to hit the deck was the back of my head. Which hurt. My pistol flew into the bushes and I heard a splash and I assumed the gun had fallen into the fake creek that gurgled through the room.

Gibbons rolled up onto the walkway next to me, and proceeded to punch me in the gut. I kicked at him, and my knee caught him on his goateed little chin and snapped his head back. He struck out blindly, hitting me in my bruised ribs with his bony fists. Yee-ouch.

I rolled away, but that hurt, too. Every time I turned over on the boardwalk, it was like someone whapping my bruises with a plank.

Gibbons crawled after me, trying to punch me some more. I kicked him again, but I used the wrong foot. Pain shot up my leg from my twisted ankle, and I figured the kick hurt me a lot more than it did him.

I rolled away some more, Gibbons crawling right behind me. Maybe I could just keep rolling, all the way to the exit, buying time until rescue arrived. But no, the boardwalk zigged to the left and I rolled right into a thick post. Ouch.

He lunged at me, but I saw him coming. I managed to throw my hands up and grab his shirt while he was in mid-air. I yanked sideways, and it was just enough encouragement to send him headlong into the post. His noggin made a hollow sound against the solid wood—one thump on a jungle drum.

He went limp all over, sprawled on top of me. I pushed him out of the way, and rolled up onto my knees.

Gibbons was out cold. I thought about punching him some while he was unconscious, but someone shouted, "Hold it right there!"

I looked up, saw the two security guards had come through the service door. They stood twenty feet away, their guns pointed at me.

I raised my hands and said, "Okay, okay, don't shoot."

They approached cautiously, looking around in the undergrowth, their pistols aimed my way. I kept very still.

A wild hooting came from high in the trees. Sounded like Mongo. Sounded like he was laughing.

Chapter 36

Naturally, it took hours to sort out.

First, the security guards had to be persuaded not to shoot me for beating up one of their curators. These day-shift guards were a different bunch from the ones who'd rescued me from the gorillas (which was just as well, really), and it took some time to explain all that had come before.

Then there were the APD patrolmen, who showed up in response to Loretta's frantic call. They'd puffed all over the zoo, from the vet's lab to Gibbons's office to the Tropical Rain Forest to, finally, the Security office, where they found us. After all that unnecessary running around, they were ready to shoot anything that moved.

While I told them my story, a paramedic taped gauze around my hand where Mongo nipped me, but gave me nothing for pain. My head pounded from whacking against the boardwalk. My ankle ached. And still the cops kept coming with their questions.

They took me and Gibbons to police headquarters, where I was required to tell the story some more to detectives. The cops told me they arrested Tedeski at his house, where they found him hurriedly packing for an unplanned vacation. Detectives interviewed him and Gibbons, too, but the suspects had wised up and wouldn't say a word, or so I was told.

I guess the cops interviewed Loretta, too, and she and the recovering ocelots offered proof that I told the truth. So did the cops finding my gun in a puddle in the Tropical Rain Forest. Hell, even Mongo, loose among the trees, backed up my story.

Still, it was nerve-wracking, repeating the facts to different detectives and hoping I got it all right. After a while, I wasn't even sure anymore who I was addressing: APD Fraud Unit detectives, district attorney's investigators, U.S. Fish and Wildlife Service officers, U.S. Agriculture Department inspectors, and some other guys in suits all trooped through my field of vision as the day crept past.

The only cop I wanted to see finally showed up around nightfall. I was hungry and irritable and tired of being cooped up in a manure-green interview room that reeked of stale cigarette smoke. Steve Romero came into the interview room, cocked one hip up onto the steel table, and grinned at me.

"How you doing, Bubba?"

"About time you got here," I snarled. "Every other cop in the world has marched through this room today. Felt like I was running a doughnut shop."

"Ooh, right where it hurts."

"Damn it, Steve. These detectives won't listen to me. They're all interested in the zoo-animal scam, but nobody seems to believe that Gibbons and Tedeski were behind the murders."

"That's because they weren't," he said.

"Huh?"

"They've both got solid alibis for the times of the murders."

"Yeah, but—"

"Give us some credit here, Bubba. Don't you think I checked the alibis of everybody at the zoo? I mean, when I'm not busy eating doughnuts, this is what I do."

"But—"

"Hell, you're their alibi for the Tapia killing. You saw them both at Tedeski's house, right? All the way across town?"

"Right, but that doesn't mean they weren't behind it," I said. "Maybe another conspirator was involved. Maybe that person killed Cristina. But I'll bet you either Gibbons or Tedeski wore that gorilla suit."

"You'd lose that bet," he said. "They both can account for their whereabouts."

"Where were they?"

"In a staff meeting in Carolyn Hoff's office. Along with a few other people, all of whom swear Gibbons and Tedeski were present at the time of the Simmons shooting. They were discussing the bear enclosures. How to make them safer. Apparently, one of the bears injured himself, banging his head against the wall."

"I know just how he feels," I said. "But if it's not Gibbons and Tedeski, then there has to be another person involved."

"Duh. Yeah, there's somebody else involved. A murderer. But that person apparently doesn't have anything to do with black-market zoo animals."

"But—"

"Tedeski cracked," Romero said. "About an hour ago. The Fraud boys wore him down. He spilled everything. And he swears nobody was involved in the scam except him and Gibbons. Naturally, he blames Gibbons for everything."

"Naturally."

"He insists neither of them killed Simmons. He says they didn't even know Simmons suspected anything until after he was dead and people started asking questions.

"Gibbons thought they could ride it out. That's why he went to Tedeski's house. He was trying to keep him in line. He was mad because Tedeski stayed home, drinking, rather than make an appearance at Simmons's funeral. The vet wanted to shut down the whole operation. That's what he was telling Gibbons when you saw them at the house."

"But they went ahead with the ocelots."

"They'd agreed to meet an order. If they crapped out on it, their buyer, a private breeder in Colorado, would be furious. Tedeski said Gibbons was worried the guy would sic the feds on them if they didn't come through."

"I don't believe it," I said stubbornly. "Somebody's lying here. Those guys killed Simmons."

"Nope. I understand, after all you've been through, that you want to pin it on them, but they're not the ones."

"But who else would want to kill Jeff Simmons?"

"Good question," Romero said. "And I'm working on finding the answer. But not you. You're done."

He got to his feet, looked down at me.

"You did a good job, Bubba. Congratulations."

There's something I never thought I'd hear him say. It stunned me.

He smiled. "It's true. If you hadn't stayed after these guys, we probably never would've turned up the animal scam. These scumbags are going away for a few years. That's something."

I frowned. It was something, all right, but it wasn't enough. I'd been doggedly barking up the wrong tree the whole time. How humiliating. And the killer was still on the loose.

"I've got a uniform waiting downstairs to drive you to your car," he said. "Go home, Bubba. Get some rest."

I slowly got to my feet. My ankle was swollen, and I limped painfully to the door. He held it open for me.

"Hey," I said. "What about my gun? I need it back."

"No can do. It's been submitted to the lab for ballistics tests."

"Why? I didn't shoot anybody with it."

"Part of the chain of evidence," he said. "You left a hole in a filing cabinet—"

"That was an accident."

"Plus a couple in the roof of the Tropical Rain Forest exhibit. We've got to match those up, account for all the shots that were fired."

He was right, of course, but damn, I hated to be without my gun. Guess that's what I get for trying to shoot Mongo.

Chapter 37

A thought waylaid me before I made it home. Had anyone told Loretta Gonzales there was no connection between the animal trafficking and her boyfriend's murder? She probably was at home, satisfied that we'd found the killers. I hated to be the one to bear bad news, but somebody needed to tell her.

I had her address from the check she'd given me. Loretta lived in an apartment off University Boulevard a mile north of UNM. Not a swank address, by any means. A place for students willing to overlook its concrete-bunker design in favor of cheap rent. Which told me Armando Gonzales wasn't footing the bill. When Loretta set off on her own, she meant it.

I found a parking place on the far side of an asphalt lot, and hobbled across to her building. My ankle hurt like hell, and I was stiff all over. But I had a duty, and there'd be no rest until it was done.

Loretta's was the corner apartment, and its door opened directly onto a sidewalk that fronted the parking lot. I rang the bell, then stood with my weight on my good foot while I waited for her to answer. After a minute, the door swung open and there she was, all glossy black hair and smooth skin and sad eyes.

"Mr. Mabry," she said. "What are you doing here?"

"I just got done with the police. There are some things I need to tell you."

She stepped back and gestured me inside. She wore faded jeans and a plain gray sweatshirt. Her feet were bare, and she wore no jewelry. Keeping it casual, home alone, mourning.

The living room was small, with an overstuffed couch and chair and a flimsy-looking coffee table crowded close around a TV/stereo cabinet. The furniture was done in a jungle print, with palm fronds and banana leaves woven into the design. I suppressed a shudder. What looked to be African art—wooden masks and bright paintings—decorated the walls. Above the sofa was a wide watercolor of a pride of lions out on the savanna, all looking off to the left like they'd just gotten wind of a fresh meal.

A student desk with a blank-screened computer was wedged into the far corner, further crowding the living room. Beyond, through an open doorway, glowed the white appliances of a small kitchen. Another doorway was cut into the left-hand wall, and a square hall led to a bathroom—more white enamel—and what I assumed was the apartment's one bedroom. Nice enough place, but tiny. Clearly not what Armando Gonzales would've chosen for his baby girl, which, I suppose, was the whole idea.

I made a beeline for the sofa and flopped down onto it and raised my injured foot.

"Okay if I rest this on the coffee table?"

"Go ahead. Can I bring you something? Aspirin? A beer?"

A beer sounded good, but then it almost always does. I shook my head. No need to get too social here. I had a message to deliver. I should get it said, then get out. Go home and rest, as Romero recommended.

She sat across from me, looking expectant.

"Guess you heard the cops arrested Gibbons and Tedeski," I said.

She nodded. "The police wouldn't give me the details. They wouldn't even tell me which of those rats killed Jeff."

I winced. Here comes the hard part.

"I talked to the homicide lieutenant right before I left the cop shop. He doesn't believe either of those guys is responsible for the murders."

"What?"

"Sorry, but that's what he said. They've got alibis. They were meeting with Carolyn Hoff and others when Jeff was killed. People can vouch for them."

"But the missing animals. You proved—"

"Yes, the cops are charging them with the thefts. The feds are involved, too, and they'll track down how many animals were sold off and all that. Apparently, all kinds of exotic animal laws were violated. But the cops don't believe the thefts necessarily had anything to do with the murders."

"I can't believe this. I thought it was over."

"Me, too. Nothing would've made me happier than proving that Noah Gibbons was behind Jeff's death. But the connections just aren't there."

"But what else could it be?"

"I don't know. I'm still working on that."

Tears welled up in her brown eyes. Oh, man.

"Don't cry, Loretta. We'll find the murderer. I promise."

She nodded and tried to smile at me, but it faltered in face of those tears. She plucked a tissue out of a box on the table beside her and dabbed at her eyes.

Poor kid. Such a tragedy. She's so young, so lovely, and her whole life's been wrecked by some asshole in an ape suit. She might get over the death of her fiancé eventually, but I had a feeling there'd always be a sadness there she'd have to overcome.

I wondered if Jeff Simmons had appreciated her when he was still alive. Had he known how lucky he was, to have a woman who loved him this much? Would they have lived happily ever after, given the chance? Now that she was all alone, would she ever find another man who could make her happy?

Goddamn, what a mess. I often feel sorry for my clients. They've got troubles, or they wouldn't come to me in the first place. But rarely had I felt so sad for anyone as I felt right now for Loretta Gonzales.

She brushed back her hair, pulling herself together. Even all red-eyed and puffy, she was beautiful. No wonder Jeff Simmons fell for her. No wonder other men found her so alluring. How many must've resented Simmons for getting in the way—

Then it came to me. Perhaps Simmons's death (and the killing of Cristina Tapia) indeed had nothing whatsoever to do with zoo profiteering. Maybe it was about something more primal and biological than theft. Maybe it was about animal magnetism. Maybe it was about love.

I stared at the wall, my brain buzzing like a beehive. Loretta caught me gawping, and said, "What is it?"

"I've got an idea," I said. "I need you to make a phone call."

Chapter 38

By the time the doorbell rang fifteen minutes later, Loretta and I had worked out a plan. It involved me eavesdropping from the little hall, so I grunted up off the sofa and limped around the corner.

Loretta went to the door, and I pricked up my ears to hear what would come next.

"Where are you hiding Mr. Mabry?" a shrill voice demanded. "I know he's here. I saw his car outside."

What the hell? I peeked around the corner, and there was the ever-effervescent Julie Keen, dressed in her usual style—an Astroturf-green suit with matching handbag and high heels—with her blond hair piled high. She bulled her way through the front door past an astonished Loretta.

"There you are, Mr. Mabry! What are you doing? Are you hiding? Why would you be hiding? What's going on here? Did I interrupt something? Are you—"

"Stop!" I hate yelling, but it was the only way to interrupt her.

Her mouth kept moving, but no sound came out, so I hurried to fill the void.

"What are you doing here?" I asked as I limped toward her. "Are you following me?"

I didn't see how that was possible, unless she'd waited outside the cop shop for hours.

"I didn't need to follow you," she said. "I figured it out on my own. I knew Miss Gonzales was your client, so I cruised by her apartment building once in a while, figuring you'd stop by here eventually. I live nearby, you know."

"I didn't know."

"Then I saw your car, that Oldsmobile? Which, I must say, is a good choice for a private detective. No one would look twice at an ugly old car like that, not unless they were like me and were specifically looking for it."

"Why?" If I could only get in one word at a time, I might as well ask my own questions. Make 'em count.

"What?"

"Why were you looking for me?"

"You never called me." She made a little pout to show she was put out. "I got you that information, but you never called to tell me what you made of it. It was supposed to be a you-scratch-my-back-I'll-scratch-yours situation, but you never called and my back still itches. That's not fair, Mr. Mabry. Then I find out today that you used that research—my research—to solve the murders! You promised me the story if—"

"I didn't," I interjected.

"—you found out the—"

"I didn't."

"Solve the murders? You most certainly did. I talked to the police. They told me that those two men—" She consulted her notes. "—Tedeski and Gibbons were under arrest. The feds are even involved! But did you tell me these men were the killers? No you did not!"

"They're not."

"What?"

"Those two are not the killers. That's what I'm doing here. I was telling my client that the murderer still hasn't been arrested."

That got Loretta going again. She sobbed into her Kleenex.

"Oh," Julie said. "Oh, I see."

I'd sidetracked her for a second and my ears could catch a little rest. Or so I thought.

"But they're under arrest?"

"For stealing animals from the zoo and reselling them," I said. "That's your story. The murders are still unsolved."

"Oh."

I gently grasped her elbow and turned her toward the door.

"You came at a bad time," I said. "You can see Miss Gonzales is upset."

"Sorry about that, but I still need the information about the arrests," she said, recovering. "This is a big story and—"

We'd reached the doorway, and I guided her outside.

"Get your information from the cops," I said.

"Now, Mr. Mabry, that wasn't the deal. I said I'd help you, but I want an exclusive—"

I jumped backward, as best I could on my bad ankle, and slammed the door shut. Turned the latch, just in case.

Wham, wham! She banged on the door with the flat of her hand.

"Mr. Mabry! Mr. Mabry!"

"Go away, Julie," I yelled through the door. "We're trying to do something here."

"What? What are you trying to do, besides get rid of me?"

"Can't talk about it," I shouted. "But trust me. You need to get out of here. Go write your story. We'll talk later."

"That is not acceptable, Mr. Mabry! We had an arrangement—"

"Go away!"

I turned toward Loretta and shrugged. She shook her head. She couldn't believe the verbal stampede that was Julie Keen, either.

"All right!" Julie shouted through the door. "I'm leaving, but I am not happy!"

"Good!" I shouted back.

"You know what you are, Mr. Mabry?"

Here it comes. This ought to be good.

"You, sir, are a jerk!"

"Thank you! Good-bye!"

"That's exactly what you are, a jerk! And I'm going to tell your wife!"

"She already knows."

A final harrumph, then the sound of her heels clicking away on the sidewalk.

I looked at my watch. We were still okay. Our unexpected guest was gone. The one we'd invited was due to arrive any minute.

Chapter 39

The doorbell rang again a few minutes later. I signaled Loretta to answer it as I limped back into my hidey-hole in the hall. I peeped around the jamb with one eye. Loretta swung the front door open and I could see past her shoulder.

Perry Oswalt waited outside, all anxious and anticipatory and adipose. He wore a loose blue jacket, a knitted brown necktie, and a plaid shirt. Both shirt and tie were tucked into his jeans under his ample belly. His eyes glinted behind his owlish glasses, and his short, rust-colored hair had comb tracks in it. The reptile curator, dressed to impress.

"Hi, Loretta," he said brightly. Then his face fell, and he said, "Oh, my. You've been crying."

"It's okay, Perry. Come in."

I ducked back, but I needn't have worried about him seeing me. He only had eyes for Loretta. As she shut the door, he turned to face her, and his back was to me as I braved a peek. He had a large red pimple on the back of his doughy neck, just above his tight collar.

"I was surprised when you called," he said. "I mean, it was great to hear from you, but I was surprised. You're still in mourning and all—"

Tears sprang to her eyes again, and it didn't look as if she were faking.

"Oh, Perry," she said as she threw herself into his arms.

He hugged her tight and held her for a long time, a little longer than seemed proper, to tell you the truth. Loretta, peering over his shoulder, raised her eyebrows at me, as if to say, "Now what?"

I twirled a finger at her, signaling her to move along with our plan.

She broke the clinch, and they went to neutral corners. Loretta sat in the same armchair she'd occupied earlier, and Oswalt plopped onto the sofa where I'd sat with my foot propped up. I couldn't see his face from my hiding place because a lampshade was in the way. I leaned out a little farther, trying to not even breathe loudly. Our plan hinged on Oswalt feeling he could speak freely.

"I needed someone to talk to," Loretta said, wiping her eyes, "and I thought of you."

Oswalt scooted back on the sofa cushions, sitting up straighter.

"Talk about what?" he said. "About Jeff and all?"

"Jeff's on my mind. You can understand that."

"Sure. I thought about calling you, try to make you feel better, but I wasn't sure it was appropriate—"

"Oh, I'm always glad to hear from you, Perry."

Loretta was pretty damned good at this, I had to say. The tone of her voice was just right—grieving, but approachable, friendly, with just a hint of something flirtatious. I fully expected Perry Oswalt to go into orbit any second. She expressed misgivings when we were hatching this plan, worried that she couldn't pull it off, but she turned out to be quite the actress.

"That's nice to hear," he said.

"Besides," she said, and I braced for the segue, "I needed to talk to somebody who works at the zoo. Somebody who knows all the players."

He stiffened. "The players?"

"You've heard about the arrests?"

"Um, sure. Everybody has, but—"

"Aren't you surprised? I never expected that Noah and Buck could be behind something like that."

Oswalt shifted on the sofa. I still couldn't see his face, but his body language told me he was nervous. I wondered if we'd made a mistake about him. What if he was involved with Tedeski and Gibbons? What if he was the other conspirator in the animal thefts?

"Those bastards," he growled. "I hope they send them to prison for life."

Whoa. Maybe I'm all wet.

"Really?"

"Absolutely." He leaned forward, elbows on knees, and I could see him a little better now. In scowling profile. I knew I must be at the edge of his peripheral vision. I stood very still.

"Anyone who would trade in exotic animals like that, zoo animals, deserves to have the book thrown at them," he said. "That's stealing! And tax dollars paid for those animals. So it's stealing from the public."

"Uh-huh." I could tell Loretta was trying not to look my way, to see how she should respond to his sudden venom.

"If I'd known about it, the cops wouldn't have had a chance to arrest those guys," he said. "I would've taken care of them myself."

"What do you mean?"

He caught himself, realized he'd gotten loud. He sat back and crossed his chunky legs.

"You know," he said, "I would've, um, gathered the evidence and taken it straight to the feds."

"Well, too late for that. The police have them now."

A long pause. Loretta stared at Perry Oswalt, waiting, but he seemed to have run out of gas.

"So," she resumed, "you never had any suspicions? About Buck and Noah."

"None at all. But I sure wonder about it now. I lost several specimens over the past year. I wonder how many of them really died, and how many were secretly sold off."

"Hmm. I hadn't thought of it that way."

"I've thought about little else all day," he said. "I know we're not supposed to get emotionally involved with the animals, but we all do, right? I get upset when I think one of my snakes is unhappy, much less sick or dying. I feel close to every one of them."

Loretta looked to be suppressing a shudder. I knew exactly how she felt. Snakes. Whew.

"I'm just that kind of guy. Emotional, you know? The things I care about, the people I care about, mean everything to me. I'd do anything for them."

Loretta nodded. "I've always thought that was one of your finest qualities."

That seemed to be pouring it on thick, but Oswalt took the bait and ran with it. He leaned toward her again.

"I think of you that way, Loretta. I always have, ever since you came to work at the zoo. I think you're just, well, just the best."

"Thank you, Perry."

"I'd do anything for you. If you need anything, ever, you just let me know."

"That's very sweet."

He wiped at his sweaty forehead.

"Do you think the zoo will be hurt?" Loretta asked. "By the scandal, I mean? You must know it's going to be on the front page tomorrow."

Oswalt looked like he wanted to spit. "I'm sure those jackals at the newspaper will see it as a big story."

Jackals? Good thing Felicia wasn't here to hear that. She'd show him jackals. She'd put a foot up his ass.

"I can't stand it when people speak badly of ZIA," he said. "We all do a great job there, a thankless job. Some people always look for reasons to put us down. But we'll come out all right. We'll weather the storm, as they say."

"I guess you're right," she said. "I mean, if two murders didn't ruin our reputation, then how could this?"

Oswalt paused, cleared his throat. "I wouldn't be surprised if they prove Noah and Buck were behind those murders."

"That's not what I hear," Loretta said. "The police don't think they did it."

"Really? I'm surprised. I would've thought they'd make that connection right away."

"Ironclad alibis." She must've not liked the way Oswalt looked at her because she added quickly, "At least, that's what I heard."

"Where did you hear that?"

"It doesn't matter. Maybe you're right. Maybe they did all those things. But it seems extreme, doesn't it, to kill people, just to cover up their little criminal enterprise?"

Nicely put, Loretta. Oswalt had no answer to that. An uncomfortable silence settled over the room.

"I'm glad you called me," he said finally. "I feel better now that we've had a chance to talk."

"Me, too," she said, though she looked pale and worried to me.

Oswalt stood up and looked around the living room. I jumped back out of sight in the nick of time.

"So this is your place. I've often wondered where you lived, what it was like."

"Really?"

"Well, I knew your address," he said. "It's on all the materials at the zoo."

"Materials?"

"You know, your personnel file and the in-house phone directory and all that. Not like it was a big secret where you lived. But I wondered about it anyway. What kind of place it was and how you decorated it and all. I like these lions."

He was referring to the framed print above the sofa, which meant he was turned my direction to look at it. I stayed very still, as if he might spot me through the wall.

"Yes, I like it, too," Loretta said. "Jeff gave me that painting."

"Oh." He sounded suddenly dejected. "Sure."

She sniffled. "Every time I look at those lions, I think of him."

"Maybe you should take the picture down."

"I couldn't do that. Not with Jeff so recently killed. Not with his murderer still on the loose."

Oswalt cleared his throat. He sounded raspy when he said, "Sure. That makes sense. These things take time."

"Finding the murderer?"

"I meant grieving. It takes time to recover. But you'll be back to your old self eventually."

"How, Perry? How will I ever be the way I was before? The man I love is dead."

"Time heals all wounds," he pronounced. "You'll find a new man. The men will be lining up for you."

Sounded like he wanted to be first in line. Little shit.

"I don't know," she murmured. "I think my heart is broken."

Hell, that was about the saddest thing I'd ever heard. My throat suddenly felt full of sand, and I couldn't even clear it. I couldn't make any noise until Mr. Snake Freak left the building.

My step backward had taken me into the doorway of Loretta's bedroom. A vanity with a round mirror stood against the wall just inside the door. The glass top was littered with makeup and eyelash curlers and lipsticks and other womanly gear. On the far wall stood a matching dresser. The bed was unmade, the covers rumpled, as if Loretta had spent much of her time there recently, writhing and crying.

I heard movement in the next room. The shuffle of feet. The sigh of a seat cushion. Loretta must've stood. I wondered whether she was ready to show Oswalt the door.

"So your apartment," he said, "it's one bedroom?"

"Yes. It's small, but it's all I need."

"Bedroom's through there?"

If he decided on the Grand Tour, we'd be nose-to-nose when he turned the corner.

"Right, and the kitchen's that way," Loretta said quickly. "You want some coffee or something?"

"I want something, but it's not coffee."

He laughed, as if that was the best joke ever, but it sounded sinister to me. I didn't like the way this conversation was going. I'd wanted Loretta to draw him out, to see if he was as crazy about her as she'd thought, to see if he was just plain crazy. She'd told me, days before, that he carried a torch for her. Everything he'd said tonight proved she was right about that, including the fact that he'd pawed through her personnel file. But was he obsessed enough to bump off her fiancé? And why kill Cristina Tapia?

I guess Loretta gave him a squirrelly look because he laughed nervously and said, "Just kidding. I would like another hug, though. Good friends like us, there's no reason we can't embrace, right?"

Me thinking: Get back, Loretta. No more contact with this guy. Things were getting sticky and strange. Maybe it was time for Bubba Mabry, sneaky eavesdropper, to reveal himself.

I sure wished the cops hadn't kept my gun.

Chapter 40

I cast about Loretta's bedroom for a weapon. Nothing there, except a fragile-looking lamp beside the bed. Good for one smack upside the head, which, I feared, wouldn't be enough to make Perry Oswalt behave himself. I needed something that would put the mojo on him.

"What's the matter?" I heard him demand in the next room. "Why are you suddenly scared of me?"

He sounded confused, angry. Uh-oh.

I tiptoed over to Loretta's makeup table, grabbed the biggest lipstick there. It was a bronze-colored tube, made of some kind of lightweight alloy. Might do the trick.

I went back to the doorway and peeked around the jamb. Perry stood with his back to me, his fists on his plump hips. I couldn't see his face, but his neck and ears were bright red. Beyond him, Loretta looked frightened.

I slipped through the doorway and stepped up behind him. Jabbed the lipstick into his lower back and said, "Hold it right there."

"What?"

"Hands up, Oswalt."

He swiveled his head around to look over his shoulder. "You? What are you doing here?"

"At the moment, I'm sticking a gun in your back," I said gruffly. "You want to ask what I'm gonna do next?"

He opened his mouth, then closed it without saying anything. He looked at Loretta, then back at me, stymied.

"I said put your hands up." I poked him with the lipstick, praying that it felt like a gun barrel through the layers of clothing and lard that separated the bronze tube from his nerve endings.

He stuck his pudgy hands in the air.

"That's better," I said. "Loretta? Are you okay?"

She nodded, but apparently didn't trust herself to speak. Her eyes were wide and fearful. Oswalt's awkward amorous attentions clearly had freaked her out. Who could blame her? This weirdo very likely was the one who killed her boyfriend. Not that I had any evidence to prove it.

I leaned close to him and talked right into his ear. "We set a little trap for you, Perry. And you fell for it."

"What are you talking about?"

"Jeff Simmons, that's what. You killed him."

"What?"

"It was you all along. You were in love with Loretta, stalking her—"

"I never—"

"You didn't like Jeff, did you?"

"He never did me any harm."

"Maybe not, but he was engaged to Loretta, and you knew that. You told folks at the zoo."

Beyond him, Loretta nodded. Some of the fear had fallen from her face. She looked angry now.

"You thought he wasn't good enough for her, didn't you?"

He'd been looking back over his shoulder at me, but his gaze shifted to Loretta now, and some of the starch went out of him.

"None of us are," he said. "Nobody's good enough for her."

"She's the woman of your dreams, isn't she?"

Loretta blushed.

"But she's beyond your reach," I continued. "Smart and beautiful and rich. Not the kind of woman who'd give a nerd like you a second look."

His breath caught in his throat, became a fat-boy rasp.

"Plus, she was already engaged to Jeff. Once they were married, all your dreams would go up in smoke."

He shook his head.

"Snakes and lizards aren't enough, are they? You needed a woman in your life. You'd found the perfect one, and now somebody else would snatch her away before you got the chance to make your move."

"You're crazy," he said, puffing. "This is all crazy. I came over here to be nice, to help out a friend—"

"Sounded to me like you were trying to seduce her."

"What? No way. She's grieving. It wouldn't be polite."

"You're worried about polite? Is that what you were doing when you put on that gorilla suit and blasted her boyfriend?"

"I didn't kill him."

"I say you did."

"Say what you want. I didn't do it, and you can't prove otherwise."

Hmm. I'd thought I could scare a confession out of him with my "gun," but he wouldn't crack. I needed more leverage, a way to buffalo him.

"The cops already have proof," I bluffed. "They've got a million ways to find a killer these days. All it takes is a hair, a fiber, a fingerprint. You made a lot of mistakes. They're already looking for you. They'll pin Jeff's murder on you, and you'll be in prison for the rest of your life."

He tensed all over at the mention of prison. Guess being behind bars would be the last thing a zookeeper could tolerate.

"I don't believe you," he said. "You've got no right to—"

Then the doorbell rang.

Chapter 41

The bing-bong froze us into a strange tableau: *Startled Trio with Lipstick and Kleenex.*

Loretta was the first to snap out of it. She turned and reached for the doorknob. I felt the urge to shout, to stop her, but why? We pretty much had to answer the door, no matter who was out there. If we tried to ignore the doorbell, Oswalt could start screaming. That could lead to all sorts of misunderstandings.

I jabbed him with the lipstick tube and snarled into his ear, "Put your hands down."

He did it.

"Now," I added, "you'd better hold perfectly still."

He nodded, his jowls jiggling.

The front door burst open, and Julie Keen came barging in, pushing Loretta out of the way, brandishing her notebook, her big handbag swinging from her elbow, her mouth already moving.

"What the heck is going on here? Who is this guy? Is this the murderer? Is that what you were doing, setting a trap for him? Why didn't you let me stay? I could've taken pictures. I could've recorded the whole thing. Imagine that, a blow-by-blow account of the capture. Well, I guess it's not too late. I can get an interview. What's your name? Why did you kill Jeff Simmons?"

Oswalt, overwhelmed, said something that sounded like, "Nrk." I knew exactly how he felt.

"Shut up!" I shouted.

Julie froze for a second, her eyebrows arched. "How dare you! Why, after all I did to—"

"Shut up now! Can't you see we have a situation here? This is no time for the press to get involved."

"The press?" Oswalt managed.

"Julie Keen," she said, striding toward him, her hand outstretched. "Albuquerque Gazette."

"Don't," I said, but it was too late. He saw his opportunity. He grabbed her hand and yanked hard. Julie stumbled on her high heels, fell headlong toward us.

Oswalt jumped out of the way, and I should've done the same. Should've sidestepped her like a matador. But no, my reflexes took over and I tried to catch her. Her blond head gored my stomach. My sprained ankle twisted and shot searing pain up my leg. And faster than you could say, "Ole!" we both tumbled to the floor.

I got untangled from her as quick as I could, but it wasn't quick enough. Oswalt was standing over me by the time I made it up onto my knees. He struck me in the ear with his fat fist, and I fell over sideways, landing on top of Julie.

She screamed. Loretta screamed. I think I might've screamed, too. Hard to tell, my ear was ringing so loudly.

I rolled off the intern and crawled away a little distance, trying to make room so I could stand up before he knocked me over again.

I'd lost my lipstick, and had no idea where it might've rolled off to. Oswalt finally noticed.

"You don't even have a gun!"

I shook my head at him, trying to catch my breath, trying to think of something to say that would calm him. Apparently, it was too late for that.

"No gun?" he yelled, astounded. "Well, hell, I've got one!"

He reached inside his jacket and pulled out a long-barreled revolver. Brown grips and blued steel. Looked like a .38. I had a feeling I'd seen that pistol before. At the Flying Squirrel café, brandished by an ape.

He pointed it at me. I sure wished I'd patted him down when I had the chance.

"Get up, you asshole."

That seemed a little harsh, but I got to my feet.

Julie had rolled to her hands and knees. Her tight skirt was hitched up around her thighs, and her blond hair had come loose from its clips. She gathered her purse and notebook and pen from the floor, apparently unaware of the gun in our midst.

"I'm okay," she trilled. "Can't believe he just knocked me down like that! Don't you have any manners? I mean, you don't want to talk to a reporter, you can just say so. You don't have to—"

"Shut up!" Oswalt was in command now, and that meant the rest of us were as good as dead. On the other hand, the apartment went blissfully silent once Julie got a look at his pistol, and that was something. If these were my last moments on Earth, I'd prefer that they be quiet ones.

"Perry," Loretta said, and her voice was calm and low. "You don't need to do this."

"You shut up, too!"

He took a step backward, pivoting so he could keep us all covered.

"You never cared about me!" he shouted at Loretta. "This was all a ruse! You wanted me to relax, so I'd let something slip, tell you that I killed your stupid boyfriend."

Had us there. That was our plan in a nutshell. Wasn't exactly working out the way we'd hoped.

"Hah! Now the tables are turned. Get over there, all three of you. Sit on that couch."

We edged around the coffee table and I sat in the middle, Loretta to my right and Julie to my left. The sofa wasn't really long enough for all three of us, and it was a tight fit.

"Hands up!"

We all thrust our hands into the air, as if we were doing the wave. Julie still held her green handbag, and it swung around and whammed me between the eyes.

"Ow!"

"Drop that purse!"

She obeyed. The purse fell into my lap, hitting me in the nuts. Felt like it weighed fifteen pounds.

"What have you got in this thing?" I squeaked. "Rocks?"

"Reporter stuff," she said. "Tape recorder. Cell phone. Camera. Notebooks."

"Shut up!" Oswalt's voice went shrill. "How many times do I have to say it? Everybody just shut your mouths. I need to think!"

He swung the gun back and forth, keeping us all covered. His face was red and sweaty and his short hair was askew and his shirttail had come untucked. He looked a little untucked mentally, too, if you know what I mean, and I clamped my teeth together rather than risk saying something else that might set him off.

Even Julie got that message. The three of us sat there, silent as the "Say No Evil" chimp, our hands in the air, our arms going numb from lack of blood flow.

The pistol swung back and forth some more, finally pointing at Loretta.

"How could you?" he asked, a quaver in his voice. "Everything I did, I did it for you."

"Oh, bullshit," she said.

I glanced over at her, saw that a certain steel had entered her expression. She'd had enough of Perry Oswalt. I tried to lean away from her, in case he started shooting, but Julie was in my way and I couldn't go far.

"How can you even say that?" Loretta demanded. "You were helping me out by killing the man I loved?"

"There was more to it than that," he said, but his voice had lost its edge. She'd taken him by surprise, standing up to him. Wish I could've showed that much backbone myself, but all I wanted was to run yelping from the room.

"What?" she said flatly. "What more could there be?"

His eyelids fluttered behind his glasses, blinking back sweat or tears.

"Jeff," he began, then hesitated, unsure how to say it. We all sat perfectly still, waiting for him to sort it out. I was pretty sure I hadn't taken a breath in minutes.

"Jeff was the kind of guy who thought everything revolved around him," he said finally.

"He was not."

"He was! You couldn't see it, but I could. He wanted attention. That's why he went to this guy here—" The gun twitched my way, which made me flinch. "—with his theories about the zoo."

"He wanted to get to the truth," she said.

Oswalt shook his head. "He wanted to be a hero. He wanted to impress you with how much he cared."

Loretta apparently didn't know what to say to that.

"Jeff told me all about it," he said. "I knew he was going to meet with this idiot."

Again with the twitch of the gun. I wished he'd stop using it for a pointer. What if it went off? Bad enough that he might murder us any minute. I didn't want to die in a freaking accident.

"Why do you think he picked you?" he demanded, and after a second, I realized he was talking to me.

"He told Loretta he'd been referred." I managed to speak pretty clearly for a man who couldn't remember how to breathe. "He said someone had spoken highly of me."

Oswalt made a face. "Oh, please."

"It could happen."

"He picked you because of your wife! He knew all about you, knew your wife worked for the Gazette. He wanted to be on the front page!"

That was a new twist. I had a little trouble getting my mind around it.

"Why didn't he just go to her?"

"That's the way Jeff's brain worked," Oswalt said. "Everything always twisty and sneaky. He was like those computers he worked with—you think it's logic and math, but they're really conspiring against you."

Okay, he'd lost me there. Computers could not conspire against anyone. Though it did seem that way sometimes. I mean, try to get anything done without first doing a reboot—

"Jeff figured you'd tell your wife all about it, and she'd go after the story," he said. "If it didn't work or it went badly, he could deny everything and hide behind his privacy agreement with you. But if it turned out he was right, he could be the hero."

Loretta began, "But I don't see—"

"Shut up! You don't see anything."

She froze, a hurt expression on her face.

"I'm sorry," he said, "but it's true. You were blind when it came to Jeff. You couldn't see the way he really was. You couldn't see that he was only after your daddy's money."

She shook her head.

"It's true!" he insisted. "He was a schemer. He told me things. He thought he could confide in me. He thought I was his friend. The harmless snake guy, the clumsy nerd."

"No, Perry," Loretta said.

"And you think of me the same way. I thought you were different. I thought you cared about me. I've seen you with the animals, how you care about them, how much you love them. Even the ones that aren't all cute and cuddly. Everybody loves the koalas and the pandas and shit, but show 'em a snake or a lizard, and they get all squeamish. You're not like that.

"I thought you could see people the same way, that you could look inside them and find the good there. That one day you'd look at me and realize we were meant for each other."

Oswalt had tears in his eyes now, and his glasses had slipped down his dripping nose. He tugged at his knitted necktie, loosening his collar. He took a deep breath and let it out slowly.

I didn't like the way he was looking at us. As if he'd made a decision about what comes next. As if that revolver held the answers to all his problems.

Then the doorbell rang.

Chapter 42

$\mathcal{T}he$ bell startled Perry Oswalt. I closed my eyes tight. The gun was pointed right at my head, and I didn't want to witness the bullet exploding from that barrel. Didn't want Oswalt's sweaty face to be the last one I ever saw.

Bing-bong, but no boom. I relaxed my squinched-up face and opened my eyes. Oswalt had wheeled toward the closed door. I felt sure bullets would splinter through that apartment door and ventilate whoever was on the other side, but he didn't fire.

His head snapped around and he looked at us, then back at the door. Then back at us again. Then at the door. I would've fallen over, dizzy, if I'd been in his shoes, but his mind apparently was whirring the whole time, because he came up with a plan.

"You," he said, pointing the gun at Loretta. "You'll answer the door. Act like nothing's wrong."

He kept his voice low, which showed an amazing amount of restraint, given the circumstances. I would've been squealing like a little piggy.

"You two go in the bedroom."

Okey-doke. Nothing would make me happier than to have a nice solid wall between me and that gun. I sprang to my feet, dumping Julie's purse on to the floor. I pulled the intern upright and we turned toward the hallway.

"Hold it," he said.

Damn. So close.

"Don't get any ideas. You make a noise, I'll shoot Loretta."

He couldn't really bring himself to shoot the woman he loved, could he? I wasn't sure. His eyes looked wild. He was sweaty and disheveled and twitchy. Walking the razor's edge of sanity. Maybe he would shoot her. Maybe he'd shoot us all.

I shoved Julie ahead of me, which drew a scowl from her, and we marched around the corner into the hall. As soon as we were screened from view, she hurried across the bedroom.

"What are you doing?" I hissed.

"Getting out of here."

"Didn't you hear what he said?"

She stopped and turned, her hands on her hips. "You're going to listen to him?" Her voice wasn't much over a whisper, but I winced anyway. If Oswalt heard us conspiring, he'd shoot us for sure.

"You want to wait around until he comes to kill us?" she said, and I could have done without the sarcasm, thanks very much.

"He's got my client," I said. "I can't just abandon her."

"Well, she's not my client." Julie bent her knee and yanked off one of her high-heeled shoes, then switched feet and yanked off the other. In her stocking feet, she tiptoed over to the bedroom's one window and reached for its latch.

"Wait a minute," I whispered. "Maybe that's the cops at the door."

"No," she said over her shoulder, "it's probably Felicia."

"What?"

Julie shushed me, then turned away from the window long enough to whisper: "I called her after you threw me out of here earlier. Told her you were being a jerk. I have to say, she didn't seem the least bit surprised. I mean, if I was married to a jerk and somebody pointed that out, I'd—"

"Would you get to the point?"

"I told her something was up with the zoo story, and she said she'd come over and help me out."

I blinked at her.

"So that's probably your wife at the door."

"And you're just gonna go out the window and forget about her?"

"I'm not forgetting anybody," she whispered tightly. "I'm going for help. Which is more than I can say for you, Mr. Bigshot Private Eye."

I stopped listening to her. It was the only way to keep from killing her with my bare hands. I went back to the hallway.

The doorbell rang again. Turns out the ringer device was on the wall there in the hall, which meant the bing-bong was right next to my ear when it went off. I about jumped through the ceiling.

"Coming!" Loretta called in the living room. Lot of whispering going on in there, too.

I edged closer to the doorway, pressed against the wall, and, as before, peeked around the jamb so I could see into the living room.

Loretta was reaching for the doorknob. Oswalt was in the corner, behind the door, pressed against the wall. He held the gun pointed skyward, but his jaw was set and he looked ready to shoot. Oh, shit.

What should I do? Should I spring into the living room? Try to distract Oswalt? Take a bullet rather than let him shoot my wife?

But what if that wasn't Felicia at the door? I might be willing to take a bullet for my sweetie, but would I make that sacrifice for anyone else? I couldn't think of anybody. For certain, it would be a pretty short list.

Should I call the cops? My cell phone was out in the car. Julie had said she had a phone in her purse, but her bag was in the living room. She's no help, halfway out the bedroom window. Even if I reached the cops, they couldn't get here in time.

Okay, I was dithering. But all these thoughts flew through my head in the seconds that it took Loretta to turn the doorknob.

Bang! The door flew open, kicked hard by someone on the other side. The impact knocked Loretta backward, but it had a worse effect on Perry Oswalt. The door slammed against him, and his head smacked the wall. The gun went off, blowing a hole in the ceiling. Shattered sheetrock rained down, and plaster dust clouded the air.

To me, the gunshot was like a starter's pistol. I leaped around the corner into the living room and raced toward Oswalt, trying to get to him before he recovered.

The front door bounced off Oswalt and slammed shut, but before it did, I glimpsed Felicia outside. She'd been the one who kicked open the door. So typical of her.

I prayed the gunshot would signal her to get the hell out of there, but I know my wife. She'd be more likely to come charging inside.

I barked my shin on the coffee table, which really hurt, but I limped between the table and the sofa as fast as I could, and launched myself at the fat man.

We crashed into the corner behind the door, and I bounced right off Oswalt's blubber. My assault knocked the air out of him, though, and he didn't have a chance to bring the pistol around. I grabbed for his gun arm, trying to keep the pistol pointed at the ceiling. His jacket was made of some slick fabric, and it was like grasping a fat eel.

He tried to muscle me backward, to point the gun at my head. I threw my body against his, hip-checking him into the corner again.

"Oof!" he said.

"Help!" I said.

But Loretta was too stunned to help. I could see her out of the corner of my eye, backing away, her eyes wide.

The door banged open again, flattening Oswalt and me against the wall. The pistol fired into the ceiling. More noise, more plaster powder. Perry was so covered in the white dust, it was like I was wrestling a mime.

Felicia scurried into the room. Jeez, hon, I thought, don't come in here. It's dangerous.

Oswalt kicked and struggled and the front door slammed shut again. I still had hold of his thick wrist with both hands, keeping the pistol aimed skyward. I bent my arm and slammed him in the nose with my elbow. Once, twice. Blood spurted from his nostrils and he made a gurgling noise.

I whammed his gun hand against the wall, and he lost his grip, and the gun went flying.

Okay. Now we were on an even footing. Now that he no longer had the pistol, I could beat up this fat fucker, show the ladies how it's done. I let go of his arm and cocked back a fist and—he punched me in the gut.

Now it was my turn to say, "Oof!"

Hadn't seen that one coming. I'd been focused on his right hand, the one that had held the pistol. That left sneaked right in there, knocked the wind out of me.

He windmilled his right fist, trying to cold-cock me, and punched me in the side of the neck. That hurt a lot, and I staggered backward. His scowling, bloody, plaster-dusted face lit up. He had me reeling. He thought he could punch his way out of the corner.

Enough of this. I kicked him in the shin, the oldest trick on the playground, and he howled. Then I popped him again in his bloody nose. His glasses went flying, and the pain made him grab at his nose with both hands.

I punched his soft stomach, and his hands fell to cover there. Then I hit him in the face again. The old one-two. Moe vs. Curly.

Oswalt bellowed. He dropped his head and charged me. I tried to dance out of the way, but there wasn't room. The coffee table caught my calves, and I fell backward. We landed on the table, which collapsed under our sudden weight. A splintering crack, then we splatted onto the floor, Oswalt on top, squishing me flat. Breathless and dizzy, I threw ineffective punches into his flabby sides, trying to get him off me.

He grabbed for my throat. Guess he planned to choke me to death while the women watched. I don't know what he was thinking. I was too busy writhing and wrestling and trying to get loose.

Boom! Another gunshot. More of the ceiling fell down on us. Oswalt and I froze in mid-grapple. He turned to look and I raised up my head to peer over his shoulder.

My wife stood by the front door in a perfect shooter's stance, Oswalt's pistol gripped in both hands, pointing at us.

"That's enough," she said firmly. "Get off him."

Oswalt obeyed, though he managed to give me a final squish as he got up. As soon as his weight lifted off me, I kicked him in the leg. Little bastard.

"Enough!" Felicia commanded.

Cowed, I rolled over, gingerly separating myself from the splinters and sawdust that had once been Loretta's coffee table.

By the time I got to my feet, Oswalt had his hands in the air, his breath coming hard. Felicia kept the pistol pointed at his chest.

"Whew," I said. "Way to go, hon."

She didn't even look at me. Unlike some of us, she doesn't get distracted when she's got the drop on a bad guy.

Loretta had retreated all the way to the kitchen. She had a telephone to her ear.

"Are you all right?" I asked her.

She nodded, then said into the phone, "Police?"

Good. Let the cops sort out the rest of it. As I turned back to my wife and savior, we were all taken by surprise once more because—guess what?

The doorbell rang.

Felicia was nearest the front door, but she said out of the side of her mouth, "You'd better get that. I'm busy here."

I stepped around her, and warily cracked open the door.

Julie stood outside in her stocking feet. She smiled brightly when she saw me. She was accompanied by a bewildered young man, whom I took to be a neighbor. He wore a red UNM sweatsuit and white sweatsocks and no shoes. He brandished a Louisville Slugger, ready to brain somebody.

"I brought help," she said. "Is it all over? Everything okay in there? What did I miss?"

Chapter 43

Felicia let me hold the pistol while we waited for the cops to arrive. She ordered Oswalt to sit on the couch, then handed the gun to me.

"Here, Bubba," she said. "Keep an eye on him."

The temptation to shoot him was pretty strong, especially now that the adrenaline was wearing off and I could feel the new bruises I'd suffered in our tussle. I sat in the armchair across from him and rested the pistol on my knee, aimed at his face.

Oswalt used his knit necktie to dab at the blood running from his nose. He glared at me, but he still didn't have his glasses, and I figured he couldn't see me all that well. Couldn't see how my own face was screwed up in pain, or how disheveled and dusty he'd left me.

Soon as she saw we had the situation under control, Julie dismissed her white-knight college boy. At first, the neighbor wanted to hang around while we sorted everything out, but Julie yapped at him until he abruptly decided he didn't want to get involved. Go figure.

Felicia and Loretta murmured together in the kitchen, my sweetie making sure my client was okay. Which was nice. We'd wrecked Loretta's living room, but that was probably the least of her worries. Much more overwhelming was that there'd been betrayal and gunfire and violence right before her eyes. And her boyfriend was still dead.

I wondered briefly whether anyone upstairs had been hit by bullets flying up through the floor. I didn't hear any noise from up there. Surely, there'd be a commotion if we'd accidentally plugged the tenant or an Avon lady or something.

Julie had disappeared into the bedroom, and she returned now, her shoes back on and her handbag dangling from her elbow. She had her pen and pad in hand as she hurried over to Felicia, looking at her admiringly with shiny puppy eyes.

"My God, that was just super, the way you took control. You're so brave, Felicia. I wish I had that kind of nerve!"

My wife looked Julie up and down. Her lip curled in that cute way it does when she sees a cockroach in the kitchen.

"How did you even know what was going on in here?" Julie chirruped.

"I didn't," Felicia said. "When the front door opened, I saw there was somebody behind the door."

"How?"

"Through that little crack between the door and the wall. I didn't know who it was, but—"

Felicia caught herself. Julie was furiously scribbling down everything she said.

"What are you doing?"

"Why, I'm interviewing you, of course."

"Don't bother," Felicia said. "You won't be writing this story. It's mine."

Julie beamed at her. "Oh, I don't think so. You can't write it. You're the heroine of the piece. You saved the day!"

"What about me?" I blurted.

They ignored me.

"It's my story," Felicia said.

"You've got a conflict of interest. Your husband started the whole thing."

"Hey, I didn't start it. Perry did."

They ignored me some more.

"What about you?" Felicia said to Julie. "You were in here before I was. You called me to the scene. If we're going to start trotting out our conflicts, then you've got as many problems as I do—"

I tuned them out. If they could ignore me, I could ignore them right back. Besides, I didn't care about the coverage or the Gazette or anything else. I just wanted this to be over.

Loretta stepped around the other two, and came back into the living room. She hesitated before crossing my line of fire, but she saw that Oswalt wasn't about to try anything. She hurried across the room and found his eyeglasses on the floor. He stopped dabbing at his bloody nose when she handed him his specs.

"Thank you." He put on the glasses, which had been bent in the fight. They sat crookedly on his swelling nose.

Loretta remained standing there, wringing her hands, staring at Oswalt as if he were some exotic creature she'd never seen before.

"You really did it, didn't you?" she said after a moment. "You really killed Jeff."

He ducked his head, ashamed. His hands twisted at his necktie and he made snuffling noises. Might've been crying. Might've just been trying to breathe through the leaking blood. I couldn't tell. But he looked guilty as hell. I hoped he still looked that way when the cops got there. Maybe they could get him to confess.

"None of this was ever about the zoo, was it?" she said. "It was never about Buck and Noah and what they did."

Okay, now I was starting to worry a little. Was my client in shock, or was she just slow on the uptake? I mean, we'd established all this earlier, before the shooting started. Oswalt looked up at her, a puzzled expression on his face, like he was wondering about her, too.

"No," she said, "this was all about me. About the feelings you had for me. Which means I'm the one responsible for Jeff's death."

"Now hold on," I said. "You didn't do anything wrong. Snake Boy here was the one who thought he could advance his romantic agenda with an ape suit and a gun. You never did anything to encourage him."

Oswalt and Loretta stared at each other, ignoring me, which seemed to be the pattern around here.

Tears filled Loretta's eyes. Aw, hell. Here we go again.

Felicia crossed the room and put her arms around Loretta, gave her a squeeze. Loretta's wet gaze never left Perry Oswalt.

"I'm sorry," he said finally, his voice cracking. "You were just being a friend to me. I took it all wrong, didn't I?"

Loretta sobbed, and Felicia turned her away, marched her off toward the kitchen. Felicia shot Oswalt a look over her shoulder, such a fierce look that I'm sure he felt relieved that she was no longer holding the pistol. Julie followed the other women to the kitchen, still writing in her notebook.

Once they were in there, I said to Oswalt, "I've got one question."

Took him a second to focus on me through his smudged, crooked glasses. Once I was sure he was registering what I said, I asked, "Why the gorilla suit? If you wanted to kill Jeff Simmons, you could've done it anytime. At his home. On the street. Why at the Flying Squirrel, with me sitting right there?"

He wiped at his eyes and answered me.

"Jeff talked to me right before he went to see you. Told me about his suspicions and how he'd use you to get the newspaper interested."

Ouch. That part still stung.

"I had that gun," he said. "In my desk. I'd been thinking about doing things with it. You know—" He glanced to the kitchen to see whether the women were listening, but they were busy consoling Loretta. "—killing him before they could get married."

I nodded, wishing I had Julie's tape recorder going right now.

"When he left, going to that café, it was the perfect opportunity. If he died while talking to you about his conspiracy theories, then everyone would think he'd been killed to shut him up."

"But you couldn't just waltz in there and shoot him," I said. "Not if you wanted everyone to believe the killer was someone else."

"Right. I thought about tying a scarf around my face, like a bandit, but look at me. Look at this body." He held out his arms, and stared down at his dusty paunch, in case I was having trouble seeing for myself. "Somebody might recognize it."

I made no comment. Now that he was talking, I didn't want to sidetrack him.

"Then I thought of that gorilla suit. I'd seen it recently, when I was in Jungle Jim's workshop, hammering together a new cage for Agatha."

Who? Oh, right, his iguana. Sheesh.

"I pulled my car around to the service entrance behind the amphitheater. Then I got the ape suit and that funny bag with the flowers on it and I hustled over to the Flying Squirrel."

He glanced at the women. Julie was looking our way, but I didn't think she'd heard what he'd said. Too bad for her, I thought smugly.

"You know the rest," he said.

I certainly did, and I knew even better than he did how close his plan had come to working. He'd wanted to steer attention to the black-market conspirators, and he succeeded in that. I'd chased off down that trail, and the cops would have, too, except that Steve Romero had done his legwork.

"I don't understand about Cristina Tapia," I nudged.

Oswalt hung his head. "That was a big mistake."

I waited him out. Finally, he muttered, "She went around ZIA, asking all of us if we'd seen that gorilla suit. I knew she'd find out it was missing, and then it might come back on me. When she went to the workshop, I followed her."

"Didn't you think shooting her would just call attention to the fact the ape suit was missing?"

"I hadn't planned to shoot her. I wasn't sure what to do. But then she saw me. She was on the phone, telling somebody about it, and she saw me peeking in the door at her. The gun was in my hand. She saw that, too. I panicked."

Now it was my turn to feel guilty. I was the one who'd sent Cristina looking for that gorilla get-up. I was the one on the phone with her when—

Then the doorbell rang.

The women wheeled around like gazelles at a watering hole, all twitchy and ready to run. But then we heard, "Open up! Police!"

The ladies hurried across the living room, walking right through my line of fire again—what was wrong with them?—and Felicia went to the door.

Oswalt said, "Loretta?"

She stopped and looked down at him. I tensed as he dug into his pants pocket. If he came out with the knife or something, I'd shoot, even if the cops were only a few feet away. But he pulled out a jingling set of keys.

"I know I don't have any right to ask," he said. "But would you look after my pets while I'm gone?"

Warm-hearted Loretta gave him a fractured smile. She took the keys as the door opened and cops spilled into the room.

I was still shaking my head in wonder when the policemen ordered me to drop the gun.

Chapter 44

We were up half the night, dealing with uniformed cops and detectives and Romero, who didn't seem at all pleased that I (and my many helpers) had solved the murders.

To recuperate, Felicia and I slept late Saturday morning. After we finally woke up, I staggered into the kitchen for life-giving coffee, and Felicia braved the chilly outdoors to fetch the newspaper from the porch.

We sat side-by-side at the kitchen table, the Gazette front page spread out before us. The lead story was about Perry Oswalt's arrest for the two homicides. An accompanying article gave details about the arrests of Noah Gibbons and Buck Tedeski and their larcenous, if apparently unrelated, scheme. The sidebar included a few paragraphs quoting Gibbons's brother, Isaac, who was out of the animal park business these days and apparently not a bit surprised that his rat of a brother had grown up to be a crook.

I figured prominently in both stories, and I wondered whether that would help my business at all, whether it would somehow cancel out the bad publicity I'd earned over the years.

Looked to me like the zoo would survive the damage to its image. Carolyn Hoff had refused to comment, according to the stories, but it was clear this was a case of a few bad apples rather than a rotten orchard. Albuquerque taxpayers will continue to support ZIA. We love our zoo.

The best quote came from Jungle Jim Johansen: "The recent events at the zoo just go to show that humans are the most deadly of animals. And the most untrustworthy." Somehow, I think that wasn't in his usual script.

Felicia didn't seem at all pleased that her newspaper had done such a thorough job of reporting the complicated events. I think that had something to do with the fact that both stories bore the byline: "By Julie Keen of the Gazette Staff."

"Your intern did a pretty good job," I said. "All the facts are there, and they're told in a straightforward manner."

Felicia grunted and got up for more coffee. She didn't offer to top off my cup.

On her way back to the table, she picked up the little digital camera the newspaper had loaned her the week before. She sat down and set the camera on the table before her, turning it this way and that, studying its buttons and dials. Something about her expression, the way she cocked her head to the side, made me think of a monkey with a shiny toy. It was all I could do to keep from laughing.

Instead, I opted to tease her some more.

"Yeah, old Julie really nailed this story. Spelled everybody's name correctly. Got the sequence of events right, which was no mean trick in this case."

"Uh-huh." Acting like she wasn't listening.

"I like the way she tells about you crashing our little party at Loretta's," I said. "Makes you sound like Wonder Woman."

"Mm-hmm."

She still fiddled with the camera. She held it up to her eye and aimed it at me. I smiled big, and was rewarded with a blinding flash.

While I blinked against the red spots dancing before my eyes, Felicia frowned at the two-inch-wide screen on the back of the camera.

"Let me see."

She turned it around so I could view the captured image. You know how people always talk about the "deer in the headlights?" That's how I looked.

"Maybe you'll get better with practice," I said.

She pushed some more buttons on the little chrome camera.

I couldn't seem to get a rise out of her, no matter what I said. But I gave it one last shot.

"Guess Julie will get a lot of attention for this story. Maybe she'll even win a journalism award."

"Good," Felicia said. "Maybe she can parlay her success into a full-time job. Then she can stop bugging the rest of us."

I grinned at her. Started to say something else, but I was interrupted.

Our doorbell rang.

Chapter 45

Leaving Felicia in the kitchen, I limped to the front door in my bare feet, my old flannel bathrobe flapping around my knees. I figured it was more media people at the door, maybe TV types come to interview the intrepid investigator and his super-hero wife. I couldn't have been more wrong.

I threw the door open, and two gorillas in black suits and black crewcuts shoved their way inside. They grabbed me by the armpits and carried me backward and dumped me on the couch.

Allow me to clarify: These weren't actual gorillas. Not even guys in ape suits. They were the other kind of "gorilla," the type regularly employed as bouncers and legbreakers. Swarthy, mus-cled-up thugs with low brows and wide jaws and thick necks. True, they were nicely dressed, but one look at these goons, and you'd never question the theory of evolution.

Before I'd finished bouncing on the sofa cushions, another well-dressed man came through the front door. Armando Gonzales. He was half the size of the beefcake boys, but he scared me worse. The thugs were all business, but Gonzales was furious. His face was dark with anger and his eyes were bloodshot and I could prac-tically see steam coming out of his ears.

The bodybuilders stepped out of his way and stood side by side, a wall of muscle. They were so pumped up in the pectorals and biceps, their arms couldn't hang down normally. Instead, their hands were out to the sides, gunfighter style. I wondered who tied their neckties for them.

Gonzales stabbed the air with an index finger, and said to me, "You son of a bitch."

"Hey, now." My Mama wouldn't appreciate that slur, but I didn't get a chance to say so.

"What did I tell you?" he demanded. "Huh? What did I say? I warned you to stay away from my daughter. I told you, if you put her in harm's way, I'd fucking kill you. Isn't that what I said?"

I tucked my bathrobe around my knees. It wasn't comfortable, sitting on the sofa, looking up at these angry men, while wearing no pants.

No chance of running. And, as mad as Gonzales appeared, no chance of talking my way out of a beating. Maybe if I just sat quietly, it would all be over soon, and I'd wake up in a nice peaceful hospital. With no doorbells.

"So what did you do?" he continued. I understood that these were rhetorical questions. If I'd tried to answer, he'd probably have his goons yank out my tongue. "You set a trap for the killer, and you used Loretta as bait!"

Okay, so that wasn't exactly it. Yeah, we set a trap. And, sure, Perry Oswalt never would've fallen for it if Loretta hadn't been there. So I guess, technically, she was the bait in the trap. But she'd been a willing participant. Wasn't like I forced her into anything. Neither of us had expected that gunplay would result; we were just trying to get Oswalt to open up. All these retorts and arguments zipped around my brain, but I knew better than to trot them out for Armando Gonzales. He was way past the point where you could reason with him.

"She told me all about it! Oh, she didn't want to. She tried to protect your sorry ass. But it became clear pretty damned quick. Shots were fired! She could've been killed!"

I tried to look contrite. I didn't expect it to help, but maybe if he saw how bad I felt about—

"You fucker!"

Okay, so "contrite" didn't work on him.

"I tell you what I'm gonna do." His voice lowered, and I thought he was really dangerous now. "I'm gonna hand you over to these boys here. I'm gonna let them do whatever they want. Puny guy like you probably won't be much of a workout for them, but they'll have some fun."

I glanced at the goons. They bared their big muscular teeth in anticipation. Oh, shit.

"Me?" Gonzales said. "I'll be nearby. I want to be sure I can hear you scream. I want to hear your bones snap—"

Bright light flashed through the room, leaving us all dazzled.

The two goons whipped their heads around, and one slid a hand inside his jacket.

Felicia stood in the kitchen doorway, still in her fluffy bathrobe, the little chrome camera up to her face. As we all gawked at her, she snapped another frame, blinding us with the flash.

"Armando Gonzales," she said, as measles of light danced before my eyes. "Remember me? Felicia Quattlebaum? I work for the Gazette?"

Gonzales still blinked and reeled, but Felicia's matter-of-fact voice seemed to settle him down.

"I interviewed you last year, remember?" she said. "Did a big feature on ArGon for the business page?"

Gonzales tugged at his shirt collar and sweat popped out on his forehead. He remembered her, all right.

"This camera belongs to the Gazette." She nonchalantly studied the little screen on the back of the camera. "Takes great photos. You should see yourself here. You and these brutes you brought with you. All tensed up and full of drama. You'll look great when I put you on the front page."

"Now hold on," he said.

"No, you fucking hold on," she snapped. "This is my house. You come here, make a lot of noise, threaten my husband. That's just wrong."

Now it was Gonzales' turn to look contrite.

"Bubba nabbed that killer," she said.

I started to say something about how Loretta and Felicia helped, but my sweetie shot me a look that would peel paint off a wall, and I clamped my mouth shut. She was in control here. No sense distracting people.

"Now you want to repay him with a beating?" she said. "Well, go right ahead, Mr. Gonzales."

Huh?

"Have at it. You and your boys. Beat the daylights out of him."

What?

"But I hope you don't mind if I take pictures the whole time. I'm going to make you famous."

Oh. Okay.

Gonzales held up his hands placatingly. Felicia rewarded him with another eyeball-busting flash. She held the camera out away from her face to study the screen.

"Wow. That's a good one."

He cleared his throat. "Okay, okay. You've made your point. We'll just be going."

"You don't want to stick around? We'll have a nice photo session."

I thought that was pushing her luck. No reason one of those bodybuilders couldn't bounce across the room and snatch the camera from her hands and crush it to dust. But Felicia had them where she wanted them.

Armando Gonzales jerked his head toward the door, and the goons, their giant shoulders slumped in disappointment, headed for the porch.

Their boss turned to me, but his eyes kept cutting over to Felicia. He plastered a big, fake smile on his face, in case she snapped more pictures, then talked through clenched teeth.

"Send me a bill and I'll mail you a check for your services. But don't go around my daughter again. You're done, do you hear?"

I nodded.

"All right then."

He turned the smile Felicia's direction and said, "Good day."

"Bye now," she said sweetly.

The door slammed behind him.

Chapter 46

Felicia and I sat on the sofa together, admiring the digital photos of Armando Gonzales and his thugs standing over me in my bathrobe. It was a nice sequence. As she flipped through the shots on the little screen, you could watch the blood drain right out of Armando's face. Even the steroid boys seemed to shrivel a little in each passing photo.

"You pulled my fat out of the fire again," I said.

"I can't help myself. It's habit-forming."

"Lucky for me."

"I swear, Bubba, the things you get yourself into. Even when a case turns out right, you've got the client's father threatening to kill you. Don't these things ever end with everybody happy?"

"Not often," I admitted. "But I'll be happy if Gonzales sends me a check."

"Think he will?"

"Would he dare stiff me? Now that he knows my wife is Flashgun Felicia?"

She laughed and gave me a playful slap on the shoulder, which hurt, and took my picture again. She needed to stop playing with that flash before I went completely blind.

Then the doorbell rang.

"Oh, no," I said. "I'm not answering it this time."

"Go ahead, Bubba."

"No way. I've had it with doorbells."

"Oh, go answer the door," she said. "How bad could it be?"

I shook my head some more.

"Stop worrying." She held up the little camera. "I'm armed."

I got up from the sofa and slumped over to the door. This time, I remembered to stoop and look through the peephole.

Marvin Pidgeon scowled back at me from the porch. Marvin's the attorney I mentioned. The slip-and-fall guy. Seeing him reminded me of all the messages he'd left on my answering machine, none of which I'd returned.

I opened the door.

"There you are!" he shouted up into my face.

Marvin's one of those unfortunate guys who's extremely hairy all over, downright furry, everywhere except on the top of his head, where he's completely shiny bald. He looks like he outgrew his hair. Right now, his scalp glowed bright red.

"I've been calling for days!"

"I know, Marvin. I'm sorry. I meant to call you back, but I've been really busy—"

"I can see that!" I hadn't noticed that he held a copy of today's Gazette in his hands. He thrust it at me, held the front page inches from my nose. "Everybody can see what you've been doing!"

"Yeah, well, I was—"

"So now you're a big shot, huh? Too busy to return my calls. Too important to waste your time with something as small-time as a physical injury case."

"Not at all—"

"I guess it would be boring to you now, tedious even, to help some poor unfortunate who has suffered tremendous pain and hardship because of a debilitating fall. Someone who's lost income and opportunity, who's unable to take care of loved ones because of the pain and suffering—"

I held up my hands to stop him. "Marvin, you don't need to make your closing argument here. I'd be happy to take on your slip-and-fall cases."

That tripped him up. "Really?"

"You bet. Nothing would make me happier right now than a little tedium."

"Yeah?"

"Sure, Marvin. Come in and have a cup of coffee and tell me all about it."

I put my arm around his shoulders and led him into the house.

"If you behave yourself," I said, "Felicia might even take your picture."

He looked at me like I was bananas.